MW01537940

BURNING ROSES

To Jaden & Gabby!

Thank you! I hope
you enjoy the
story!

[signature]

BURNING ROSES

A NOVEL

KATARINA ARRUDA

authorHOUSE®

AuthorHouse™
1663 Liberty Drive
Bloomington, IN 47403
www.authorhouse.com
Phone: 1-800-839-8640

© 2013 by Katarina Arruda. All rights reserved.

No part of this book may be reproduced, stored in a retrieval system, or transmitted by any means without the written permission of the author.

Published by AuthorHouse   01/07/2013

ISBN: 978-1-4817-0291-1 (sc)
ISBN: 978-1-4817-0290-4 (e)

Library of Congress Control Number: 2012924282

Any people depicted in stock imagery provided by Thinkstock are models, and such images are being used for illustrative purposes only.
Certain stock imagery © Thinkstock.

This book is printed on acid-free paper.

Because of the dynamic nature of the Internet, any web addresses or links contained in this book may have changed since publication and may no longer be valid. The views expressed in this work are solely those of the author and do not necessarily reflect the views of the publisher, and the publisher hereby disclaims any responsibility for them.

To Miguel; without you, I would not know the meaning of love,
nor would I be able to write about it.

CHAPTER ONE

WONDER

I remember when I first fell in love with her. It wasn't a hard thing to do. Loving her was easy. Loving her was never a risk, it was never a daring chance, it was never a leap of faith. And when I did fall in love just a short period of time after I met her, I fell hard. The beauty of her laughter struck me; her dark brown, soulful eyes made me drop to my knees. Her flawless skin was as soft as her gentle heart. I could not withstand the force of fate because destiny knew that once I laid my eyes on her, I'd never be the same. And destiny was right. Destiny was dead on.

She had a dimple on her right cheek. It was always the first thing I noticed when she smiled, laughed or scrunched her nose the way she did when she was pretending to be mad. She was so cute. Sometimes as life moves on, you forget to notice the small things. You forget to remember the subtle things, the things that shouldn't even make a difference. It was just a dimple to her. It was just a dimple to me. It was just a dimple to the whole entire world. But that dimple came out after a smile, and that smile only happened when she was happy. And when she was happy, I was at peace. Her happiness meant the world to me. The entire world.

I worked outside during the first snowfall of the season. It wasn't too cold outside, and our foreman needed us for the day, so we just decided to zip up our sweaters and continue working. Of course, some people left, but I chose to stay. I was standing on the twelfth floor of the building watching the snow fall. I tried following the same flake until it hit the ground but I was interrupted from my thoughts. "Wanna grab a beer after work?" Cam asked. Cameron Fitch was a friend I'd known since kindergarten. I had been working with him for three years. He was taller than me, about six feet three inches, and because of his hectic workout schedule, he was built as well. Cam took off his hard hat and scratched his head. His green eyes glared right through me. I could tell by the way he looked at me that he understood. He knew I wasn't okay and that I hadn't been for a long time. Still, I didn't talk to him about any of it. Working was what I did to keep my mind off her. Working there was my only escape; I could not be reminded. I needed her out of my head or I would have gone insane.

I realized then that I had not answered his question. "Not today, Cam, I just wanna get this shit done and go home," I said.

"You sure, man? You look like you need to loosen up," Cam responded.

"Who cares what I look like? I just wanna get this shit done and go home. Traffic is gonna suck," I said.

"For sure," he said. "But traffic will be a lot better after a beer or two." *What do I have to lose?* I asked myself. I had already lost everything. *Might as well try to forget what is missing for a few hours.* "Fine," I said.

The day seemed to drag on slowly. It felt as if I had been there for 12 hours. As much as I hadn't wanted to go at first, getting drunk in a bar seemed more and more appealing as the day went along. By the time we had lunch, I could barely feel my fingers because of the freezing temperatures. But my hands loved holding that hot cup of coffee as I sat down in the trailer with the rest of the guys. They all talked about sports, hunting, fishing and women. I never said much but just sat there and listened most of the time. Or, at least, pretended to listen. I'd catch bits and pieces of their conversations and try to laugh when it seemed appropriate, but my mind always wandered. When I worked and rushed, she never crossed my mind. But while everyone else looked forward to lunch time, I feared it. I got bored at lunch, and when I got bored, my mind drifted to another world. Was she alive? Out of all the goddamned questions I had, that was the one I needed answered the most. Every single day of my life since the disappearance, I had been haunted by that question. Was she alive? It had been 11 weeks. She couldn't possibly still be alive. But I had hope. And as delightful as hope seems, it can be the worst thing in the world. It kept me holding onto something that my reason knew was unrealistic. Hope was a fishing line that hooked into my lip and dragged me across the lake, leading me nowhere. Would I be someone's dinner or a catch-and-release? I'd never know until I got there. And waiting for my fate was one of the worst feelings in the world.

I felt guilty most of the time. I felt terribly guilty. I should have been with her. I should have prevented the situation. Her car was a piece of shit; we both knew this. She had gotten a cheap car because it was all she could afford at the time. I had wanted her to have a car so she wouldn't have to rely on public transit to bring her everywhere, especially at night. So she worked one summer, saved money and bought herself an old Jeep Wrangler. But just like every other used car on the planet, her car had a problem. Sometimes, the car just wouldn't start. It was a simple fix; I knew this and so did she. I told her I would fix it myself and I told her not to bring it to the mechanic because she would be wasting her money. She shouldn't have listened to me. Of course I didn't fix the stupid car. I was too busy; everything else came first. She stopped asking me to do it, probably because she got used to the words, "Not now, babe." She went to work one night and according to the surveillance footage the police showed me, she got into her car, then about a minute later, she got out. She opened the hood of the vehicle and started touching things. She didn't know what she was doing. She had never understood the mechanics of anything, let alone a car. She was alone with only street lamps and the moon to light her way. A truck pulled up beside her about a minute later. A man came out. A big man. They started talking. He seemed friendly towards her. She was naive at times. I tried telling her to walk away. I shouted at the screen. "Don't talk to him, baby! He wants to hurt you. Just walk away." The investigating officer stared blankly at the screen. "I'm sorry," he said. It was hard to see, but what happened next sent an eerie vibe through my bones. She started walking backwards. He followed her. And then he punched her, knocking her to the ground. She was on the ground, and he was on top of her. We couldn't tell what was happening because her car was in the way of the camera. My eyes filled with tears. I wanted to kill him. Whoever the fuck he was, I wanted him dead. I didn't want to watch the rest, but my tortured heart wouldn't let me take my eyes off the screen. I just watched as my baby suffered endlessly. After a few long minutes, he dragged her into his truck. And my strong baby girl was still fighting. My heart was shattered, my breath jammed in my throat. There is no feeling like watching the only person you love being beaten in front of your eyes. She was being abducted and there was not a goddamned thing I could do about it. But I had a little inkling of happiness when I saw her still fighting. I was proud of her. She tried her best to get away. And that was why I still had hope. There wasn't an ounce of flesh in her body willing to give up when times got hard. And that is why I still believed she was alive and fighting. There was nothing capable of bringing her down. I was proud of her but ashamed of myself. If I had fixed that fucking car, none of this would have happened. *The day they find her body is when it will hit me,* I thought. It's because of me that she was killed. I took her for granted every single day of my life.

After the work day was done, Cam and I drove to Sport's Kitchen, a bar we often went to. When we walked in, the bartender was wiping down the counter to our right. The dim lighting made it hard to see. There was a crowd of people huddled around the bar watching a hockey game. They started hollering as a puck went into the net. I immediately wanted to get out of there. As if Cam sensed my energy, he looked at me and said, "Don't worry, we'll get a booth."

A young waitress led us to our table. She was very vibrant and upbeat. We sat at the table and she asked us if we wanted to get started with drinks. "Two Coronas," Cam said. He looked at me. I had a blank expression. "Keep them coming."

"Kendra" was the name on the waitress's nametag. She nodded her head, smiled, spun around with a bounce and walked away. I watched her from behind as her long brown hair swayed with the bounce of her steps. She was happy.

"So," I heard Cam say. I didn't turn my head. I kept my eye on Kendra until she was out of sight. "How are things?"

I turned to face Cam. "They're all right," I lied.

Cam looked at me as if to say, *You don't gotta bullshit me; I can see right through you.*

I rolled my eyes. "What do you want me to say, Cam? You want me to tell you things are great? That would be a lie. Or do you want me to tell you that I can't even fucking breathe normally anymore?"

Cam opened his mouth to respond, but Kendra came back with our beers. Cam closed his mouth quickly without taking a breath.

Kendra placed our beers on the table and smiled. "Anything else, boys?"

I shook my head and Cam smiled at her. She smiled back and walked away with the same bounce in her step.

"Fuck, man, I can see it in your eyes." Cam said.

"See what?" I snapped.

Cam leaned into the table and whispered. "She looks like Rosie. She reminds you of Rosie, and it's written all over your face."

"Fuck off, Cam." I said. "You're making shit up."

"C'mon, Ethan. I don't want to pester you about this, but you're a wreck. You need to talk to someone. Anyone."

"No, I don't," I responded, frustrated. I came to have a few beers, not a therapy session. Nervously, I took a long sip of my beer. I saw Cam nod his head and chug his beer. *This is going to be a long night,* I thought. Cameron Fitch, as much as I loved the guy, was stubborn as a mule. And alcohol is a strong poison. Cam knew the more he fed me, the more I'd open up.

After three beers and random conversation, I started feeling the buzz. I'd never been a huge drinker; I was something of a lightweight. Every time Kendra came with a new round of beers, I felt my heart tear a little more. What was it about her that reminded me of Rosie? Was it her hair? Her smile? Her laugh? Was it the way she walked with a cute bounce in her step? Was it her vibrant energy? Whatever it was, it was killing me. I needed more drinks to numb the feeling. I needed alcohol running in my blood to dull the pain. But fate was twisted, and Kendra brought the beers. She was the darkness that was tearing me apart, but she brought the poison that made it feel better. She was somewhat of a contradiction. I wanted her to leave but I needed her to stay. She was just like Rosie in a way. She was right there in front of me, but I couldn't have her. She wasn't mine. Just like Rosie was no longer mine. She belonged to someone else. Something else. An entire entity separate from myself. She was no longer tangible. She no longer lingered in my senses. And then it began to hit me. No matter how many times I stared at her photo under my pillow, no matter how many times I replayed the sound of her laughter in my head, no matter how many times I placed her sweater near my nose and inhaled her sweet aroma, no matter how many times I screamed her name at night, I would soon forget her. I was starting to forget how her lip curled up when she smiled. I was starting to forget which spot on her neck was so sensitive that by blowing on it, I could send little tiny bumps all over her body. I was starting to forget the softness of her skin. I was starting to forget her. She was slowly slipping through my fingers. And it seemed that the tighter I held on, the faster she'd go. Every single moment of every single day, she was slipping away, and I would eventually lose her once and for all. I didn't know how I would live my life without her. I just couldn't do it.

Suddenly, my voice interrupted my thoughts. "I can't live without her, Cam," I blurted out. I knew it was the alcohol talking, but it spoke the damned truth. The alcohol was saying all the words I've been dying to speak.

Cam was caught off guard by the bluntness of my statement. He shifted uncomfortably in his seat and cleared his throat. "What? Who?" He asked.

He was playing dumb, which angered me. "Are you fucking kidding me?"

Cam looked down, embarrassed. "Sorry, man. I know you miss her."

I laughed out loud when he said that. "Miss her?" I repeated. "Cam, I missed her when I drove away alone after dropping her home at night. I missed her when I was at work and she was at school. I missed her on the weekends when she was at work. I missed her when I woke up in the middle of the night and she wasn't lying next to me. I don't miss her now, Cam. The fucking feelings I have now are nothing compared to missing her. There was sweetness when I missed her because I knew I'd be seeing her again. I am not going to see her again, Cam. Is that fucking hard to understand? I'm tortured every day—not because I miss her, but because I'm dying without her." My voice cracked and tears blurred my vision.

Cam couldn't look me in the eye. He looked down at his hands as he twiddled his thumbs.

"Great, Cam, just fucking great. You get me drunk, you get me talking, and all of a sudden you're mute. This isn't a fun game to play. I was doing well, you know. I was getting on with my days just fine."

"That's bullshit, Ethan. You think I don't see through that? You think we all don't notice how depressed you are?"

"We all?" I repeated.

"Yes, Ethan. All of us. They guys at work, your brother, your parents. You haven't even touched your guitar in three months. We're all worried about you, Ethan." Cam looked at me sympathetically.

Just then, I realized we were talking a little loud, so I lowered my voice. "I'm not the one you should be worried about, Cam. Rosie is out there with some stranger—if she isn't already dead. We all should be worried about her. Not me."

"Don't be ridiculous," Cam said with frustration in his voice. "You don't have to accuse us of not worrying about Rosie. Of course we all worry about her. But Rosie is out of our hands. And because you're my friend and I have access to you, I think I am morally obligated to make sure you don't drive yourself off a fucking cliff. Don't peg me as the bad guy, Ethan. There is no harm in trying to help someone."

"No harm for who, Cam? For you? Or for me? Because this isn't the kind of tea party I was looking forward to. I wanted to drink so I could forget. Forget about everything for a couple of hours. Forget about her. You don't know what I'm going through, Cam. You have no idea."

"No, of course not," he said sarcastically. "I may never have loved a woman. But you're forgetting one huge detail, Ethan. I lost my baby sister. Remember her? Leah? Does her name ring any bells? Because I remember the day she died in a car accident. I remember that day really well. And I know exactly how it feels to have my heart ripped out of my chest. And it sucks. It hurts, a lot. And I know what it feels like to not just miss someone but go crazy without them. I know how it feels." The frustration escaped his voice at this point. "But you gotta talk to someone about it, Ethan. It's almost been three months and you haven't said a single word to anyone. Not even me."

I tried my best to stop my tears from falling. They fell onto my lips and I tasted the saltiness of my pain. I brought my hands to my face and wiped it dry. I took a deep breath. "How can I talk, Cam? Rosie was the person I talked to all the time. How can I talk? I can't even get comfort out of my own home because the house I live in is not my escape. The people I live with are not my escape. When things got tough, I went to her. She was my escape. She was my home." My lips were quivering as I was talking, and I suddenly became self-conscious. I was a grown man crying in a public place, in front of my best friend. But when I looked Cam in the eye, I saw that his eyes were glistening, and suddenly my insecurities disappeared. "I don't have a home anymore. She was my whole life. I have nothing, Cam. Absolutely nothing. Don't get upset or offended when I don't talk to you. There is nothing for me to say." I stood up and grabbed my coat. I threw some cash on the table to help pay for the beers. I turned around and walked away. I left him waiting in the bar struggling to carry the heavy words that I had spoken.

I heard him call my name a few times as I left the bar. I drowned out the noise. That's all it was now, just noise. My name didn't mean anything anymore. I didn't jolt when I heard it. It didn't faze me. I was nothing. The only way I'd ever feel anything again when I heard my name would be if her angelic voice were speaking it. And I did hear a voice; every single night, I heard the voice say my name. It was always reassuring when I heard it, so I believed it was hers. She said my name in a way that made me believe everything was going to be okay. "It's okay, Ethan. I love you," she'd say as I slowly drifted off into sleep. Her voice was my lullaby. As my name danced off her lips, I would close my eyes and lie in peace with a small smile across my face. Her voice sang me to sleep. "Everything is going to be fine. Ethan . . . Ethan . . . Ethan."

I tried to take my car, but I was so drunk, I couldn't get the key into the ignition. Frustrated, I got out and decided to walk home. I wasn't okay to drive. I probably would have ended up killing myself in an accident. It was cold outside and snow fell as I walked home to an empty house. As I stumbled into my cold bedroom, I knocked Rosie's picture off of my dresser. I watched it fall and the frame shatter. I fell to my knees and broke down from all the day's pressures resting on my shoulders. I held onto her broken photo for dear life, begging her to come back. The alcohol burned, running through my blood. I finally got into bed and tried to fall asleep, whispering her name. I spent that whole night waiting for a response. Waiting for an answer. Waiting for my lullaby. She didn't show up. It was the first night since her disappearance that I couldn't hear her voice. And I knew then that I would never hear it again. After 11 weeks, it had finally happened.

I looked at my lonely guitar now nesting a family of spiders. Dusty and neglected, I imagined myself strumming that thing again and singing my own pathetic lullaby.

I stand alone in this darkened town;
The streets are bare and no one's around.
My devoted heart knows the truth,
But my desperate eyes still search for you.

I had completely forgotten her. I would never have her back.
I should have taken the car.

CHAPTER TWO

ANXIETY

My heart pounded loudly in my head. Its regular rhythm gradually increased in speed. The pain started to become evident. I was in a state halfway between my nightmare and my dream. I kept my eyes closed, afraid of waking up to reality. My dreams were usually pleasant, and I enjoyed the time that I dreamt. My dreams were painless and carefree. But as soon as my dry eyes opened and saw the real world, everything came crashing down in front of me. My reality was not what I had expected. My life was not what I had dreamed.

I opened my eyes in a panic, quickly checking the time on my cell phone. I thought I was late for work—until I clued in that it was Saturday morning. After my nerves relaxed, I slowly sat up in bed and rubbed my eyes. I had a sudden head rush; it felt as if my brain were trying to escape my skull. Of course it wanted to leave. Just like my heart spent its time trying so desperately to rip through my rib cage and taste freedom. Unfortunately, my organs wouldn't betray me like that, though I often wished they would. I rubbed my temples, trying to massage out the pain. After concluding my fingers were not the cure to this godawful hangover, I got out of bed, walked out of my room and walked to the washroom.

My washroom was severely outdated and equipped with a blue toilet and sink. The vanity doors were squeaky and the hinges needed some grease. My mother had asked me to fix them many times, but I had never gotten around to it. I grabbed a bottle of Aspirin and popped two pills. I chased them down with a glass of water. I saw my reflection in the mirror, and I was suddenly appalled by the image staring back at me. My hair was overgrown and messy. Of course, I had just woken up, but I looked like this daily. I needed to shave because my five o'clock shadow was long enough to shade a flock of birds. My dark eyes were swollen, my skin was dull and my face was drained. I suddenly looked ten years older than I was. I stared at myself in disgust. How had I let myself become like this? I always used to take care of myself. Rosie definitely wouldn't approve. Rosie would want me to be happy. She wouldn't have understood. She wouldn't have realized how impossible it was for me to be even a little happy without her. It wasn't something I could do. I splashed some water on my face, sparing me from another argument with myself. Every day was a constant battle, and no matter how many times I fought with my thoughts, I still lost. I grabbed some Colgate and my toothbrush and brushed my teeth. I started to feel a bit better.

I was about to take off my clothes and step into the shower until I heard a knock on my door. *Unusual*, I thought. *Three bathrooms in the house and all of them are occupied?* I rolled my eyes and slowly opened the door only to see my mother standing there, phone in her hand, tears in her eyes. My heart stopped. *This is it.* I was either about to receive the best news of my life, or the worst. But I couldn't tell from my mother's green, watery eyes. Until a faint smile moved across her face and three simple words escaped her mouth: "They found her."

It's weird how fast life can turn around. One moment, you can speak as many words as you want. The next moment, it seems impossible to find words. Impossible to express what you feel. Words are suddenly not something you own or maintain or control. It's like you've spent your whole life soaring through the sky, then all of a sudden, evil cuts off your wings and you are no longer able to fly. You plummet to the earth, expecting to die. With a snap of a finger, circumstances can change for the worse or the better. You've spent your life running through trails like the Road Runner from Saturday morning cartoons. All of a sudden, you're brought to a halt; there's a fork in the road and you don't know which way to turn. And when you finally make a decision—you want to go right—you can't move your feet. Paralyzed, you remain in the same spot. There's nothing you can do. Everything you've been taught since you were an infant suddenly escapes you. You can't talk, you can't breathe, you can't walk, you can't even move. You're trapped in a moment in time. Unable to react. For some people, it doesn't last long; for others, it can last forever. The news about Rosie's return took a long time to sink in. My mother at the washroom door didn't faze me, I still didn't believe it on the way to the hospital with my parents, it still didn't hit me when I saw her family in the waiting room, I still didn't believe it when the cops showed up. I had no idea what I was doing. I had no idea what I should expect. I had no idea what had happened. I just sat there in the hospital, extremely hungover, waiting. Waiting for something. Waiting for anything. What would happen when I saw her? What would she look like? Was she okay? Was she happy? What had happened to the man who took her? Had he hurt her? Of course he had, but billions of questions ran through my mind as I sat there and waited. Waited for what? What in the world was I waiting for? I was scared. Holy fuck, was I ever scared. I'd never thought this day would come. I thought she had died, for Christ's sake! I hadn't heard her voice last night. I had thought she was gone. But she wasn't; she was here. The only thing that separated us was a door. A goddamned fucking door. What would I say when I saw her? Would I hug and kiss her? Should I hug or kiss her? Or should I give her space? *I don't want to make her uncomfortable,* I thought. *But she won't be uncomfortable around me—she loves me.* She still did, right? What if she didn't love me anymore? What if she didn't even know who I was? *Maybe she has severe memory loss and doesn't remember me?* I thought. What if she did remember me? What if she blamed me for not fixing her car? What if she hated me? What if her parents found out that I hadn't fixed her car and they blamed me too?

I guess it was obvious that I was panicking, because Rosie's dad, Phil, patted me on the back, interrupting my thoughts. "You okay there, Ethan?" he asked. He took a seat next to me.

I noticed I was sweating profusely through my shirt.

"You're pale. Do you want some water?"

I shook my head. "Thanks, anyway," was the only thing I could mutter.

Why wasn't he freaking out like I was? His daughter was in that room and he didn't know what to expect either. *Is everyone calm except for me?* I started to freak out again, so I took a deep breath and closed my eyes.

I don't know how much time had passed, but I was awoken from my sleep or daydream by Phil. He looked like he had just been crying as he held his wife by the waist. Phil and Anne were really good parents to Rosie. Phil was tall and slender. He owned his own successful landscaping business. He made a decent amount of money, enough to put Rosie through school. Rosie's mom, Anne, was smaller like Rosie. She had dark hair and dark eyes like Rosie did. Anne worked as a tutor at a recreational centre for underprivileged kids. She didn't make a lot of money, but she and Phil were both smart people and never struggled for anything. Phil nodded his head and I knew it was time for me to go in. *Oh no, can I do this?* I slowly stood up, trying to find my balance on wobbly knees. My hands were shaking. I took a deep breath. I walked up to the door, placed my hand on the cold doorknob and turned it.

She looked different, a lot different. She had lost a lot of weight. Her face was sunken in. She looked pale and ill. She had old, faded scars across her face and arms. Her body was covered with old bruises and some fresh ones. Her hair was matted and had lost its lustre. Her eyes were swollen. Her lips were swollen. Holy shit. An immediate rush of anger and sadness hit me like a freight train. I didn't have a clue how it was possible that I remained steady on my own two feet. It was hard to keep standing when everything behind me was falling apart. A river of tears started falling from my eyes but I brought my hand to my mouth so she wouldn't hear me cry. Our eyes made contact. Something deep inside me itched to touch her. My skin wanted to taste her skin. But her eyes were different, cold and empty. She seemed distant, removed from this room. Not a part of this life. Fighting back temptation, I kept my hand at my side, forcing myself not to touch her. She was so different. I had no feedback from her; I had no idea what she wanted. She didn't look at me. She stared ahead, watching the wall. Her eyes watered and she blinked away tears. She slowly brought her hand up to wipe her face. I watched as a tear fell onto her lips. Oh, how I missed them. I needed so badly to kiss her. I wanted to make her feel better. But there was nothing there, no *Hello*, no *I miss you*, no *I love you*, no smile. Nothing. What did I expect to happen? Had I believed she would jump for joy as soon as she saw my face? Had I actually believed that or just hoped it? Had my hopes and dreams disrupted my vision of reality? I had wanted her so badly. I had wanted Rosie to come back in one piece, unharmed and untouched. I wanted it to go back to the way it was. How had I expected it to be any way but this?

She pursed her lips together, and hesitantly, she asked me to leave.

Was it selfish for me to be angry? Was it wrong for me to be mad? Because I was. It was so quiet in the room I heard my heart break. It was as if I had embraced her soul and sharp thorns tore right through my heart. I heard the blood flow through the crack of my beating heart. I felt the blood pour through and I thought it was going to leak through my skin. I thought I would bleed to death and die right there on that floor. Unfortunately, I was not that lucky. I nodded my head, fighting back tears. I picked up what was left of myself and walked out of that room. Walked away from her. Walked away from everything.

If I could only imagine what she was feeling. If only.

There were so many questions I wanted to ask. I'd been in the dark about the entire situation for eleven weeks. I didn't know what had happened at all. Where was her abductor? What had happened to Rosie? She was obviously hurt—maybe she had even been tortured. I suddenly wanted to know everything. Rosie needed to stay in the hospital overnight for observation, so the nurse requested we leave so she'd have time to rest. My parents and I waited a long time while Phil and Anne spent over an hour talking to the investigating officer. What was he saying? What were they talking about? I nervously shook my leg and chewed my fingernails until I saw Phil shake the officer's hand. The officer walked away and Phil and Anne turned towards us. They both came over and greeted us. "She's been through a lot," Phil said, trying to break the silence.

I heard my mother clear her throat. "We're all really upset about the situation," she said. She stood up and my father did the same. "We're going to head home." She looked at me as if to ask whether I was going to join her and my father or stay at the hospital.

I looked at Phil and he nodded. I was going to stay.

"All right then, have a good night." My mother hugged Anne and Phil and my father did the same.

I watched my parents walk away.

"Anne, darling," Phil said. "Will you take my wallet and grab us some sandwiches and coffee? It's already almost four o'clock and none of us have eaten."

Anne nodded and took his wallet. She walked out of the waiting room towards the deli shop. I watched her walk away. That was all I could do, all I could manage. Just watch.

"I would completely understand if you left Rosie," Phil said, breaking the silence. I was shocked by his honesty. I shook my head at the thought. "What are you talking about?" I asked as politely as I could.

"Look," Phil said, placing his hand on my shoulder. I pulled away from his touch. Phil noticed my reaction and changed his approach. No sugarcoating from here on out. "She's been through hell, Ethan. The police officer only shared the facts; none of us know what actually happened to her. We don't know the true details. You're a nice kid, but I think it would be best for the both of you if you just forgot about everything. Pretend nothing ever happened between you two. She can't overcome this in a healthy way while she is romantically involved with you."

I was angry. I was upset. I was hurt. How could he just ask me to walk away? After everything Rosie and I had been through, he just wanted me to forget it all? Rosie was my whole life. And I was hers. We had our future planned out, we had ideas and memories. We had love. "I can't do that," I said, choking on my tears. "You can't ask me to do that. I can't do that."

Phil looked down and ran his hands through his salt-and-pepper hair. "Listen, Ethan," he said.

"No! You listen to me!" I interrupted. "Rosie is the best thing that ever happened in my life! I will not give up on her or on us. I love her, Phil. You should know what that means. You have a great wife. Put yourself in my shoes and imagine if this happened to the person you love. Don't ask me to walk away from this."

"It did happen to a person I love: my daughter. I know what is best for her. And you are not what she needs right now."

I was no longer able to handle the conversation. I needed to get out of there. I needed to get out of his face. "Maybe that is what you

17

believe. But if Rosie wants me out of her life, let her tell me that. Until then, I will be by her side every single day until she wants me to leave. This isn't up to you." I said. I stood up and walked away just as Anne walked in with a few sandwiches.

"Ethan? Where are you going?" she asked.

"Home," I said.

The look she gave Phil showed me that she and Phil had already spoken about me. And the look she gave me showed that she agreed with him and wanted me out of Rosie's life.

When I got home, I couldn't eat or think. My world was spinning behind me and I was losing all control. I quickly went to my room and slammed the door. I sat on my bed, put my head in my hands and just let it all go. All the tears, all the worries, all the anger—everything that had built up inside for the past three months—finally poured out of my eyes and into my hands. I watched a river of pain slip through my fingers and onto my floor. It felt good to cry. It was a release. One like no other.

Just then, I heard a knock on the door. "Honey, are you all right?" I heard my mother ask from behind the closed door.

What a stupid question. Was I all right? Of course I was not all right. My whole life was ruined. All my hopes and dreams were shattered. The love of my life was lying in a hospital bed, probably contemplating whether or not she ever wanted to see me again.

My mother came into my bedroom. She saw me crying and took a seat next to me. She put her hand on my knee and said, "I know it's hard, honey. But it's going to get better. She's alive—we know that, right? She just needs time to settle. She's been through a hell of a lot."

I didn't respond. It was not that I didn't want to; I didn't know what to say. What was I supposed to say?

"Talk to me," she said. "Tell me what's on your mind."

I looked into my mother's eyes and told her the truth. "It's my fault this happened."

My mother was taken aback by my statement and looked at me in shock. "What do you mean? How was it your fault? You didn't do anything wrong."

I interrupted her. "You're wrong, mom." She looked at me in utter confusion. "Do you know how guilty I feel, every single day of my life?" I started to cry again.

A mother's automatic response was to cry as well. "What did you do, Ethan?" she asked as her eyes begged for an answer.

"I was supposed to fix her car." I said. "There was something wrong with her car and I was supposed to fix it. I told her not to go to a mechanic so she wouldn't waste her money. But I didn't fix it. Her car didn't start that night because I didn't fix it!"

My mother let out a laugh of relief. She quickly covered her mouth, hoping that I wouldn't realize she was laughing, but I noticed her eyes, and they were smiling.

Without a word, I stood up and headed for the door.

"Ethan, wait," she begged. I stopped. "I didn't mean to laugh. But this is absolutely not your fault. That nasty man kidnapped her and did this to her. You didn't."

I faced my mother. "I wish it were that simple, mom. I really do." I turned back around, grabbed my keys and headed for the front door. I walked downstairs and passed my dad in the kitchen. He called my name, but I ignored him. *They don't know how guilty I feel,* I thought. *They will never know how hard it is knowing every day that your actions directly ruined the life of the only person you've ever loved.* They would never understand how hard it was to live with the guilt that I possessed.

Noticing that my car wasn't in the driveway, I remembered last night and Cam. I looked at my cell phone and saw that I had six missed calls and eight text messages from him.

Did u get home ok last night?
Dude u ok?
Call me pls.
Ethan!
I just saw the news! R is ok??
CALL ME ASAP
HELLLLOOOOO
Im going to kick ur fucking ass whenever I see u.

I couldn't help but smile when I read the last one. I really didn't feel like talking to him, so I just texted him back. *Im fine.* Message sent. I put my phone in my pocket and started to walk to Sport's Kitchen. I felt my phone vibrate in my pocket. I pulled it out and saw it was a text from Cam.

Where r u??
Walking to the bar. 4got my car.
WTF man! call me
Don't feel like it
Where's R?
Hospital
Is she ok??
I guess
U guess?
I guess.
Fuck u.
U too.
I'll meet u at ur car.

I didn't respond to his last message. Knowing that he would otherwise get there before I did, I picked up the pace. I cut through lawns, went through an alley, and for the last two minutes, I decided to jog. It was cold out and my lungs started to burn. When I turned onto the street, I saw Cam leaning against my car. Too late.

He noticed me right away and started to approach. I had lost the battle. "What the hell is wrong with you?" Cam asked as he walked up to me.

I walked past him and continued to my car.

He walked behind me. "Ethan, why won't you say anything?"

I stopped suddenly and turned to face him. "What do you want me to say?" I yelled.

"Anything!" he yelled back. "Where is Rosie?"

"I already told you, Cam. She's at the hospital. She is with her parents. She's fine." I unlocked my car and got in. Stubborn ol' Cam got in the passenger side. *Of course*, I thought. "What are you doing?" I asked.

"Let's drive," he demanded. "I've got all night, and I've got all day tomorrow. Let's just get out of here. I'm not leaving until you start talking. Let me know what's going on with you." One thing about Cam was that he was very persuasive. I did as I was told and we were off. Off to somewhere, going nowhere.

After maybe about twenty minutes of silence, I decided to speak. "They want me to leave."

"Who does?"

"Her parents."

"Why?"

"I don't know. They don't think it's a good idea we carry on a relationship."

"Because of what happened to her?"

"Yeah," I said. "They don't think she can heal properly. They think she needs alone time to forget about everything. To get over everything."

"Maybe they're right."

"What?" I asked. "You can't possibly be on their side."

Cam sighed. "Ethan, it's not about taking sides here. When it comes down to it, all that matters is Rosie."

"But how do they know what's right for her?" I asked.

"They don't."

I stared at him with a confused look on my face.

"Only she knows what is best for her," he finally said.

I let out a sigh of relief. "So that means what?" I asked. "What do I do?"

"You gotta be there for her, man. Show her that you care and that you're not going anywhere. Remind her every day that you love her. Until she tells you she wants you to leave. Then I guess you'll have to leave."

Suddenly remembering what had happened earlier today, I confessed what she said. "She already asked me to leave. Does that mean she doesn't love me anymore? That she already wants me out of her life?"

"Maybe," he said. "But try looking at this from her point of view. Put yourself in her shoes. Maybe she loves you so much that she doesn't want to put you through all of this. What if she doesn't want you to see her in pain? Maybe it hurts her to know that you're suffering too. I'm sure if she could, she'd ask her parents to leave. Unfortunately, she depends on them. You can be sent away. She can save you from all of this. Remember, Ethan, you don't know what happened to her. Maybe she knows that she's eventually going to have to tell you everything that happened with that man. And maybe she doesn't want to go there now. Maybe she doesn't want to revisit that nightmare."

I didn't respond. He read my hopeless expression.

"You know what I would do if I were you?"

"What?" I asked.

"I just wouldn't give up. I'd be by her side through it all, no matter what. She is going to try to push you away. She will with all her might. You just gotta hang in there. You'll only prove to her that you love her. And no one can fight love. As much as she tries, just remember that love will always be there. Even when the people in love are lost."

I considered Cam's words. Was he right? Did Rosie just need time? Regardless of what anyone else said, I knew for sure that I was going to stand by her side, no matter what. I wasn't sure, though, if she needed me or if it was just that I needed her. I definitely needed her. I knew I couldn't live my life without her. But did she feel the same way? I hoped to God that she did, because I wouldn't be able to live with myself if she were able to live without me. I shook my head at the thought.

When I got home that night, my stomach was burning with hunger. I hadn't eaten all day. And, to my surprise, my brother's car was on the driveway. He must have heard about Rosie and decided to pay a visit. I walked through the front door and into the kitchen where my parents and brother were just about to have dinner. I quietly took a seat, showing no interest in talking to anyone. I started to fill my plate up with salad when my brother greeted me.

"Hey Brad, nice to see you," I said. I noticed he was about to say something, but changed his mind. I decided to stay quiet. My mother gave me a don't-be-like-that look, so I started some small talk. "How school?" I asked as I placed some chicken breasts on my plate. I was starving.

"It's good," he said. "I just started my reading week."

"Really? It's not even three weeks until Christmas," I said.

"I know. That's just how it worked out."

My brother and I were very different. My brother had always had the brains; he studied, did well in school and was always the good one. I, on the other hand, had hated school. I hated going to class, I hated doing my homework and I hated studying. My brother graduated high school at the top of his class, whereas I had barely gotten by. So eventually, our lives took different directions. He went off to college and I went straight to work. Ever since then, we hadn't been as close. Sure, I still loved the guy—he was my baby brother and we always got along—but life changes sometimes. And people begin to drift away and start creating their own paths. My brother had been on his own path for a long time, and he was happy about it. And I was happy for him.

"Rosie's parents called," my dad said, breaking the silence. "They want to talk to you."

"Pass the mashed potatoes, please, mom," I said, ignoring what my dad had said. She looked at my father and passed me the mashed potatoes anyway.

"Are you upset with me or something, Ethan?" my father asked.

"No, I'm not. I just don't want to talk about them right now." I said.

"Did something happen?" my mother asked.

I ignored her question.

"Ethan," my father said. "Your mother asked you a question."

I rolled my eyes. "Can we just drop it? Please!" I begged. "I don't want to talk about them or the situation or Rosie. Just leave it alone!"

Suddenly losing my appetite, I got up quickly and walked upstairs to my bedroom. Quietly closing the door behind me, I let out a sigh of relief. I shut off the light, got into bed and tried to get some sleep. Under usual circumstances, my father wouldn't have let me get away with that kind of behaviour, but because of the particular situation, I knew I wouldn't be disturbed.

I woke up the next morning to a knock on my bedroom door. I looked at my cell phone to check the time. It was 7:30 in the morning. I groaned. "What?" I yelled to the person at the door.

"It's Brad," he said from behind the door. "You're not naked, right? Is it safe to come in?"

"Uh huh."

Brad opened the door. He was already showered and dressed. I still wanted to sleep. Was he crazy? "What do you want?" I asked, as I got up and put on a pair of pants.

"Just wondering if you wanted to go to Betty's Diner for breakfast?" he asked. "Like old times?" I didn't really want to go out, but a big greasy breakfast sounded amazing. I put on an old sweater and we left.

The smell of fried bacon, eggs and hash browns brought back old memories. The cushiony pleather seats were coloured a vibrant yellow and the diner was bright. The big windows allowed natural sunlight to come through and create a warm atmosphere. It wasn't too crowded that day, but there were enough people to make a dull roar of conversation. Brad and I used to go there every Sunday morning for some artery-clogging meals. The coffee was cheap, but it was the best coffee I'd ever had in my life. Brad and I took a seat in a booth next to a window. The waitresses were great and fast. Our coffee cups were filled only a minute after we sat down. The waitress asked for our order. I always got the same thing every time we went there. "Bacon, eggs, sausage and hash browns, please." I said. The waitress wrote down my order in her notepad and nodded. She looked at Brad and he told her he'd have the same.

"So how have you been?" Brad asked as he put some sugar in his coffee.

"Good," I said. "How's school?"

"It's good. I'm done this year, you know."

"Yes, I do know. That's exciting. Any internships lined up?"

"I have a few. I still don't know what I want to do yet. There is one company, RTG Incorporated, that I'm really interested in."

"Yeah?" I asked. "How come?"

Just then, the waitress came with our meals. My stomach was dancing with joy. I was starving. Brad took a bite out of his bacon. "They have better opportunities for me to move up in the company than the other places," he said with his mouth full. "And they have better benefits. And I'd be able to choose my own hours once I became permanent."

"Nice," I said, wolfing down a mouthful of hash browns. "What would you do there?"

"I'd be responsible for the plans. I'd plan where all the hydro poles would be placed. And they are also working on a new design. I think they want to reconstruct all the hydro wires and poles. It will create a lot of jobs and, according to the research, more efficient energy will be used."

"Interesting," I said, completely disconnected from the conversation. I was so hungry I had already almost finished my meal.

"And eventually, I'd be in charge of the team of designers. I'd make a hell of a lot of money."

I smiled. "I got another raise." I said.

"Great!" he said. "That's awesome."

"Yeah," I said. The conversation got quiet. The waitress came back and filled our cups. When she left, Brad said, "I need to tell you something."

"Yeah," I said. "Sure, go ahead."

"You know Rosie's parents called while you were out yesterday. I wasn't there yet, but they told mom and dad what happened. They told me and they wanted me to tell you. They said they thought it would be better if I told you."

Feeling hurt and betrayed, I said "Why the hell did they involve you anyway? You're never here. You're never around. Quite frankly, this is none of your business!" I stood up and picked up my coat.

Before I had a chance to leave, Brad said, "Don't punish me for getting an education, because that is not fair. Now please, sit down."

He was right. I had no reason or right to say that. It wasn't his fault that his school was quite a distance from our home. And he did come back home for every special occasion and when he was off in the summer.

What was I thinking? I sat down. "Sorry," I said. "I've just been going fucking nuts lately. I'm going insane."

"It's okay. I completely understand," He said. "How should I do this?"

Panicked, I asked the first thing that came to mind. "Was she raped?" I shut my eyes and prayed that he would say no. I hoped that he would laugh and tell me I was crazy. I begged and pleaded, I asked God to send a message to Brad. A message that said no, no one touched her that way. I held my breath.

"Yes," he said. "She was raped." I could tell by the look on his face that it pained him to answer that question. Trying my best to cope with the answer, I moved along with my next question. "Where is he now?" I asked.

"Rotting in hell, I hope," he said. "He's dead."

I liked the answer to that question. I was glad he was dead. I really was.

"How?" I asked.

"He was shot in the head."

"The cops?"

Brad shook his head. If not the cops, then who would have shot him? Who would have killed him? And suddenly it hit me. Rosie? My Rosie shot him? *It isn't possible,* I thought.

Brad read my expression and simply nodded his head.

Rosie killed him. Holy fuck. A wave of emotions crashed through me. I was shocked, of course. But I was proud. She killed the man who tortured her. It sounded terrible, but I was happy that she had.

"It was self-defence. He was attacking her and she got a hold of his gun and shot him. She thought he was actually going to kill her that day. She noticed that he was stalking a few other girls over the web, and she thought he'd gotten sick of her and found someone else. That's what she told the cops, anyway."

"Holy shit," I said. I ran my hands through my hair. Nervously, I chugged my coffee. I got up and grabbed my coat and keys.

"Where are you going?" Brad asked, grabbing his coat as well.

"I have to see her. I gotta go see Rosie."

We left the diner. I needed to see her. I had a sickening feeling that what Brad had told me was just the gist of the situation. I knew Rosie had a lot more to tell me. A whole lot more.

CHAPTER THREE

LAUGHTER

After driving Brad home, I took the quickest route to the hospital. I had no idea if she would still be there, but I thought it was worth a shot. I had not yet wrapped my mind around the severity of the situation. I was in a state of shock. I still couldn't believe that Rosie had killed him. I still couldn't believe Rosie had been raped. The thought of her being taken advantage of angered me. *Who thinks they have the right to do that to anyone?* I thought. I started to get really angry, so I turned up the radio in attempt to tune out my thoughts.

Rosie and I met the summer after she graduated high school. She had gone to the same school as Brad but she was a year older. One night, Brad really wanted to go to a party. The only way my parents would let him go was if I went with him, but I didn't want to spend Saturday night partying with a bunch of teenagers. My brother begged me to take him and promised that I didn't even have to go to the party; all I had to do was drop him off, go somewhere else and then pick him up when he called me. I said no at first, but the look he gave me broke my heart. Besides, when I was in high school, I was a lot worse than him. I went to parties every weekend. I drank a lot of booze and smoked a lot of weed. Who was I to deny my younger brother a little fun? So I decided to suck it up and drive him to the stupid party. We arrived at a mansion with drunken kids hanging out on the driveway and the front lawn. The look on Brad's face was priceless. His eyes lit up as I pulled up by the sidewalk. He quickly got out of the car and shouted a rushed thank you. He was out of my sight in seconds. I sat in the car and pulled out my phone and sent him a text message. *Call me when ur rdy to go. And don't get 2 drunk or I'll kick ur butt.*

As soon as I had pressed send, a girl opened the car door, got inside and said, "Just take me home."

I blinked and stared at her in confusion.

She looked at me and her face went completely red. "Oh my God! I am so sorry!" She grabbed her purse and started to leave. "I thought you were my mom. She said she was picking me up. I am sorry. You guys have the exact same car."

"Don't worry about it." I laughed as she opened the door. "Happens to me all the time. You're probably the fifth person who has done it tonight."

She turned back to face me and laughed. I noticed she had a dimple. I was fascinated. "You don't need to lie to me," she said. "I know I'm an idiot."

I smiled and told her not to worry about it and wished her a good night. She sat there for a while staring at me. She looked down and bit her lip and quietly asked me if I wanted to go for a walk. It was an unexpected question. She was obviously a very confident person to ask a complete stranger to hang out.

"It's only 10:30 and I didn't want to go home just yet," she explained. "But I just can't handle this party."

I sat there for a while. What did I have to lose? There was no danger for me. The situation was more risky for her. I shrugged my shoulders, took my keys out of the ignition and said, "Let's walk." She pulled out her phone and sent a message to her mother letting her know that she was staying.

We walked down the sidewalk and admired all the beautiful houses on the street. She was shorter than me, about five feet two inches. She had long, dark brown hair and dark brown eyes. She wore a white summer dress with knee-high cowboy boots. She had a cute bounce in her step and she walked very quickly.

"So," she said, stepping in front of me and walking backwards, "I'm Rosie. Rosie Lutine." She stuck out her hand and I shook it.

"I'm Ethan Hobbs."

"What brings you here, Ethan Hobbs?" She turned back around and returned to my side.

"My brother was dying to go to this party," I said. "My parents didn't want him to go without me, so I'm pretending to go. I dropped him off."

"Oh, who's your brother?" she asked.

"Brad. Brad Hobbs."

She smiled. "I know him. He's a year younger than me."

"You do?" I asked. "Why hasn't he ever mentioned knowing such a pretty young lady such as yourself?"

She smiled at my comment. I saw her cheeks flush red and she looked down at her feet.

"You know, this is the second time you've blushed in front of me. What's up with that?" I joked.

"I'm blushing again?" She panicked, bringing her hands up to her cheeks. "Sorry, I have a disorder."

"A disorder?" I asked, raising an eyebrow. "What kind of disorder?"

"A disorder that makes me blush. The doctor said it's serious and life-threatening. If I blush too much, I may just die."

"Wow, that's some serious stuff."

"It really is. So you can't make me blush," she said. "You wouldn't want to be responsible for my suffering or even my death, would you?"

Never, I thought.

Her phone started to ring. As she pulled it out of her purse, I saw the name on the screen: Liam. She looked up at me.

"You can take it." I said.

"No," she said. "It's okay. Nothing important." She ignored the call and put her phone back in her purse. "Anyway,"—she looked around as if to find something to say and looked down at my feet—"I like your shoes."

I looked down at my own feet, not remembering what my shoes looked like. I looked back up and laughed. "Thanks."

Her phone started to ring again and she fumbled to get it out of her purse. It was Liam again. "Sorry, I'm gonna take this one." She stopped walking. I stopped too. It suddenly occurred to me that perhaps she didn't want me too close as she spoke to this Liam person, so I started walking around. She noticed and held up her finger, signalling for me not to move. She answered the phone. "What do you want?" she snapped. "Yes, I did leave . . . No, I am not coming back . . . Because you're an asshole . . . You're drunk . . . Shut up! . . . I saw you dancing with her . . . Yes, but you told me you would never talk to her again . . . It doesn't matter . . . Okay, I'm hanging up now . . . Bye, Liam . . . No . . . Bye." She put the phone back into her purse and rolled her eyes. We started to walk again. "Sorry about that. My boyfriend is an asshole."

I was disappointed to find out that she had a boyfriend. I had kind of had a feeling that she was interested in me. "Boyfriend?" I asked.

She must have noticed my facial expression because she laughed. "Yes . . . No. Well, sort of."

I looked at her, puzzled.

She let out a sigh. "He's an asshole," she said. "A very big asshole. He treats me like crap. He probably cheats on me all the time. He is a spoiled brat with a big trust fund." She looked up at me and the sadness in her eyes caught my attention. "The party is at his house," she confessed. "I saw him dancing with his ex-girlfriend, so I left."

"Oh," I said. "Want me to kick his ass?" I joked.

She let out a loud laugh. It was a refreshing sound. It was sort of musical; the kind of music you listen to when you need your day to brighten up. The kind of music that gives you hope and dreams. Dreams for a better world. I liked the sound of her laugh. "That would be really, really nice," she said. "But he's not worth it."

"So why is he worth your time when he's not worth mine?" I asked.

I heard her breath catch in her throat. I could tell by the look in her eyes that she was searching for an answer. She shrugged her shoulders and said, "Sorry, bud, I don't even know the answer to that question."

"Do you know why he treats you like crap?" I asked.

"Probably because I don't sleep with him," she confessed. "He can get it from any other girl, so he chooses to go after them."

I let out a little laugh. "Typical," I muttered.

"What's typical?" she asked angrily. "I'm a virgin. What's so bad about that?" Her voice started to get louder. "See, it's people like you who mess up society! Guys like you make girls like me suffer and feel bad because we don't want to give ourselves so quickly. And some girls aren't strong enough to stand up against the pressure of society! You're a jerk!"

"Whoa! Whoa! Slow down!" I matched her tone. "I wasn't talking about you! I was talking about him!"

She pursed her lips together and looked down at the ground. I saw her face go red again. "Sorry," she looked up at me. "I thought you were mocking me."

I smiled. "I made you blush again."

"Oh no!" she yelled. She brought her hands to her throat and pretended she was choking. "You're—" She started coughing. "You're killing me!"

"Oh no!" I panicked. I took her hands off her throat while yelling, "I know CPR, I know CPR!"

She started to laugh hysterically.

I started laughing too. "You're cute," I said.

She stopped laughing and looked up at me. Her eyes were glistening. She had such a vibrant personality and some magnetic force was drawing me to her. She smiled and looked down at her feet. I placed my finger gently under her chin and lifted her head up so her eyes could meet mine. "You can do so much better than waiting around for someone who doesn't go crazy every time you smile."

After a moment or two, she said, "What are you trying to say?" She stepped away from me and spun like a ballerina. She stopped and her face met mine. She showed me her silliest grin, and her smile stretched from ear to ear. "Does my smile make you crazy?"

I playfully shoved her and started walking ahead. "No," I joked. "I never said it makes me crazy. I'm just sure some weirdo out there might actually like your smile."

She walked quickly as she tried to catch up to me. "Hey," she said. "Why are you being such a bully?"

I stopped and turned around. "I am *not* a bully!" I said. "And it offends me that you think so."

"Cheer up," she said. "I was just joking. You're not a bully. You're actually quite nice. And cute."

"Cute?" I asked, pretending to be shocked. "I'm not cute. I'm sexy!"

She tilted her head back and let out such an exhilarating laugh. It was a great laugh and suddenly I had a hard time figuring out if it was real or sarcastic. "Wait a minute," I said with a raised eyebrow. "That laugh wasn't real, was it?"

She flirtatiously spun around and her hair grazed my face. The scent of her shampoo made my senses go insane. She grabbed my hands and said, "You'll never know," and then she gently kissed my cheek. If we lived in an animated film, my heart-shaped eyes would have popped out of my head. I barely knew her, but she had such a hold on me. I found myself going crazy for her. She was confident and sure of herself. She was full of life, vibrancy and energy. She was contagious and I found myself wanting to be with her all the time.

The night continued with playfulness, flirting and laughter. I drove her home, wished her good night and ended our date with a kiss on her cheek. She did blush again, but I liked it. I loved it, actually. She saved my number on her phone and she told me she'd call me. She had the upper hand and left me waiting and tortured. And after three weeks I thought the call would never come. But it did. When I had finally given up hope, she called me and told me she was no longer with Liam and that we should hang out again. After three weeks of thinking what I wanted to happen would never come, it did. And it was the best phone call I ever received in my life.

Second-best, actually.

I wanted to hear her laugh again. I would give up many sounds just to hear her. I would trade the sound of spring birds chirping in the early morning. I would give up the sound of the ocean reaching the shore. I could live without the sound of music. I'd give up the sound of fire crackling and burning while you roast marshmallows over it. I would throw away the sound of wind whistling through tall grass. I would give up the sound of rain hitting a tin roof. I would give it all up just to hear her laugh one more time. Because when she laughed, the world and everything around me suddenly turned to dust. When she laughed, it meant that she was happy. When she laughed, I didn't care about anything but swooping her up in my arms and planting a kiss on her soft lips. When she laughed, the world suddenly became something I believed in.

At the hospital, I went to Rosie's room only to find it empty. I quickly found a nurse and asked her where she was. She told me Rosie had left about an hour ago with her parents. I thanked her and ran out of the hospital to the parking lot and got in my car. I drove to her house. When I turned onto her street, I noticed a news van and a small crowd of people on her lawn. The press must have wanted to see her arrival. I found room to park on the street and walked to her house. The news crew were already packing up their equipment and the crowd was dispersing by the time I reached the front porch. I knocked on the front door. I heard footprints and some shuffling, and then finally, the door opened. Phil stood there, surprised to see me. "Ethan," he said, stepping onto the porch and closing the door behind him. "What're you doing here?" he whispered.

"Phil, I need to talk to her," I said. "Please."

Phil frowned. "I don't think she wants any visitors at this time, Ethan."

The way my name slipped off his tongue made the hair on my back rise. "I am not a visitor, Phil." I said. "I'm her boyfriend."

"Listen," Phil began.

"No!" I said, suddenly feeling brave. "I need to see her. I'll wait out here all night until I do. This isn't fair. Let her tell me herself she doesn't want to see me, because I don't want to hear it from you!"

All he could do was blink and clear his throat. "She's, she's," he stuttered. He cleared his throat again and opened the door, letting me into the house. "She's in her room."

"Thanks," I said without missing a beat. I quickly ran upstairs to her bedroom and stopped at the closed door. She never used to keep her bedroom door closed.

I knocked and waited for an answer. I heard a little bit of shuffling behind the door, so I decided to open it slowly.

"Rosie?" I slowly peeked into her room. I saw her sitting on her bed with her back towards me. There was an open box beside her and pictures spread across her bed. She sniffled and wiped her face, then she cleared her throat and told me to come in. I closed the door behind me and walked towards her. Getting a closer look, I saw that all the pictures on her bed were of us. "Holy shit," I said.

She looked up at me with red, swollen eyes. She wiped her face again and sniffled. "Crazy, isn't it?" she asked.

I slowly sat down beside her. There were so many pictures of us. I had no idea she had developed so many.

"What is?" I asked.

"Life," she said.

I nodded. "It is crazy, isn't it?" I smiled and placed my hand gently on hers.

She pulled her hand away and stood up. "Listen," she said. "I don't know anything, okay?" She started pacing back and forth. She ran her hands through her dull, lifeless hair. "I don't know anything."

I stood up and gently held her arms. "It's okay, Rosie," I said. "Calm down."

She pulled herself out of my grip. A pained look came across her face. "Please, Ethan," she said. "Just let me talk to you the best way that I can."

37

I put my hands down and sat back down on her bed. She began to pace again. Her mind seemed jumbled. "I don't know what I'm doing anymore, okay?" she began. "I was really scared living with that man." She sat down beside me. "I was scared every single day. I missed you so much. That man took everything from me. He took my dignity and my security. He even took my happiness," she said as she struggled to choke back her tears. "And I have no idea how to get it back. I know I just got back home and I need time to get over it all, but I have no idea how it will turn out." She started picking up the photographs of us. "Remember this one?" she asked, showing me the picture we took when we went on our first road trip. I had stopped for gas and she stuck her head out of the window and stuck her tongue out at me. She had no idea I had a camera. I had quickly snapped the picture.

I smiled. "Yeah," I said. "I do. You look so cute."

She had a blank expression. She quickly put the photo down and grabbed another. "And this one?" she asked. She showed me the photo of us at her cousin's wedding. It was the first time Rosie had gotten drunk. The photograph was of us dancing the night away. I was dipping her and she had the biggest smile on her face. I could still hear her laughter from that night. "I love that one," I said.

She remained expressionless. She put that photo down and picked up another one. A photo of when we went camping together alone. We were sitting by the fire when I pulled out the camera and took a picture of our faces. The whole time I had thought she was smiling, but when I looked at the photos later on that night, I learned that she had put on a sulky face. Even when she pretended to be sad, she was cute. That was also the night we first made love.

"That was *our* night," I said, knowing that the photograph would spark some reaction. I was hoping for a smile. I desperately searched her bruised face for one, but she didn't even move.

She put down the photo. "These pictures used to make me happy," she said. "When I looked at these pictures, I would laugh or smile and feel something here." She pointed to her heart and started to cry again. "Like this one." She picked up the picture of me with Stitch, her favorite Disney character. The photo was from when we went to Disneyworld together one summer. "I used to love this picture. I used to laugh at this picture. Now, I feel nothing." She put the picture down on the bed. I could feel my heart breaking in my chest. It was pure, raw pain, with no anesthetic or morphine. And I wondered how many times one heart could break before it would die. Because at that moment, that was exactly what it felt like I was about to do: die.

She picked up another picture. It was the two of us holding the litter of puppies that her cousin's dog had had. I held three of them and she held two. I remembered that day very well because she begged her parents to let her have one. They said no, but she was desperate for one. She kept the picture as a reminder that one day we'd have our own family, our own rules and our own dogs. "Puppies!" she yelled. "Who doesn't like puppies?" She began to get hysterical. "Because it sure feels like I don't. This picture does nothing for me! Now it's like these fucking pictures mean nothing to me." She grabbed the box of photos and threw them on the floor. She let out a loud yell that startled me. I held my breath and tried hard not to move. She grabbed our photos in a frenzy and threw them all over her room. She was yelling and crying. I quickly got up and begged her to stop. I tried grabbing her but she continued trashing the place.

"Get out!" she yelled. "Just get out."

I stopped suddenly in my place. She shoved me and told me to get out again. I tried to stand my ground. She shoved me again. Tears started to fall from my eyes. I tried to fight it, I tried to keep still. But she raised her hand and slapped me. My eyes widened in shock and I brought my hand to my face, struggling to believe what she had done.

"I hate you, Ethan," she whispered. "Get out."

I walked out of her room and out of her house.

I made a promise to myself that day. I promised myself and Rosie that I would keep coming back. No matter what, I would keep coming back until she told me she loved me again.

Driving home that afternoon, I realized that I missed not only the sound of her laughter, but also the sound of mine. I couldn't remember the last time I had had a true, genuine laugh. A laugh of healing and joy. A pure laugh. It felt like the ground beneath me was crumbling and I was about to fall into the deepest pit on earth. I had been certain that if Rosie returned, life would get easier, but I was wrong. I was happy that she was back and extremely happy that she was alive, but she had me trapped. What had happened in her room really scared me. In three years of dating, I had never seen her act that way. I had no idea what to do. I needed to be with her, I needed to comfort her, I needed to show her that I cared for her and loved her. *It's going to be hard when she tries to push me away*, I thought. But I needed to do it. I needed to see her smile again. I needed to hear her laugh. And I so desperately wanted the reason for her laughter to be me. *Whatever it is, I just want her laughter to be the result of me.* I wanted her to be the way she was before. I needed her to be the Rosie that I fell in love with. I needed to hear her laugh just one more time.

CHAPTER FOUR

MADNESS

It was hard to sleep, hard to eat, hard to work, hard to focus, hard to concentrate, and hard to talk. It was hard to do anything. The week at work went by painfully slowly. I went to work, did what I needed to do, went home and spent the rest of the evenings in my bedroom alone. The world was a dark place for me. I had lost all hope for anything being normal again. I had no idea what I could do to make everything okay again. I was helpless. I wanted Rosie to run straight into my arms, but I knew she wouldn't. She didn't want to see me again. She hated me. I tried praying to a God. I prayed and prayed until my knees started to bleed. Obviously whatever God was in charge of this planet enjoyed playing with my heart. It was a game for him. He thought it was a great idea to create messed up people and put them in a world with beautiful people. He thought it was funny that these messed up individuals hurt these beautiful people. He obviously didn't care about Rosie. No, he didn't. Because this Holy God of ours created cancer. And He gave cancer to innocent children and to nice grandparents. He spread diseases to people who deserved to live and then watched them die. But the people who hurt others, who abused others, and who murdered others didn't get any of that. Actually, you know what those murderers got? They got to live in a prison. They got to stay warm in the winter. They got to eat food paid for by taxpayers. The same taxpayers whose children were abused and murdered. The same taxpayers who worked hard and got cancer and didn't have enough money to pay for medication because they were not insured. Oh, but those murderers stayed indoors in winter, they ate for free, played for free and lived for free. And the people who deserved to be killed and to rot in hell stayed in prison. With no worries in the world.

And now I'm in my cold room, I thought, my pillow soaked with tears, angry at the world while the love of my life is living in a nightmare.

Do I believe in God? I think so. Do I believe he is all-loving? No. Because any God who can watch the news and not do anything about this world is not all-loving. Any God who can watch Rosie suffer is unkind. A very, very cruel God.

I was in a bad temper for the rest of the week. My mind was working on very little food and hardly any sleep. My blood boiled and I just needed to disappear. I tried to block everything and everyone out. And I tried my best.

On the last day of the workweek, I was working with an older carpenter and another apprentice. When it was finally lunch time, I put down my tools and headed towards the trailer.

I heard Cam call my name. I turned around and saw he was walking up to me. "Want to go to the Peaches bar tonight?" he asked. "A lot of the guys are coming."

"No thanks," I said. "Next time." I turned around and opened the door to the trailer. I went to grab my backpack to get my lunch, but it wasn't on the hook. I looked down on the ground but couldn't see it there. *What the hell?* I thought. The trailer started filling up with people. Then I noticed someone in the far corner sitting with my bag by his feet.

Enraged, I walked up to him and demanded to know what he was doing with my bag.

"This is your bag?" he asked, looking completely puzzled.

I grabbed the bag from his grip and said, "Yes, it's my fucking bag." I opened the zipper to show the man my belongings. "What the fuck are you doing with it anyway?" I asked.

He stood up to meet my gaze. "Calm down, bro," he said. "I have the exact same bag. It was a mistake." He backed away and started towards the door.

"You're obviously a fucking idiot then," I said. "Don't touch my shit again." I'd attracted the attention of the guys in the trailer. All eyes were on me.

The man suddenly turned around and walked back up to me. "What the fuck is your problem, man?" he asked.

I felt threatened by his approach. "You need to get out of my fucking face," I threatened.

Cam unexpectedly got in between us, trying to prevent a fight. "You need to calm down, Ethan," Cam whispered in my ear. "Let's go." He grabbed my arm and started directing me towards the door.

I pulled my arm from his grip.

The man who took my bag started laughing and said, "Listen to your boyfriend, Ethan. Get the fuck out of here." And then, out of nowhere, the man spit in my face.

It's difficult to explain my emotional and mental process at the time, but it felt like all the anger that had built up in my mind since Rosie was kidnapped rushed to my fist, and my fist decided to plant itself into that man's jaw.

He dropped to the ground and was out cold. I don't remember the specific details exactly, but I remember Cam grabbing me and leading me out of the trailer. I remember people rushed to the man's aid. Some people thought it was funny and other guys were mad.

When the foreman noticed the commotion, he walked up to Cam and I and asked what happened.

"He deserved what he got," was the only thing I could say.

Cam rolled his eyes but our foreman walked into the trailer to see for himself.

After a few moments, the foreman walked out again. He looked angry. He quickly grabbed my arm and directed me towards his office. "What the fuck do you think you're doing, Ethan?" he asked. "You can't go around punching people."

"He spit in my fucking face. What the hell was I supposed to do?"

We stopped at his office door. "I'm pretty fucking sure he just didn't walk up to you and spit in your face. That man has worked for me for many years and he's not the type to do that."

"What are you trying to say, I started this?"

"I know you started it," he said. He looked around and lowered his voice. "I know what's happening with you, okay? I know about your girlfriend. We all know about your girlfriend. And we are all trying really hard to be nice to you. But you can't go starting fights for no fucking reason. I could fire you for this, you know."

I bowed my head like a first grader being yelled at by his teacher. "I know."

"Listen to me," he said. I met his eyes. "You need to take time off. Take a week off. Get settled. Get your mind around things. You're a great worker, but I don't need this bullshit on my job site. Things need to get done. This isn't the sixth grade where you go around punching people. This is real life."

"I can't. I need to work," I said.

"This is not negotiable. I am obligated to suspend you for a week."

"And what about him?" I yelled. "Spitting is an assault!"

"I'm sure he learned his lesson," he said. "I know you don't need the money, but I'll pay you for Monday and Tuesday. The rest of the week is out of my hands. Come back to work next Monday with a brand new attitude, okay?"

"Fuck," I muttered as I kicked the ground. "You're killing me."

"No," he responded. "You're doing that to yourself."

I rolled my eyes in response.

"Get out of here," he said as he shoved me. I guess he needed to pretend he was actually mad at me.

I walked to my car and drove around for a bit until I found myself sitting at a bar on the other side of town, wasting my money as I drowned myself with poison.

I needed something to dull the pain in my fist and to drown out the pain in my life.

I don't remember how long I had been sitting at the bar, but I was already slurring my words by the time Cam showed up. It was already dark outside and the moon was up. I stood up to greet him, but I almost lost my balance, so I sat back down. He took the seat next to me and asked where I had been.

"I called you like ten times, man. Why don't you answer your phone?" he asked.

"What are you?" I slurred. "The phone police?" I started to laugh.

Cam rolled his eyes, "Fuck, Ethan, you know I worry about you."

"Worry less," I snapped. "I'm fine. I am totally capable of taking care of myself." I slurred.

"You're wasted," he said.

"Ding! Ding! Ding!" I yelled. "Ten points for Cameron, he's a fucking genius!" I started to laugh, and then I asked the bartender to get me another drink. "And get one for this guy too." I turned to face Cam. "What do you want to drink?"

"Ethan, what are you doing?" he asked. The bartender placed two shots of tequila in front of me. I grabbed one and chugged it back.

"I'm drinking." I burped up a bit of vomit. "I'm drinking tequila." I offered him the other glass but he looked disgusted. So I took his shot as well.

"Why are you doing this?" he asked.

"Doing what?" I yelled, annoyed at his behaviour.

"Why are you drinking?"

"What do you mean, why am I drinking?" I slurred my words. "You're the one who wanted to go to a fucking bar." I turned to face the bartender. "Another one, please."

The bartender nodded his head disapprovingly, but he poured me another shot anyway.

He placed it on the counter and Cam grabbed it before I could. "Aren't you going to cut him off?" Cam hissed at the bartender.

The bartender smiled and said, "That was his last one."

I looked at Cam with sad eyes. He slid the glass my way and I took the shot. The hot liquid went down my throat and sent a rush through my veins. Hard liquor was pure magic.

"Why are you being such a party pooper?" I asked.

Cam rolled his eyes. "You know Rosie wouldn't like seeing you like this, right?"

The sound of her name struck my heart like a bolt of lightning. My anger suddenly came back and escaped my mouth. "Who the fuck cares, Cam?" I slurred. "She hates me. She doesn't love me anymore. I don't care anymore."

"Of course she loves you, Ethan." Cam said trying to reassure me. "She's just going through a difficult time."

46

"You don't know shit," I said as I stumbled to my feet and lost my balance. I leaned against the bar and pulled my keys out of my pocket. "You don't know what she said to me. She hates me. I'm leaving, this place sucks." I started walking, knocking over a barstool in the process. Cam got up and helped me out the door. We stood outside in the cold air. It felt so good to have hot alcohol flowing through my body while the cold air crawled on my skin.

"Let me drive you home," Cam offered. "You can't drive like this." He tried to grab my keys but I pulled out of his grip.

"I'm fine," I told him. "I can drive. I'm not an idiot."

"No," Cam said. "You cannot drive. And yes, you are an idiot." He tried grabbing my keys again. I stumbled, trying to escape him, but he got my keys and put them in his pocket. "C'mon," he said. "You need to go home."

"No," I said. I started walking away from him. I was walking in zigzags and it was hard to keep my balance. "I'm gonna go to Rosie and kiss her goodnight. She likes when I kiss her goodnight."

"Ethan," Cam said as he caught up to me. "Are you crazy? You can't walk to her house. It's probably an hour from here."

"Time doesn't exist, Cam. Time is just a little figment of our imaginations." I poked the rim of his hat and started to laugh. Cam shook his head disapprovingly. "I remember when I had an imagination," I continued. "I used to imagine my life with her. I used to imagine her on our wedding day. I used to imagine her with a big belly, carrying my kids. I used to imagine her with flour dusted in her hair and chocolate on her nose. I used to imagine kissing the chocolate off of her face, carrying her upstairs and making love to her." I spun around and stopped in front of Cam. "You know what I imagine now?" I asked, leaning in close to his face. He backed away. "I imagine my death. I imagine it coming soon and coming fast."

"You're fucked," Cam said. "You can't think like that."

47

"I am, Cam!" I shouted. "I'm thinking about it now, and now, and now, and even now! And I'm really angry at the whole world right now. I'm mad at you, I'm mad at my mom, and my dad, and Brad, and Phil, and Anne, and God and everyone." I started to whisper. "I'm even mad at me." I laughed. "Isn't that fucking crazy?"

"Okay!" Cam shouted. "Calm down."

"I'm going to see her. I'm going to kiss her. I'm going to kiss her lips. And then I'm going to kiss her nose. And then I'm going to kiss her forehead. And then she's going to go to sleep and then I'm going to watch her. Because she looks like a beautiful angel when she sleeps. And I like looking at her when she sleeps."

Cam nodded his head. "Fine," he said. "I'll walk with you, Ethan. But I know you're up to no good. And you might mess shit up even more if you do this."

"Life is fucked," I said. "It really can't get any worse."

"Suit yourself," Cam said. "But don't blame me when it doesn't go well. Because I am not responsible for you losing your mind. You are responsible for that."

"No," I said. "I'm not. She is. She is the reason why I've lost it all."

It took about an hour to reach her house. Cam wanted me to hurry up because it was already almost midnight. I stepped onto her lawn, looking for her bedroom window.

"Ethan!" Cam hissed. "They're all sleeping. Let's come back tomorrow."

"No!" I hissed back. "I already told you, I need to kiss her goodnight."

"What are you gonna do?" Cam asked. "Throw a rock at her window?" he said sarcastically.

I turned around and smiled. "What a great idea!" I said excitedly. "Help me find one." I got down on my hands and knees and began searching for a stone.

Cam remained on the sidewalk. "Ethan!" he said. "Get up! You're acting like a fool."

"Are you going to help me find a rock or not?" I asked. "If not, you can just go."

Cam let out a sigh and without even moving an inch, he found one. "Here," he said as he tossed the stone towards me. "Now hurry up, it's fucking freezing out here." Cam wrapped himself in his own arms and shivered.

I picked up the rock and held it in my hand. It was cold. There was no way she hated me, I thought. She couldn't. I was supposed to be the one who comforted her. She wasn't supposed to hate me or fear me. She was supposed to love me and remember all the good times we'd had. She was supposed to remember the good moments. And she was supposed to have gone crazy when she first saw me. She was supposed to hug me and kiss me. She was supposed to smile and laugh and cry. She was supposed to dance and spin. She was supposed to have gone insane when she saw me, wasn't she?

Well, I guess she had gone a little mad, right? And I guess I had as well.

Without hesitation, I threw the rock at her window and waited. I saw my breath in the cold night. I should have been cold, but all the alcohol in my bloodstream felt hot. It made me feel daring and dangerous. Impatient, I found another rock and threw it even harder.

"Ethan!" Cam hissed from behind me. "Calm down, you're gonna break her window."

I ignored him. I grabbed another rock and was about to throw it but I saw the light in her room go on. "Rosie!" I yelled. "Rosie, I'm down here!"

"Shut up!" Cam said, scanning the area to make sure we were not attracting any attention.

I waited for her to open her window, pop her cute head out and tell me she'd be right down. She didn't open the window. However, the light stayed on. A few moments later, I heard movement at the front door and redirected my eyes to the sound. Cam did the same. Rosie walked out the door with a loose baggy sweater wrapped around her shoulders. My sweater. I smiled.

"Hi, baby," I slurred as I wobbled up to her. I reached out to hug her. I opened my arms and she stood still, allowing me to embrace her. She didn't hug me back. When I pulled away I saw tears in her eyes. "What's wrong?" I asked, as I almost lost my balance.

"What are you doing to yourself?" she asked and started to cry.

"What do you mean?" I asked. "You think I'm doing this to myself?"

She wiped her eyes and sniffled. She noticed Cam standing behind me and waved at him.

"Rosie," I said and then laughed. "Rosie! Fuck, I'm drunk." I turned to look at Cam and he shook his head. I couldn't understand why. I turned back to Rosie. "What do you want me to do?" I asked.

She looked down and shook her head. "I want you to leave me alone," she said. "Please, just leave me alone. I'm asking you nicely."

I looked down, pursed my lips together and pointed my finger at her. "You're really going to do this?" I asked. "You're really going to fucking do this?" I snapped. The intensity in my voice made her flinch. I immediately felt bad. I quickly turned around and yelled at the top of my lungs. "Fuck!"

"Ethan!" I heard Cam yell. He walked up to me and shoved me. "What the fuck are you doing?" I shoved him back until I heard Rosie command us to stop. I quickly turned around to face her.

"Stop what?" I snapped. "What do you want me to stop?" She took a step away from me, probably appalled by the smell of my breath.

"You're acting crazy," she cried. "You're scaring me."

"I'm scaring you?" I yelled. I started pacing back and forth. "You're scared of me? Holy fuck, Rosie. All I want to do is love you. That is all I want to fucking do." I ran my hands through my hair. I looked into Rosie's eyes and I saw fear. Pure fear. Her eyes looked as if she thought I were a wolf and she were a rabbit. My prey. Her eyes looked like they were scared of being hurt. Scared to die. I wondered if that was the same look she had had every single day while she lived with that man. The thought of the man brought me to a whole new level of anger. I grabbed her by the arms and I heard Cam tell me to stop. I ignored him. "I'm sorry, Rosie." I said as I held her tight. She winced in pain, so I loosened my grip. "All I want to do is love you. And you won't even let me do that."

"You're a monster," she whispered.

"I'm not the monster here," I snapped. Before I could continue my sentence, she interrupted.

"Don't you dare!" she snapped. "Get out of here. You disgust me."

My breath become fast and sharp. I almost felt steam blowing out of my ears like a train whistle followed by a scream. I felt Cam grab me from behind, but I shoved him away. Rosie locked her eyes on mine. She wanted me gone, and she was dead serious. But I wasn't ready to give up this fight. I didn't deserve any of this. "Look, Rosie, you've got me acting like a damned fool," I snapped. "Does this make you happy? Look, I'm standing here on your lawn drunk out of my mind. I punched someone today at work for something so fucking stupid. I'm yelling at you now. Is this what you want? Do you want me to be angry and pissed off? Is that what you want?" I yelled. "Because you sure know how to make me mad!"

"You're not supposed to be mad!" she yelled even louder than me. I was startled and completely shocked. "I'm supposed to be mad! Don't you get that? I was the one who was kidnapped, I was the one who was beaten. I was the one who was raped!" Tears started falling from her eyes. I felt a lump in my throat and I tried my best not to cry. "I was raped, Ethan. Every single fucking day I was raped. And you'd think it would get better. You'd think I'd get use to the abuse. But you don't, Ethan. You don't get used to it and it never gets better!" She took a step towards me and leaned close to my ear. "I had to kill him, Ethan. I killed him." She took a step back and wiped her face. "Do you know how hard it is to fight off these demons every day, Ethan? I can't sleep anymore. Every night, I wake up coughing and choking from the same nightmare. I dream about how he used to wrap his hands around my neck because he told me he had to control my breathing. He reminded me every single fucking day that I was alive because of him. And he was right. He could have killed me, Ethan. He could have killed me whenever he wanted. Now please, next time you show up on my lawn drunk out of your mind, remind me how hard it is for you to be hurt. Please, remind me. Because I *know* what it is like to be hurt, Ethan. I know what it feels like to hate the whole world. I don't want to hate everyone, Ethan. But I do, and I can't help it." Her anger turned to sadness and her face was dripping with her sweet tears. "Madness has been my only companion for three months now. I have nothing else."

I stood there in shock and in silence. I couldn't think, I couldn't move and I couldn't feel. How was I to respond to that?

"I'm asking you to get out of my life so this can be easier for me. Please stop thinking about what you want and what hurts you. Because this hurts me a whole goddamned lot too. Just leave me alone. Please, because I can't handle this anymore."

The lump in my throat felt like a beach ball. The pain was horrendous and I couldn't hold my tears any longer. I cried right there. Right on her lawn. My eyes met hers and I was looking for an expression. An emotion. A feeling. I found nothing. I found absolutely nothing. And I immediately felt pathetic. She was right, I thought. She was absolutely right. She asked me for space, and I couldn't even give her that.

Just like I couldn't even fix her car.

I woke up the next morning on top of a cold, ceramic surface. I opened my eyes and found myself staring at a white porcelain toilet bowl. My head was pounding and I cringed at the intensity of the pain. My stomach was empty and my throat burned. The smell of vomit filled my senses and reminded me that I had spent another night drinking. As everything began to kick in, I remembered getting extremely drunk. I had memories of Rosie, but they were unclear and foggy. And I quickly remembered that my toilet bowl was blue, not white, so where the heck was I?

I rolled over onto my back and groaned. Sleeping on tile is a good way to have a neck cramp in the morning. My movement made the room spin. The sunlight peering through the window was hard to bear, so I covered my eyes with my hands. Where the fuck was I?

Just then I heard a knock on the bathroom door. I mumbled and groaned and kept my eyes shut. When I finally opened them, I saw Cam standing over me, staring at my face. "You okay?" he asked.

I rolled over onto my stomach again and let out a groan. "I'm alive, right?" I asked.

Cam laughed and stuck out his hand to help me up. I stumbled to my feet and rubbed my neck. "Why did you make me sleep in here?" I asked.

"I didn't," he said. "You were on the couch. Until you started vomiting."

"Oh," I said. I looked over to the couch and noticed a trail of vomit leading towards the washroom. As I began taking in my surroundings, I noticed that I was in Cam's newly renovated basement. I had never visited before. "I like the place," I said, giving him an impressed nod.

"Thanks," he said. "Too bad you didn't see it when it was clean and organized. You never came around while Rosie was missing."

The mention of Rosie triggered a flashback. I started to remember what had happened the night before and began to panic.

"Rosie," I said, rushing to grab my things. I fumbled around his living room picking up my shoes and my shirt.

"Relax," Cam snapped. "You need to get your shit together, man. You're losing your mind."

I suddenly stopped in my tracks. I sensed frustration in his voice. He was right, I had gone crazy. I put my shoes down and slumped down on the couch. Cam sat beside me.

"I ruined it, didn't I?" I asked.

Cam shrugged his shoulders. "I don't know, man," he said. "What do you want me to say? You were out of your mind. You were an idiot, but you were also drunk."

"She hates me." I said. "She hates me, Cam."

"I don't know," Cam said. "I think she's trying to hate you."

"What do you mean?" I asked. "Why would she try to hate me?"

"Okay, Ethan, look," he began. "There is no denying that this girl loves you. There is no doubt in my mind that she's crazy for you. Now I know this sounds twisted and backwards, but try to follow me here. Again, I'm not sure if this is exactly what is going through her mind, but it makes sense to me. So just listen."

I nodded my head in anticipation of his wisdom. "Okay," I said. "I'm listening."

"She loves you. She does. I could tell by the way she used to look at you. I could tell by the way she smiled as soon as she saw you. I could tell by the way she spoke to you that she did love you and she did care for you. She has been through hell. We all know this. And I can't begin to fathom how she is feeling right now. Look, Ethan. She was raped, okay? You were the first and only person she had ever been with. And I don't consider rape to be sex, but technically, now you're not the only person she's been with. That is mentally, emotionally and physically scarring on its own. Now imagine that happening every day. Imagine being beaten every day and treated like you were nothing. Imagine being alone and scared. Imagine asking yourself every day if this is the last time you'll wake up. She went through a crazy ordeal. She is not okay, and she won't be for a while. And I know I told you not to give up on her, and I did mean that. Don't give up on her. Because even though it's hard, I know she'll come around. I just have this gut feeling that she'll be okay. She'll walk with her head up again one day. She'll smile again."

I began crying. Cam hated seeing me cry, but I couldn't help myself.

"And you know what, Ethan? I know this is hard for you. The girl you're madly in love with doesn't want you around. I can't even imagine how you feel. But you gotta think of her. Respect her wishes. I know you don't hurt her intentionally, but the thought of you kills her. She wants you to back off because she doesn't want to burden you with her problems. And she's scared. She's vulnerable. She's afraid. She needs time. But she doesn't hate you. If she hated you, she wouldn't act the way she does. What happened between the two of you yesterday—that wasn't hatred. That was passion and anger. It was pure fiery love."

He made complete sense. Rosie did love me. She loved me in a passionate, fiery way.

But fire is hot, and it burns.

CHAPTER FIVE

JOY

It was a hot and humid the first time Rosie and I went out together. The sun was hidden by dark grey clouds, and the moisture in the air was enough to make anyone feel sick. I finished work that day, went home, and took a shower. She had asked me to pick her up from her place at 7:30, so I had quite some time to kill. My mother knew right away what I was up to.

"Cologne?" she asked, looking impressed as she walked past my room carrying a basket of laundry. I heard her laugh as she continued down the hallway. I rolled my eyes as I stood in front of my mirror and fixed my hair. I straightened out my shirt and took one last look at myself. I took a quick breath, grabbed my keys and headed for the door.

I pulled up on Rosie's street fifteen minutes early. She lived just outside of Caledon, a small town whose buildings mainly consisted of my dream: country-style homes. I parked the car, got out and stretched my legs. I felt a bit nervous, but who didn't get nervous on a first date? I pulled out my phone and sent her a quick text. *Hey I'm early, I'll be outside. Come join me, whenever you're ready, of course.* I placed my phone in my pocket and leaned against my car facing her home. It was an older house but it stood strong. The grass was trimmed and the flowers were blooming. A pebbled path led from the sidewalk to the front door. The door and shutters were painted white and stood out against the dark brick. Three trees stood tall and provided cool shade. I felt beads of sweat form above my lip and on my brow. I suddenly wished I could stand under those trees, absorbing the cool air while I waited. I felt my phone vibrate in my pocket and I quickly grabbed it. It was a text from Rosie. *Be out soon.* I put my phone back in my pocket and took a deep breath. I tried using my sleeve to dab away at my sweat but was not successful. The sun was burning hot through the clouds. Good thing I wore shorts, I thought.

I was preoccupied watching a squirrel climb a tree when I heard the front door open.

"See you later," a voice yelled. I looked up. It was her. She noticed me looking and our eyes met. She was beautiful. She wore light blue, faded jeans with a simple white T-shirt. Her hair was still wet from her shower. As she got closer to me, my smile grew wider. There was no trace of makeup on her face. It was different from the last time I saw her, but it was refreshing. I liked it.

Before I could stop them, the words escaped my mouth. "God, you're beautiful," I muttered.

She stopped in her tracks and tilted her head sideways.

I cleared my throat. "Uh, hey," I said. "Nice to see you." I reached in for an awkward hug. She patted my back and pulled away. *I'm such an idiot.* And like a big goof, I stood there and stared at her for a while. She smiled and I noticed her dimple. I returned the smile. I was looking for words, but I couldn't find any. I froze, until she finally spoke.

"Sorry about my hair, I just got out of the shower when you texted me. I would have dried it, but I didn't want to keep you waiting."

Are you kidding? I thought to myself. I loved the way the ends of her hair soaked through her white shirt and her black bra became visible. "Don't worry," I said. "My fault. I was early." And like an idiot, I couldn't take my eyes off her breasts.

I felt her fingers touch my chin and she guided my face to meet hers. "Ready to go?" she asked as she smiled. All I could do was smile and nod my head up and down really quickly.

She got into my car herself and closed the door. *I didn't even open the door for her,* I thought, and began to panic. I stood there contemplating whether I should open her door, pull her out and do it all over again, or if I should just get into my car and drive. And as I was thinking, she honked my horn. I rushed to the driver's side and got in.

We started driving and I blasted the air conditioning. It was a cool and refreshing drive. The weather was ridiculous and the cold air felt amazing on my skin. I was quiet the whole time, but Rosie wasn't. She sang along to every song on the radio. I saw her hand reach for the volume knob and she turned it down. "Are you okay?" she asked.

Oh crap, she's talking, I thought to myself. I shifted in my seat and cleared my throat. "Uh, yeah, I'm fine," I said as I kept my eyes on the road. I waited for a response but she looked straight at me. "I was enjoying your singing." I said.

She pursed her lips together and narrowed her eyes. She didn't believe me.

"Okay, I'm nervous as hell!" I confessed.

Rosie began to laugh. It was music to my ears. "Why?" she asked. "You were fine the other night."

"Yes, but the other night was different." I explained.

"How so?" she asked.

"Because it was." I looked her way and noticed she wasn't satisfied. She waited. "I don't know. You had a boyfriend last time. You were off limits. It's like I was talking to a friend. Now you're single and we're on a date and it feels like you're an exam I need to pass." I looked at her and she had her eyebrow raised. "No," I said.

"Not like that. I mean, uh, I want to make sure this day is perfect for you and I feel like I keep messing up."

"You're doing great," she said. She smiled and gently placed her hand on my knee. "You're sweet, and I like that."

I didn't respond. I stared ahead at the road. What was I doing? I thought to myself. All I was going to do was break this girl's heart. Once she found out my history and how many girls I'd hurt, she was going to walk away. She removed her hand from my knee and looked out the window. Her smile faded.

I cleared my throat. "Look," I said. She turned to face me. "I just think you're beautiful. And you make me nervous. Because you're beautiful and sweet and funny. And I'm thinking you shouldn't be with a guy like me."

"Whoa!" she said. "Ethan, need I remind you this is the first date? Whatever past demons you're dealing with do not come up now. First date. Relax. We'll have fun. We don't have to get married just yet."

I was relieved and I let out a sigh. She was right, I was in way over my head. It was only one date, one night, one time. It was nothing serious.

I had decided on a typical dinner and movie date. We pulled into the packed parking lot where crowds of teenagers hung around the entrance of the theatre. As I began driving towards the restaurant, I saw Rosie was smiling to herself. I wondered why. "You seem happy," I said as I parked the car.

She sighed and shrugged her shoulders, but she didn't reach for her seatbelt.

"You ready to go?" I asked as I reached for my buckle. She quickly grabbed my hand and I immediately felt tense.

She held a painful expression as her eyes met mine. She pursed her lips and said, "I don't want to be rude, but we can't spend the evening here."

I tried to think of a reason she wouldn't want to spend the evening at the restaurant. "You don't like Italian?" I asked.

"No, it has nothing to do with that. I have a better idea. Let's go."

"But I'm hungry," I whined, though I started the car. "Why can't we eat here?" I put the car in reverse and began to drive.

"No offense, but dinner and a movie?" she said sarcastically. "Where are we? In the world of clichés?"

"Whoa!" I said. "Sorry, Miss Hotshot. Too cool for clichés? I see how it is."

Rosie started to laugh and she placed her gentle hand on my knee. "No, that's not it at all. I just have a better idea."

"Oh yes? Please, tell me what is better than some pasta and a comedy?"

"Trust me," she said without removing her hand from my knee. She gave it a firm squeeze and said, "Just drive."

I did as I was told.

We ended up on a dirt road near abandoned train tracks. The sun was almost out of the sky and I couldn't help but wonder if this was the part where she murdered me. I parked my car beside a tree and we got out. I looked around. There was a cool breeze in the air and I was comforted by the cooler temperature. It was a refreshing end to a hot day. "Really?" I said. "This is better than dinner?" I kicked the dirt.

I noticed her head tilt up towards the sky as she closed her eyes and inhaled. The way she stretched her neck made me want to kiss her. I looked up at the sky and realized she was admiring the beauty of the sunset. I took a deep breath of pure air. The evening was warm and my body was relaxed. I was suddenly interrupted from my thoughts when I felt a soft hand grab mine. "Let's go," she said as she led me onto a set of train tracks.

I followed her, trying to keep my balance.

She skipped along the tracks gleefully. Her hair blew in the wind and she turned around and smiled.

"Isn't this dangerous?" I asked.

"What?" she asked. "Walking on train tracks?"

I gulped and nodded my head.

"No," she said as she slowed down. "I think they're abandoned."

"You think?" I asked as we walked side by side.

She smiled.

"So is this where you kill me?" I asked.

She immediately stopped and stared at me with her mouth open. Then she frowned and said, "How did you know? Am I that obvious?" She kicked the dirt beneath her feet and looked disappointed.

I laughed. I thought she was adorable.

"Hey, c'mon," I begged. "I'm too young to die."

She punched me on the arm and I almost fell over. I started rubbing my arm and accidently revealed a tattoo I had. I hoped she wouldn't notice, but she noticed right away.

"Hey." She held up my sleeve. "Nice tattoo."

I immediately pushed her hand away and covered it up. She shot me a concerned glance and asked me what it said.

"It's nothing," I said, badly wanting the conversation to end. I pretended that I had noticed a rabbit, pointing in a different direction and diverting her attention. She knew what I was doing, but I guess she realized I didn't want to talk and stopped pushing.

It got quiet and I could tell she wasn't happy. "You're the one who said we didn't have to talk about dark demons, right?" I said, trying to cheer her up.

She looked into my eyes and smiled. "Fair enough."

"So what are we doing here, anyway?" I wondered why we had been walking along those tracks for so long.

"Nothing, really," she said. "I just really like it here. My dad used to bring me here all the time. We'd catch toads and bugs." She looked at me to see my reaction.

"You?" I asked. "You actually touched toads and bugs?"

She nodded her head up and down with a big smile on her face.

"Never would have thought you'd be the type."

"Well," she responded, "I am. Well, I was."

"What? You don't catch bugs anymore?"

"Ew." She laughed. "I do not."

"So why did you do it back then?" I asked.

She inhaled and looked down at her feet. "To make my dad happy, I guess," she said.

I stared at her, waiting for more.

She let out a sigh and said, "He wanted a son."

I nodded my head so she knew I understood. However, I kept quiet. The evening was calm and peaceful.

"I guess he wanted to do all the boyish things with me because he had no one else to do them with," she said. She let go of my hand and tied her hair up into a loose ponytail. I had always wondered how females could tie their hair so quickly and so accurately without even looking.

"Why didn't your parents try for a boy?" I asked.

"They did," she said. "Apparently I was a miracle baby and shouldn't even have been able to survive past conception. They tried and tried and tried again, but I guess miscarriage after miscarriage made them give up."

"Tough," I said as I looked at my feet.

"Gosh!" she said. "I'm sorry. I was the one who said no gloomy sad stuff. And here I go and open my mouth anyway. I'm sorry."

"Hey," I said. "No need to apologize."

"You're just so easy to talk to," she said as she looked into my eyes. Her eyes were round and dark. They were the most beautiful eyes I had ever had the fortune to gaze into. As we both lost ourselves in a trance, I heard the whistle of a train. I almost froze but Rosie jerked her head to the left and let out a scream. I immediately looked the same way and saw the train heading straight for us. I placed my hand on Rosie's back but she'd tensed up. Instinctively, I pushed her into the bushes beside the tracks. I quickly jumped in after her. We both landed on soft grass. Rosie shut her eyes and clamped her ears as the train went by. I tried to ask if she was okay but I couldn't even hear my own voice. I took her in my arms and held her tight against my chest. It felt like the train was taking forever to pass, but I didn't want it to end. I loved the feeling of her against my body as she breathed heavily. As the train finally passed by, I slowly released my grip. She looked up at me and uncovered her ears.

She was so cute. "Is it all done?" she asked with her eyes closed.

"Yes," I whispered. "All done."

She let out a sigh of relief and lay back in the grass. I did the same. I took her hand and faced her. We both looked at each other and burst out laughing. I was laughing so hard I had to clench my stomach.

"You were so scared!" I said.

"I know," she said, trying to catch her breath. "I thought they were abandoned!"

"Wow! What a thrill!"

We were both still catching our breath when she leaned in and kissed me. Right on the lips. I gently pushed her to the ground and kissed her hard on the mouth. She placed her hand on my head and tugged at my hair. My inner lion was awoken and my insides started to go crazy. Before we could get any further, she pushed me away

and I fell onto my back. She sat up and leaned in to kiss me one more time. She stood up and reached out her hand to help me up. Why had she stopped? I stood up and faced her. I placed my hand behind her head because I wanted to kiss her again. I waited for a signal. I waited for a smile. Anything. All she did was move my hand away. She turned around and started walking towards the car. I had no choice but to follow.

"Hey," I said as I caught up to her. "What was that all about?"

"What was what about?" she asked.

"That," I said. "You just kissed me and then we made out and then you stopped."

"And?" she asked.

"Why did we stop?" I asked.

"It's getting late," she said. "I think we should head out."

Okay, I thought to myself. She was walking ahead of me and I couldn't help but feel confused. Was she having fun? Why did she want to leave all of a sudden? She stopped abruptly and I almost bumped into her. She remained in front of me as I stared at her back. What was she doing? She quickly turned to face me and kissed me hard on the mouth. I lost my footing and took a step back. She pulled herself away from me and covered her mouth. Her eyes widened.

"Sorry," she said. "I'm sorry." She turned around and started walking again.

I grabbed her arm and stopped her. "Rosie, what's wrong?" I asked.

She turned to me but her eyes remained on the ground.

"Why do you keep apologizing for kissing me?" I asked. "I'm not gay, you know. I like when you kiss me."

She groaned and stomped her feet. "I know," she whined. "I'm sorry, I just can't help it."

I tilted my head sideways and gave her a confused look.

"I'm not a whore, okay?" she said.

"What?" I spluttered. "A whore? I never said you were a whore, nor did I think it."

"I know," she said as she looked down.

I wrapped my arms around her and kissed her head.

She hugged me back.

"You gotta tell me what's on your mind." I whispered into her ear.

She let out a sigh and stepped away from me. She looked into my eyes and confessed. "I'm never like this," she began. "Well, I never had the chance; I was stuck with Liam for like ever. But I never just kiss guys. I don't take guys to the tracks." She looked down and held my hands. I loved the feeling of her soft skin against mine. "My dad wanted me to date Liam because Liam is rich," she continued. "And I know that sounds terrible, but my dad isn't a bad guy. He's just looking out for me. But he never saw the bad stuff. He saw the gifts and the dinners and my smile. My fake smile, I guess. But I was never happy with Liam. He cheated on me, he yelled at me all the time when I messed up on stupid things. And he didn't want me going to school. There was no way in hell I'd give up school to satisfy him. I wanna be able to depend on myself, you know?"

I stared at her and smiled.

"What's so funny?" she asked.

I let out a little giggle and said, "Nothing."

"Liar." She shoved me. "What is it?"

"It's just that you said this is the first date and we weren't gonna let out any demons."

She playfully shoved me again. "Shut up," she said. "I just don't want you to think I'm easy because I kissed you."

I laughed again. "I never thought you were easy. I can imagine how hard it is to resist my sexy lips," I said as I puckered them up.

She stood on tiptoe, rested her hands on my shoulders, and pressed her lips onto mine. Her gentle kiss nearly knocked me off my feet. My heart was screaming with joy. This girl was everything I had ever imagined the perfect girl to be. I was falling for her. And I was falling hard.

I was really hungry by the time we left the tracks. I decided to drive to an old burger joint Brad and I used to go to. It was still owned by the same people; I had become acquainted with them while I was growing up. The restaurant was empty because they were just about to close. The owner, Vladimir, noticed me right away and called my name.

"Ethan!" he yelled out with his heavy Russian accent and his arms spread open. He placed his dishcloth over his shoulder and embraced me like a bear. He was a big, heavy-set man with huge arms. He almost lifted me off my feet. He noticed Rosie and let get of me right away. "And this is?" He took her hand and kissed it.

"Oh," I said, clearing my throat. "This is Rosie, a friend of mine," I explained. He nodded his head, but his eyes showed me that he knew that Rosie and I were more than friends. "It is very nice to meet you," he said.

Rosie smiled and said, "The pleasure is all mine."

"Please guys, take a seat," Vlad said. "Choose anything you want. It's on the house."

"Thank you," Rosie said as she held my hand and led me to a table. We sat down and Vlad handed us our menus. "I'll get you two birds of love some drinks," he said as he walked away. Rosie and I started to giggle.

"Gosh, is it that obvious that I'm crazy for you already?" I said as I opened up the menu. I noticed Rosie blush, but my menu hid my smile.

"You're just a bad actor," she said. "You have to learn how to keep your cool."

"Oh," I said. "And I suppose you know how to do that?" I asked.

"Yes," she said. "As a matter of a fact, I do."

"I'm sure," I said sarcastically. "I already saw you blushing."

She looked at me, her eyes wide with shock. Her face flushed red and she brought her hands up to her cheeks.

"See." I laughed. "Not as cool as you thought."

"Shut up," she joked. At that moment, Vlad showed up with our drinks.

"What do you birds of love want to eat?" he asked.

I smiled at the sound of his accent. I was about to order when Rosie spoke up. "How about you cook us something special tonight?" she asked. "It's our first date you know, and I'm sure you know exactly what we'd like."

Vladimir's smile stretched from ear to ear. He excitedly grabbed our menus and said, "For sure, I know exactly what to feed you! I'll be right back, birds of love."

We both giggled as he walked away.

"What a cutie-pie," Rosie said, grinning. "I like him."

"Good," I said. "He's great."

"How do you know him?" she asked.

"I used to come here all the time with Brad. We were regulars."

"Oh," Rosie said. "You only came with Brad?"

I guess eventually we'd have to start talking about me. "No," I said, smiling. "Not just Brad."

Rosie narrowed her eyes. "You brought girls here?" she asked, also smiling.

"Yes," I explained. "Just a few."

"I'm sure," she said sarcastically.

"Hey, you're the best girl I've brought here," I said, trying to save myself. "And I mean it."

"I'll pretend to believe you," she whispered as she winked.

"I know you won't believe anything I say. You girls always have your guard up like you have targets on your heads," I said. "But I won't try to convince you. Just let me show you that I mean everything I say. Please?" I asked.

"You bet," she said. She gave me two thumbs up.

I smiled.

Vlad came back with our food. He placed two plates on the table. A giant burger sat on my plate, while Rosie's held a smaller one. He placed a tray of French fries on the table for us to share. The smell of the food entered my nose and my stomach began to dance. The fries were topped with gravy, cheese, bacon and sour cream. I saw Rosie close her eyes and inhale. "Thank you," she whispered. Vlad nodded his head and dismissed himself. I grabbed my burger right away and planted my teeth into it. The juices from the burger poured into my mouth and my taste buds began to jump for joy. *I've missed this place,* I thought.

As I awoke from my food trance, I noticed Rosie staring at me. She was smiling and she asked if I was okay. I nodded my head and with a mouth full of food, I told her I was starving. She started to laugh and took the cutest little bite out of her burger. I stopped chewing my food and found myself watching. I watched as she closed her eyes and allowed the taste to take over her senses. She was enjoying the burger as if she were in paradise.

"Holy shit," she said with her mouth full. "This is amazing."

"Isn't it?" I asked as I felt joy bursting out of my eyes.

Rosie started to giggle. "Thanks," she said.

"For what?" I asked as I took another bite.

"For the date. I had a lot of fun."

"Well, we'll just have to do it again."

"Promise?"

I crossed my heart. "I promise."

And we did do it again. We had more dates, more laughs, and more kisses. And I knew we'd continue on like that for the rest of our lives. I had fallen in love that summer, and my life would never be the same again.

As the days went by, it was difficult to find even the simplest pleasure in anything. I didn't want to allow myself to believe it was over with Rosie. I was too much of a coward to come to any sort of finite answer. I couldn't explain what was keeping a little fire burning in my heart. Tiny embers still held their light and energy. If anyone were to ask me what I thought would happen with Rosie, whether I thought she'd eventually return, I would have said yes. Why did I hold on so tightly to something that would end up destroying me? Because I knew her. I knew her eyes, I knew her mind and I knew her soul. And I was certain that what went on between us was pure. There was no way that I did not love that woman. And there was no way she didn't love me back. Her smile was real. Her smile was bright and energetic. Her smile showed that she was happy. The way her soft hands rubbed my shoulders after a long day of work showed her compassion. And the way her beautiful lips gently touched the tip of my nose as she whispered, *I love you.*

I loved her too much to smile. I loved her too much to laugh. I loved her too much to even breathe. And I felt sick to my stomach every single day. Why had I been given a normal chance at life? Why was I able to live? I couldn't be anything without her. I couldn't be happy knowing that she wasn't. I couldn't smile knowing that she wasn't. I couldn't feel joy, I couldn't laugh, I couldn't dance, I couldn't run. I couldn't do anything she couldn't. But I had to. I had to keep breathing. I had to keep living. Because the tiny embers in my heart, even amongst the ashes and debris, still burned. And no matter how many times I tried to drown them out with my tears, I was unable to. Because the embers were bright. Rosie lived in my heart, and as long as she was alive, the flame burned brightly.

And I wanted so badly to run from everyone and from everything. I wanted to run from it all. I wanted to run home. But when I tied up my shoelaces and took off, I always found myself running to her.

She was my forever home.

CHAPTER SIX

RESENTMENT

Vanilla-scented candles and nutmeg filled the air in my home. Christmas was a few days away and my mother was getting the house prepared for her fantastic feast. She started by putting up and decorating an eight-foot tree. After that was done, she placed tiny Christmas ornaments and knickknacks all over the house. She hung stockings above the fireplace and filled them with candy canes. She wrapped all the railings in our house with garlands and lights. Christmas music was always playing on the radio, and when commercials interrupted her cheerful spirit, she'd play her Christmas CDs. There was a heavy snowfall that week and the temperature dropped. The fireplace was always lit, keeping our home warm and cozy. My mother tried her best to make gingerbread cookies every day so we could enjoy them with eggnog. Christmas was her favorite time of the year. I didn't get all the hype, but hey, it was her thing and she was having fun, so why did I care?

My brother was home from school for two weeks. It was always weird having him around now. Sometimes we'd still set three plates instead of four. At other times, my mother would take the bedsheets off all of our beds except for his, forgetting that he was here. This always happened when Brad came back. But once we finally got used to the routine, he'd leave again. My mother loved it when we were all here; Christmas was her favorite season because it was the only time of year we were all together. The happiness my mother had in December was contagious. It was impossible not to absorb her delight while she was around. It felt like she could make the whole world happy if she could only come in contact with everyone around Christmas. That year, however, was different. It was the only year in my entire existence that her happiness didn't move me. It was the only year that I ever felt hatred towards my mother for being happy. I envied her ability to move on. And I resented her for it. How could she even consider being happy knowing the truth about Rosie? How could she dare? But I couldn't help my feelings. I knew I was wrong and that I shouldn't hate my mother. I felt guilty at the same time, but my hatred took over. Nothing was in my control anymore.

I was grabbing a jug of juice out of the fridge when Brad walked into the kitchen. I pretended not to notice him so I could get a cup and go back to my room uninterrupted. Getting away from Brad was never that easy, unfortunately.

"What's up?" he asked as he took the jug out of my hands and chugged it back like an animal. He had just gone for a run and he was sweating profusely. My stomach turned at the sight. I decided to forget about the juice and just go back into my bedroom. "Nothing," I said. I started to leave when he grabbed my arm. I turned around. "What?" I snapped.

Brad looked shocked as he let go of my arm. "Jesus, man," he said as he placed the jug of juice onto the counter. "What the fuck is wrong with you?"

"You want to know what is wrong?" I said. "I come here to get juice, and I'm holding the juice and you rip it out of my hands and drink it like a psycho. And obviously I have no reason to be in the kitchen anymore because your sweaty hands and face touched the juice and infested it. So I want to go back to my room, where I was before, without being interrupted. But that's impossible when Brad is around. Because when Brad is gone, everything is fine, but when Brad is here, everyone goes crazy trying to turn the house around for him. Mommy does everything for Brad when he's here. Brad got all the good grades, Brad goes to school, Brad is such a good boy. Ethan is a wreck. Ethan is dumb. Ethan sucked at school. Ethan is an asshole now. Mommy and Daddy love Brad, even though Ethan was first. Brad took them from Ethan."

Brad stared at me with a blank expression.

"All I wanted was a cup of fucking juice," I continued. "And you took that away too."

I kept my eyes on his. His heartbroken expression was as plain as day. He simply shook his head, turned around and walked away. I spent the rest of the day in my room. Just as I did every day.

My home felt like a prison. I spent most of my time alone in my room looking through old albums, surfing the web and trying to read books with little success. Most of the time, I'd hold Rosie's picture to my face and stare at her beautiful smile. My quiet cries were drowned out by the cold winter just outside my door. I battled with myself and I tried to convince myself that something good would come of all this. *Something is going to change,* I thought. She just needed time to heal and then she'd be back in my arms. I really needed something to become of this, because if Rosie didn't come back, I couldn't live. If Rosie woke up one day and knew she was happier without me, my world would shatter into a million pieces. And I'd fall onto my hands and knees picking up the pieces of my world, and I would try to put them together. They'd prick me and poke me, but my bloody hands would be restless. I'd continue putting the puzzle together. Despite my despair, despite my exhaustion, I would put everything back together again. I'd fix it again. Even if I bled to death, I'd find a way to make things perfect again. I'd create a perfect world for Rosie to live in so I could see her smile and hear her laughter every single day until the end of my existence. And I'd have it no other way.

I was awoken from the dream I'd dozed off into by my mother singing "Joy to the World." I tried putting my pillow over my head to block the sound of her voice, but it didn't work. A rush of anger began to flow through my body. *Why is she singing?* I asked myself. *Why is she so fucking insane?*

"Why are you so fucking angry?" I heard a voice say.

I quickly sat up and opened my eyes to see Brad sitting at my computer desk. I must have said those things out loud. Nonetheless, I was pissed that he was in my room. "What the fuck are you doing here?" I snapped as I got out of bed.

Brad stood up and told me to calm down.

"Get out of my room!" I snapped as I pointed to the door.

Brad's eyes started to fill with tears. "Why are you acting like this?" he yelled. "You're my big brother and I just want to talk to you! But you hate the whole fucking world! You don't have to hate us, Ethan! We didn't ask for this to happen to you! I just wanted to talk to you!" Brad started to walk out of my room.

My blood was boiling and a surge of anger caused me to push him into the wall. I pointed my finger in his face and said, "When will you guys get the fucking clue that I don't want to talk to anyone?"

Brad shoved me back and I almost lost my balance. "I don't want to talk about *you*, Ethan! I want to talk about me!" he snapped. "I just want to talk about me. I have a girlfriend now. She's amazing and I'm happy. She's coming over for dinner tonight. I was gonna tell you about her, but fuck it. You can stay in your room for the rest of your life, for all I care." And he left my room without another word.

And it was then that it hit me. I had turned into a monster. I was destroying my family. I was destroying my friends. I was destroying my career. And I was destroying my life. I was surprised no one had tried to destroy me.

And then I thought of Rosie.

I hadn't spoken to Rosie in a week and it was driving me insane. When she was missing, I hadn't spoken to her for three months. But the only reason I wasn't speaking to Rosie now was that she didn't want anything to do with me, and that killed me. I checked my phone every two minutes, hoping that I had a missed call or a text message. I just really missed her voice. I wanted her to be with me. I wanted to cuddle with her and watch a movie. I wanted to smell her hair. I wanted to touch her soft skin. I wanted to make love to her. I wanted to trace my finger over every curve of her body. I wanted to see goosebumps on her skin. I wanted to see the small blonde hairs on her arms rise when I whispered into her ear. I wanted to kiss her eyes. But most of all, I just wanted to save her. I wanted to make her happy again.

I decided to attend the eventful dinner. Brad was bringing his girlfriend over for the first time so I chose to get over myself and join them. I felt terrible for the way I had acted. Brad was right, I was being selfish. Everyone's else's life had moved on while mine remained in the same spot and I had to accept that. When Brad went to pick up his girlfriend, I helped my mother set the table. I could tell she was avoiding me, so I left her alone. Why was she avoiding me? Was she actually angry with me or did she just not want to ignite my short fuse?

I was getting two bottles of red wine from our liquor cabinet when my dad walked into the kitchen to help. He looked me dead in the eye and whispered, "Don't ruin this for Brad, please." A part of me wanted to be angry with my father at that moment. But the love and respect I had for my brother and family were enough for me to enjoy the night. I just wished my father blew out his birthday candles one year and asked the heavens not to ruin it for me.

A few minutes later, Brad walked in with his girlfriend. He had his arm wrapped around her waist and a brilliant smile on his face. He was as happy as he could be. Kimberly, as I learned her name was, was taller than Rosie by a few inches. She was slim but beautiful. Her golden blonde hair shone in the light and her smile was enchanting. They looked happy to be together. I watched my mother glow with delight. She was so happy to meet her youngest son's girlfriend. She excitedly shook Kimberly's hand and welcomed her into our home. My father seemed pleased, as well. He shook her hand, took her coat and hung it on the coat rack. The mood shifted when she faced me. Her smile disappeared. She nodded her head and shook my hand. She knew about Rosie—Brad must've told her. The energy in the room went from rich to dull. I began to get nervous, so I quickly turned around, found my spot, and sat down. I saw Kimberly look up at Brad. Brad nodded and pulled out a chair for her. As she sat down, her eyes met mine. And they said with pity, *I'm sorry for your loss.*

I didn't want pity. I wanted Rosie. I hadn't lost Rosie yet. And I knew I wasn't going to. I knew I'd get her back somehow. Someday, somehow.

The dinner went smoothly. My parents, Brad, and Kimberly all enjoyed the food and drink. They talked about Kimberly and her life, weather, sports, school: all the typical stuff. And of course, just like every parent does, my mother brought up embarrassing stories about Brad's childhood.

"One time," my mother said as she chewed her food, "when Brad was about five or six years old—" My mother let out a loud chuckle. Kimberly sat there in anticipation, waiting for my mother to finish her story. "He came home from a friend's house in a rush. He blasted through the front door with his hands on his butt." My mother elbowed my father in the side. "Remember this, honey?" she asked him. My father just nodded and smiled. He seemed reserved that evening, and I had no idea why. He looked at my mother as if he were begging her to calm down. She didn't. She continued. "We had just moved into this house so I guess he forgot where the washroom was." She started to laugh again. Brad rolled his eyes and asked her to stop. But as persistent as she was, she continued. "He finally decided to open a door. I guess he thought it was the washroom, so he quickly pulled down his pants and went right there. It wasn't the washroom though, it was the closet!" My mother burst into laughter. *A little wine went far with this woman,* I thought as I rolled my eyes. "Anyway," my mother went on, "he pulled up his pants and looked down and realized what he had done. He covered his mouth, and of course, I couldn't be mad. It was funny and cute, so I started to laugh. He was so embarrassed he turned red and starting crying. As I went to comfort him, Ethan came inside and noticed what had happened." All eyes were on me at the sound of my name. It was as if my whole family had just been reminded of my existence and wanted to make sure I was still around. Unfortunately, I was. "Ethan stuck his head into the closet and noticed Brad had pooped in his shoes!" My mother's eyes were watering at this point. "Ethan said, 'Hey, what did you do that for?' and pushed Brad right into the closet. Brad fell onto his little bum, right onto the shoes." Finally, my mother clapped her hands hysterically as she laughed. Thank goodness the story was over Kimberly laughed as well, though I wasn't sure if she was laughing because the story was funny or just because she was being polite. I had no clue. All I knew was that my mind started to wander off as my mother spoke. I started thinking about Rosie. I remember when my mother had told that exact same story to Rosie. Rosie had loved it.

Rosie used to sit at this table with us when we had dinner. Rosie was the well-treated guest. Rosie's coat was hung by my father. My mother told Rosie all of the embarrassing stories. Rosie sat by my side and I stood tall with pride knowing that she was mine. I had the good life. I had the girlfriend, I had the plans and I had the future. It was mine and it belonged to me. I hated Brad that evening. I knew it was wrong, but I could not help myself. How dare he bring home a girl when I couldn't even see mine? How dare he bring a stranger into our home and sit there and laugh? How could he come home whenever he wanted to and just change things? I hated him for that. I envied him for that. I was starting to resent him and the rest of my family. I hated Kimberly for no good reason. She was a complete stranger to me, but I hated her.

Then I began to wonder why it had to happen to Rosie. Why Rosie? With so many people in the world, it had to be Rosie. For what reason? I begged for an answer. I needed to know why. It should have happened to someone else, I thought. And as I blinked my tears away, hoping no one noticed, I asked myself why it wasn't Kimberly who had been kidnapped. I knew it was wrong. Nobody deserved Rosie's fate. No woman should ever be put through what Rosie had. But the monster in my mind was powerful, and I began to hate. A flame burned through my eyes. I wished all the harm that had been done to Rosie had been done to someone else. It wasn't fair. I sat at the table and watched my family laugh while I cried. I wanted Brad to know how it felt to have someone he cared for so much endure what Rosie had. Maybe even just an ounce of it. Then he would know how I felt and be a little less judgemental. As Kimberly sat at my table, I felt like Rosie was being replaced. My napkin rested on her lap and she drank out of my cup. She held my cutlery and ate my food. She sat on my chair and breathed my oxygen. She was in my house. Rosie should have been enjoying that dinner, not Kimberly. And while I was lost in this trance of hate, wishing ugly things upon innocent people, I heard the little angel on my shoulder who sounded a lot like Rosie say, "Don't hate the world, Ethan. Once you're consumed by hatred, you cannot be consumed by love."

She was absolutely right. I needed to conserve my energy for loving Rosie. And I needed to stop hating the people who loved me.

But it was hard to act like everything was okay when my heart was torn apart. *I don't think I can do it,* I thought. *Not without Rosie.*

"Ethan," my father said, interrupting my thoughts. "Help me in the kitchen for a second, please." My father placed his napkin on the table and stood up. As I rose, I felt all eyes burning through my body like lit cigarettes. I realized then that they all saw my tears. I quickly turned around and headed for the kitchen. With his back towards me, my father filled up a glass with water from the sink. He quickly chugged it back and turned to face me. He placed the cup on the counter. "Listen, son," he began. I quickly rolled my eyes, turned around and headed for the dining room but he stopped me with a firm grip on my arm. "Just listen to me, Ethan!" He begged.

My lip began to quiver and I so desperately wanted to hide my pain from him. I couldn't let my father see me cry. But this whole thing wasn't about pride or being a man. This was about Rosie and how crazy I was for her. I took a deep breath and turned to face him. I couldn't help but grab my father, bury my head deep into his shoulder and weep. He wrapped his big arms around me and held me tight. "Let it go, son," he whispered into my ear. "Just let it go."

"I can't live without her, dad." I cried. He held my body tight against his. "I can't live without her and I hate everyone else for being happy!" I sobbed. "It's not fair, dad! I'm hurting Brad, I'm hurting mom, I'm hurting you and I'm doing nothing good for myself."

My father released his grip and grabbed my shoulders. I wiped my eyes and whispered, "I can't live without her, dad. I love that girl way too much to let her go. I can't do this anymore, dad. I never used to hate life, and now all I wanna do is die!" And as I stared into the eyes of my hero, the strongest man on earth, my idol and my rock, I noticed a glint in his eyes. After staring at them for a while, I saw that it wasn't just a glint; his eyes held beautiful tears. The strongest and bravest man I had ever known began to cry in front of me. And it suddenly felt as if the ground underneath me were about to collapse. But before I could fall into the earth, my father grabbed me again and whispered in my ear, "You can't die, son. True love is the strongest force on the planet and death is no match for it. As long as Rosie is still breathing, your heart is still gonna beat."

It was then that I made my mind up. I was going to see Rosie. And she was going to love me again.

"Go get her, son," my father whispered. "Go fight back with all your heart." And with a gentle shove, he pushed me out of the kitchen. His guiding hand was all the support I needed. Without a word, I walked back into the dining room, grabbed my coat, and headed for the door.

"Where is he going?" I heard my mother ask. I turned around and saw my father standing beside her, showing a proud smile. "He's gonna get his life back," my father said to my mother. He gently squeezed her shoulder. "He's gonna get Rosie back." I saw my mother smile as I walked out the door.

I walked out into the cold night. And I walked into the first day of a new life.

When I got into my car my hands were already frozen. A sudden blaze of excitement burned through my bones. *I'm going to do this,* I thought. I rubbed my hands together to warm them up. Just as I started the car, my phone started ringing.

I picked up. "Hello?" I reversed out of the driveway and began to drive.

"Hey, man," said the voice on the phone. It was Brad. "I bring my girl over for the first time and you leave? That's nice," he joked.

"Sorry, man," I said. "You've got yourself a beautiful girl there, but I have to go get mine."

"Good luck, big bro. I love you."

"Thanks," I responded. "I love you too."

I pulled up beside Rosie's house. The snow on her lawn stood out in the dark night. I noticed that there were no cars in the driveway except for her Jeep. Were they out? I hoped that at least she was at home. I parked the car and slowly got out. *What am I doing?* I asked myself. *She specifically asked me to leave her alone, and I'm doing just the opposite.* I began to get nervous. I took a deep breath and slowly closed my car door. As I walked up her driveway, I heard the snow crunch underneath my feet. I suddenly felt like turning around, getting into my car and driving off, but I couldn't. Something was holding me back. The little angel on my shoulder was guiding me to her front door. It led the way. Gathering up all the courage I could find deep within my heart, I pressed the doorbell. I heard footsteps from inside the house, but they didn't come to the door. It sounded like they ran up the stairs. I rang the doorbell again, but this time, I heard nothing. Did she know it was me? I thought. I took a few steps back and looked towards her bedroom window. It was dark, but her lamp was on. She was home. I shivered in the cold night. I pulled out my cell phone. My numb fingers had a hard time dialling her number. It rang once, twice, then went to a busy signal. She had ignored the call. I took a few more steps back, brought my hands to my mouth, and shouted her name. "Rosie!" I yelled, trying to get her attention. "It's me, Ethan. Let me in, please!" The light in her room turned on and I immediately felt anxious. I walked to her front door and knocked a few more times until she opened it.

It's hard to explain, but when I saw her in the front door light, it was like I was looking at her for the first time in my life. Her hair hung loose around her shoulders. It had finally gotten back its shine. She wore a loose grey sweater that hung off one shoulder and baggy track pants, and her feet were bare. Her eyes were red and she looked tired. But she was still the most beautiful woman I had ever seen. I smiled.

"Hey," I said. "Can I come in?"

She hesitated, but a big gust of wind blew cold air towards us so she let me enter. As I stepped into her warm house, I inhaled a sweet fragrance. Her home was warm and inviting. I closed the door behind me and took off my shoes. She crossed her arms and looked down, as if she was afraid to meet my eyes. I wanted so badly to kiss her, but I knew I had to restrain myself. I gently lifted up her chin so she could face me. She quickly turned away, and that was when I noticed the tears falling down her beautiful face.

"Hey," I said, taking a step closer. "It's okay, Rosie. It's me, Ethan." I reached out and took her hand. "You can trust me."

Finally, her beautiful eyes met mine. She brought her hand up to her face and wiped away her tears.

"I miss you so much, Ethan," she whispered.

And in just a few words, the weight of the world rolled off my shoulders and onto the ground beneath me. I felt a lump in my throat, but instead of fighting back my tears, I just let them go. "Oh, baby," I cried as I held her in my arms. "I'm going crazy without you." I held her head in my hands. Her hair was soft and smelled sweet. Her soft skin, her sweet smell, and her arms wrapped around me sent me straight down memory lane. I missed her so much! And I couldn't believe I had survived being without her for so long. As I held her in my arms I knew that I would never let her go. No matter how much she pushed me away, I would never give up. She was my entire life. I gently held her face and started kissing her sweet tears. My lips traced her forehead, her eyes, her cheeks, her nose, and finally, her lips. And without hesitation, she was kissing me back. In just a flash of a second, the tiny little embers burning in my heart suddenly sent a blast of heat through my body. I gently ran my hands through her hair. She grabbed my wrists and pulled my hands down. She took a step back and looked at me. Her eyes burned right through my soul.

"You okay?" I asked.

She closed her eyes, took a deep breath, turned around and headed for the stairs. I stood there in confusion for a moment, but decided to follow her.

She went upstairs towards her bedroom and I continued to follow her. Before she opened the door, she took a deep breath and looked back at me. She looked worried. She opened the door and walked in, and I followed close behind her. She stopped in the middle of room, which gave me a chance to look around. Her room was completely different. It was empty, cold, and lifeless. The bare shelves on her wall no longer held her collection of books. The frames that had once held photographs of us were empty. Her bedsheets were plain and boring. Her stuffed animals were all in a bag inside her closet. Her clothes were all over her floor, and I couldn't see any separation between the dirty and the clean. Her wardrobe and nightstand were covered in dust. A gust of cold air hit me and I shivered. I looked at her window and realized it was open. In the middle of winter. Before I had a chance to speak, Rosie told me to make myself at home. I was comforted by the idea that she was finally welcoming me back into her life, but the state of her bedroom was beginning to tell me a lot more about her. She was a different person. She was not the Rosie I fell in love with. I needed to get that Rosie back.

I took a seat on her bed and she sat down beside me. "Where are your parents?" I asked.

She looked down at her hands and I saw warm breath escape her mouth. "Christmas party."

Oh God, how I had missed her voice. Her cold room sent goosebumps all over my body and I shivered. She noticed, but didn't say anything.

"They left you alone?" I asked. She nodded her head and pulled her sweater over her bare shoulder. She was cold too. I so badly wanted to close the window.

"I told them it was okay," she said. "They didn't want to go, but I made sure they did."

I nodded my head. "You wanted a bit of time for yourself?" I asked.

"No," her voice cracked. She looked at me and tears were filling her eyes. "I'm so scared, Ethan."

I had to fight hard at that moment. I tried my best not to cry with her. And in that instant I realized that not all of my Rosie was missing, but only some of her. She knew she'd be scared on her first night alone, but just like the Rosie I once knew, she didn't want people worrying about her. She wanted people to have fun, even if it was at her expense.

My only instinct was to hold her in my arms. She felt warm against my body. And as her head rested against my stomach, she peered up at me and asked me to turn on the TV. I did as I was told. She curled up beside her pillow and I did the same. With the remote in my hand, I put on some cartoons. And after she was comfortable, she rested her head on my shoulder and I wrapped my arm around her. And there I was, just like old times, watching late night cartoons on Rosie's bed as she cuddled up against me and I held her in my arms. This was what life was about. This was all I ever wanted.

When I woke later, I had to take a moment to remember what I was doing there in the first place. I quickly looked around in a panic when I remembered where I was. Rosie wasn't beside me anymore. I sat up and rubbed my eyes. I checked the time on my phone. 12:16 a.m. I got up and peeked into the hallway. The rest of the house was beginning to get cold because her bedroom door was open. The light in the hallway was on and I heard something in the washroom. I knocked on the door. "Rosie," I said. "You in there?"

I heard her sniffle and shuffle things around. She cleared her throat and opened the door. "Sorry," she said. "I forgot to take my meds."

"Meds?" I asked as she walked back into her bedroom. Before she entered, she pulled her sweater up to her neck and turned around.

"Yes," she said. "Meds." She turned back around and went into her room. I decided not to press the topic. She sat down on her bed and put her head in her hands.

"Rosie? Are you okay?" I asked as I sat down beside her.

"I want you to go home now," she said. She must have seen the disappointment in my face. "Don't worry. This isn't the end."

I let out a sigh of relief. *Thank God,* I thought. "Okay," I said as I twiddled my fingers in my lap. "I'll call you tomorrow. We should do something." I tried to read her face and hoped for a good sign.

She was expressionless. "Sure," she said. "Good night." She leaned in and kissed my cheek.

"Good night, Rosie." I whispered. "I love you." I sat there and waited for her to say it back. I was hoping she would. But she just crawled into her bed, wrapped herself in her blanket and turned her back to me. "I love you so much," I whispered again as I left her room and closed the door behind me. I stood there for a moment and watched my tears fall from my face and land on her cold hardwood floor.

She was going to say it, I thought. One day soon, she was going to tell me she loved me back. And I couldn't wait for that day.

CHAPTER SEVEN

HOPE

I was just about to get into my car when Rosie's parents showed up on the driveway. I thought about getting in my car as quick as I could so they wouldn't notice me, but as soon as that thought crossed my mind, their headlights beamed right into my face. *Shit,* I thought. So I didn't move and waited for them to park the car. They got out and Phil told Anne to go inside. As she walked to the front door, he approached me. "Ethan?" he asked. "Is that you?"

"Hey, Phil," I said as I offered my hand for a handshake. His hands remained in his pockets.

"I thought Rosie didn't want you around anymore."

And then it hit me. "*You* put that idea into her head?" I asked.

"Listen to me," he said. "She's my daughter and I already told you I don't think it's a good idea if you come around here anymore."

"She never wanted me to leave?" I asked, trying to wrap my head around the situation. Phil didn't respond. "Did she?" I pressed.

"She makes her own decisions. But as a father I try my best to advise her. I care about her and her well-being. All right? So I told her I think it best if she relaxes for a while so she can heal in a healthy manner."

"Relax?" I began to raise my voice. "Are you blind? She sleeps with her window open in the middle of winter. She is not herself anymore, Phil! Can't you see that?"

"Don't be cross with me, young man!" His voice was tough and threatening. "She is my daughter and I know exactly what is going on. She is not herself because she will never be the same again. Not after what she went through. Not ever again. I've already lost my daughter and I know I am not ever getting her back. Now I want to protect the rest of her. I need to protect her. And you're no good for her, Ethan. She can never be happy with you."

I couldn't restrain myself anymore, so I freaked out. "Are you crazy?" I yelled. "She *was* happy with me! I never put ideas into her head that would make her second-guess every decision she had to make! Do you even know her at all? All Rosie ever wants to do is make everyone happy! That is all she wants," I said. "I completely understand now. You told her she should stop seeing me and to make you happy, she did just that. It all makes sense now." I started pacing back and forth and ran my cold hands through my unruly hair. "No one can deny how happy we were together. How happy she was with me. What kind of father would make his daughter have to choose between his happiness and hers? Especially in a situation like this! All I want is for Rosie to be happy. And I don't care what makes her happy. I just want her to be at peace. But you, you just want what you *think* is best for her, even though you don't really know. 'Cause you don't really know her at all."

Phil took a step towards me. "I know my daughter more than anyone else!" he said as he poked my chest. "You got that?"

"You do?" I tested him. "Please Phil, tell me what her favorite movie is." I waited. No answer. "*August Rush.* Maybe that one was difficult. Maybe you know her favorite dog breed." I waited. Nothing. "Siberian Husky. She prefers when they are light grey with blue eyes. What award did she win when she graduated high school?" I waited. Again, he had no idea. "Of course. You wouldn't know that because you didn't attend the event. She won the Hope and Faith Award for being the sweetest person in her grade."

"I couldn't go to her graduation because I had to work. I had to work to support this family."

"Oh yes, that reminds me. Money. You thought it was in her best interests to date Liam for so long. Why? Because he had a nice fat trust fund. Was Rosie happy with him? No, she wasn't. He cheated on her. And he treated her like crap. But you shut your eyes to that, didn't you?" I asked. He was expressionless. "Didn't you?" I snapped. I saw him flinch. "And now here I am, a guy who actually truly loves and cares for your daughter, and you want me out? Suddenly I have a feeling you're looking out for *your* best interests, not hers."

"Get off my property," he demanded. "Now!"

"No problem, sir," I said. "See you around."

I opened my door, got in my car and drove off.

Rosie's father was the least of my worries. I would not let him get in the way of Rosie's happiness. Not a chance in hell.

There was a new sky above my head in the morning. A big blue sky held a bright golden sun that spread its light through my bedroom window. I woke up with a thrill in my bones and hope in my heart. Obviously, it wasn't exactly smooth sailing from here, and I knew things could change in a split second. But Rosie had told me she missed me. She had let me in her room and we cuddled and kept each other warm. I finally figured that perhaps it wasn't Rosie's idea to leave me. Instead, maybe her father had influenced her judgment. All I could do was hope. There was nothing else I could feel. I wanted so much to be in her life again. And there I was, getting up and taking a shower, debating whether or not I should call Rosie at eight in the morning or if I should wait until we could go for lunch. I was so excited that I wanted to call her that minute. But

I decided to take things at a moderate pace. Rosie was delicate and needed to be handled with care. And I planned on doing just that.

Everyone in my house was fast asleep so I decided to cook myself some breakfast. I was in the mood for some pancakes or French toast, but I had no intention of waking up my mother this early. Especially after she'd been drinking the night before. However, I did know how to make me some damn good eggs. As I was preparing the kitchen to cook this magnificent feast, I heard my cell phone ring. It was Cam calling. "Hello," I answered.

"Hey," Cam said. "What's up?" He sounded terrible.

"Hey man, are you sick?" I asked. "You sound like shit."

"Nah," he said. "I just drank too much. Anyway, what are you doing?"

I held the phone against my ear with my shoulder as I cracked two eggs into the frying pan. "Making breakfast. Wanna come over? You know, I can cook a mean egg."

I heard Cam laugh on the other end. "Yeah," he said. "Sure. What's up with you anyway? You sound—" Cam hesitated, "happy."

I didn't want to update him over the phone. "Just come over."

"Okay," he said. "See you in ten."

"Later." I hung up. I decided to grab a pack of bacon out of the fridge and make it an actual feast.

Cam walked in the door just as I finished cooking. I had set the table and made coffee. My family was still sound asleep. Cam hung his coat on the coat rack as he entered the kitchen.

"Wow." He laughed as he walked towards me and shook my hand. He looked around at the complete breakfast display on my table. He then looked me up and down and said, "You make a sexy housewife."

I laughed and shoved him. "Don't get so emotional on me, Cam. I was hungry. A man's gotta eat, and when a man's best friend comes over, that man's gotta eat too."

"I agree," he said as he sat down and started filling his plate. "And I am a starving man."

I sat down at the end of the table and filled my own plate. I was really hungry that morning.

"So," Cam said with his mouth full, "what's new?"

"Brad has a girlfriend." I responded. I didn't know if I should talk about Rosie or not.

"So I heard," Cam said as he dipped his toast into his yolk.

I didn't respond. I was focused on my breakfast, and my mind wandered off into the future. What would come of today's date with Rosie? I wondered what was going to happen?.

"Heard from Rosie yet?" Cam asked. When I looked up at him, it seemed as if he regretted asking his question for fear of my reaction.

I toyed with my eggs, pricked the yolks and watched them flow out like a volcanic eruption. "I went over last night." I said.

I saw Cam's eyes light up. "You serious?"

"Dead serious."

"And what happened?" he asked as he sat on the edge of his seat.

"A lot."

Cam waited for me to continue, but I wasn't sure if I should give him all the details.

"I went to her house," I said. I saw Cam's mouth open in shock. "I wasn't drunk this time," I joked.

Cam didn't care about the humor but pressed on. "And?" he asked. "What happened?"

"It was surreal, man."

"And?" Cam said impatiently.

"I don't know, man. I went to her house. She let me in. She started to cry and she told me she missed me. Can you believe that?" I asked.

"That's great, man!"

I hesitated. "But—I don't know."

"What do you mean you don't know?"

"It seems like she's battling these dark demons. She so explosive. One minute she's one way and the next moment she's another way. It's like I have to tiptoe around her because she is so unpredictable."

"So? She went through a lot of shit, man. How do you expect her to be?"

"Dude," I continued, "her room is different. No more books, no more colours, no more stuffed dogs. Nothing."

"Again, what do you expect?"

"She keeps her bedroom window open. In the middle of winter."

"Okay," he said. "That is weird. But again, you don't know what's going on in her mind. Stop trying to figure that out and just go with it. Just be there for her. She doesn't need you to fix her. She needs you to accept her."

Another set of wise words from Cam. They sent my thoughts into a vortex. He was right. Did I have the wrong idea the whole time? I wasn't capable of fixing her life, no matter how much I wanted to. I just needed to be there for her.

"You're absolutely right, man," I said. I looked down at my plate and realized how much I had eaten. I was beginning to feel full. "I'm gonna see her today," I said. "I think."

"Oh yeah?" Cam asked. "What are you gonna do?"

"I have something in mind."

Cam wiped his face with his napkin and put it on his plate, signalling that he was done his meal. He chugged his lukewarm coffee and stood up. "Sorry dude, I don't want you to think I just came here for breakfast. I just wanted to make sure you were still alive and well. And I'm glad you are. It's weird not seeing you at work."

I stood up and shook his hand. "Good timing too. I get two weeks off now for Christmas." I laughed. "Thanks, man."

"No," Cam said. "Thank you. Breakfast was delicious." Cam grabbed his coat and he was off.

I looked at the time on the stove and saw that it was already 9:15. The perfect time to call Rosie. She knew I was an early riser. But suddenly, I had a hard time dialling her number. I was nervous. It felt as if I were calling her for the first time and we were planning our first date. I had to keep reminding myself: It's Rosie. It's Rosie. So I summoned all my courage and hit call. The phone rang once, then twice, and then she answered.

"Hello?" she sounded tired.

"Hey Rosie," I said. "It's me, Ethan."

"Oh," she said, clearing her throat. "Hey."

I sat down on a chair. I felt like I was going to fall over. "Did I wake you?" I asked.

"Not really," she replied. I waited for more but she said nothing.

I cleared my throat. "Uh, I was just wondering if you still wanted to do something today."

"Sure," she said. Again, I waited for more.

"Okay," I said. "What time?"

"Whenever."

"Well, are you up and ready?"

"Yeah."

"Okay," I said. "I'll pick you up now?"

"Sure," she said. "See you."

And click. She hung up. She was so withdrawn.

And so distant.

I chose to go right away because I wanted to be out of the house before anyone woke up. The drive to Rosie's seemed to last an eternity. When I finally pulled up to her house, she was standing on her front porch in the same attire she had worn last night, except this time she was equipped with a pair of old boots. I stopped the car and just stared at her in shock as she made her way toward me. She got into my car and mumbled a hello.

"Good morning," I said, trying to keep a positive attitude.

She faced me and said, "Good morning." She looked tired. Her face was sunken in and she had bags under her eyes. I knew then she wasn't sleeping well at night—if she got any sleep at all. I put the car into drive and we were off. I had a surprise in mind for her and I was anxious.

"Where are we going?" she asked. Her voice was quiet and timid and her eyes remained on the road ahead of her.

"It's a surprise," I said with a smile. I looked at her but she was still looking at the road. And her face, her beautiful face, held no emotion at all. I took a deep breath and decided to raise the volume on the radio. Maybe she would react to some good music. I continued driving along but her eyes still didn't move.

"So, what's up?" I asked, trying to start a conversation.

"Nothing really," she said as her eyes held onto the dark asphalt.

"Do you want to listen to a CD?" I fumbled through my glove compartment. "Pick one if you want." I left the glove compartment open so she could go through her options. She grabbed the first one she saw and placed it in the music player. As the music filled the car I was satisfied with her choice.

"Coldplay," I said. "Good choice."

She just closed her eyes and nodded her head. Finally, I thought. She was reacting to something. It felt peaceful. She was lost in her own musical trance. She looked settled and relaxed as she bobbed her head around to the song "Yellow."

Without thinking, I placed my hand on her thigh like I usually did when we drove around. She flinched unexpectedly and shot a fierce look at me. Her eyes were wide with fear.

I quickly pulled my hand away. "Sorry!" I panicked. "I didn't mean to startle you."

She turned her back to me and looked out of the window. "It's fine," she muttered. "Forget about it."

I placed both of my hands on the steering wheel and decided to just drive. Maybe she'd lighten up when we reached our destination.

After about thirty minutes of silence we finally arrived. I pulled up on a dirt road, stopped the car, and lifted the emergency break. We both sat in silence. Rosie began to look around.

"Where are we?" she asked.

I smiled, opened my door, and got out. I walked around to open her door and gently help her out.

She walked right past me and observed the area. In a firmer tone, she asked me again, "Where are we?"

I stood beside her and took a deep breath of fresh air. "You can't tell where it is with all the snow on the ground, can you?" I asked.

She looked straight at me. "Where are we?" she demanded.

"You don't even wanna guess?" I laughed.

"Ethan!" she yelled. I was startled. "Please don't tell me we're at the tracks."

Completely puzzled, I put my cold hands in my pocket. "Yeah," I said. "We are. What's the matter?"

She looked around again, then turned to face me. Her eyes were filling up with tears. "Anywhere but here," she said. "Please." Her lip quivered and I felt a deep pain in my chest. I had never wanted to hurt her or bring her to tears.

"I'm sorry, Rosie," I said as I led her to my car. I opened the door and she got in. I got into the driver's side and started the car. "I didn't know," I continued.

"Of course you didn't," she interrupted me. "How could you know?"

I sensed a bit of spite and anger in her tone.

"That's just it, Rosie," I said. "I don't know. I don't know what goes on in your head! Why can't you let me in?"

"Because!" she snapped. "I'm fucked up. I don't even wanna be in my own fucking head, why would I put you there?"

I didn't say anything. I decided to focus on my driving. Cam's voice repeated over and over again in my head. *She doesn't need you to fix her; she needs you to accept her.* And I needed to follow his words. As much as I wanted to fight back, I chose to stay quiet.

"I'm trying, okay?" she said a while later.

I was actually surprised. I was about to give in and apologize for bringing her to the tracks. "I know," I said.

"So where are we going now?" she asked.

"No idea," I said. I looked at her. "I'm honestly just driving around. Did you eat breakfast?"

"No," she said. "But I'm not that hungry."

"You sure?" I asked.

She smiled at me. "I'm sure," she said. "Thanks."

And I saw it. Her dimple. Whenever she smiled, her dimple just jumped out at me. I had missed that dimple so much. I loved that dimple. And her smile sent a wave of happiness through me. I missed her smile. *Finally, she did it,* I thought. It was a relief to know she was still capable of smiling. She was coming back to me. Slowly but surely, she was coming back.

That was all we did for the rest of the afternoon. We just drove around the country for a few hours. It was quiet for most of the ride, but through the silence I was able to observe Rosie. I was able to study her. And I saw her existence flash before my eyes, moment after moment. In one instant, a song she loved played on the radio, and I noticed a change in her eyes. Energy and drive flashed across her eyes and I just imagined her mind carrying flashbacks and memories, reminding her why the song meant so much. My Rosie was in there somewhere just dying to get out. And I knew she wasn't okay yet, because normally, she'd be holding my hand and singing at the top of her lungs. But I was okay with the silence. Before the kidnapping, her happiness had become such a regular thing to me that I hardly noticed it anymore. I stopped caring when she sang in the car, I stopped caring when she held my hand. But now I learned to appreciate every single detail about her. And her laughter wasn't easy to find anymore. Her laughter wasn't simple. It was like pure gold: a rare and treasured thing. I did want to hear her laughter, I really did. But I didn't mind waiting for it. I didn't mind working for it. It was as if I were yearning for a well-deserved prize, and the anticipation made the prize even greater. Because when I finally did hear her laughter, I knew I would have to listen well and take in the sound of purity. I had taken her laughter for granted and I promised myself I never would again.

So I only got a smile. But I was ecstatic to have it, nonetheless.

I took her home at about one o'clock in the afternoon. She left me with a soft kiss on my cheek. "Thank you," she said as she closed the door and walked up her driveway.

"Anytime," I whispered so only I could hear. "Anytime."

And just like that, she was out of my sight. Once again. On my drive home, I felt hopeful. I was happy with the day I had had. Even though it hadn't gone as planned, and I had no inkling why she had so desperately wanted to leave the tracks, I let it go. I had let her be and that was exactly what she needed. And she had left with a smile on her face. That was all I wanted. Her happiness. There was no way that she didn't still love me. There was no way in hell that our love would end. It was there. The love we had had for each other was obvious and certain. It was powerful. And I was happy. My dad was right. Love always wins. Always.

I was anxious and hopeful. The rest of the day I spent at home with my family. They knew something good had happened, but they didn't ask me about it. I'm glad they didn't. Things with Rosie had to be treated with tender care. They didn't need to worry about us. I was going to deal with it on my own. I decided not to be so uncaring to my family. I knew very well that I had treated them poorly for the past week or so, and they didn't deserve it. But they didn't need an apology with words. They knew exactly how I felt about them when I decided to put a movie in the DVD player and watch it with them. They knew I was okay. I knew I was okay. And I knew everything was going to be okay. Rosie and I were going to be just fine. It was going to take a lot of work, especially for Rosie. But we were going to make it. No matter what happened, I would not let her go.

I went to bed that night with a dream in my heart. A dream for Rosie to make it through this tough time. And a promise. A promise that I'd stand by her side, no matter what she faced.

CHAPTER EIGHT

NUMB

Christmas Eve finally arrived on a cold winter's night. The weatherman predicted a blizzard and strong winds. The shutters on my window kept opening and closing, which kept me wide awake. Screaming winds blew by the house and howled through the trees. I felt a rush of cold air come into my room and brought my covers up to my chin and shivered. *I hate winter,* I thought. I tried to close my eyes and ignore the storm, but even with the pillow on top of my head, I couldn't fall asleep. I was lying flat on my back when I heard my cell phone vibrate. Weird, I thought. Who would text me at this time? I looked at my phone and a smile drew itself on my face. It was Rosie.

> *I can't sleep. Can you tell me the story of our first Christmas?*

I'd do anything for you, my love. Anything in the whole world.

> *I'd love to.*

Rosie showed up on my doorstep in a red wool turtleneck with a giant snowman on it. She held a bottle of wine in her hands and she had snow in her hair. Her cheeks were dusted pink and her nose was bright red. She smiled and shivered as I stood in the doorway. I saw her dimple. *How could anything be so cute?*

"Hi," she said as she leaned in to kiss me. Her nose was frozen. I held her head in my hands and kissed the tip of her nose. She wiggled it and chuckled.

"You look beautiful, Rosie," I said.

She stepped into the house and shivered. "Even in this sweater?" Her big eyes looked up into mine.

"I love the sweater." I laughed. "You look good in red."

She looked down at her sweater and back up at me, grinning from ear to ear. "My grandma made this for me. I wear it every Christmas," she said.

"I love it." I grabbed her hand and led her into the kitchen.

My house was warm and bright. When we walked into the kitchen, Rosie inhaled the savory aroma of turkey and stuffing. "Mmm," she said with her eyes closed. "It smells delicious." Her statement caught my mother's attention. She quickly turned away from the stove to face us.

"Rosie, my love," she said excitedly. She held open her arms and hugged Rosie. My mother was still wearing her Frosty the Snowman oven mitts.

"Merry Christmas, Mrs. Hobbs," Rosie said as she hugged my mother.

My mother held Rosie away and studied her. "I absolutely love your sweater, Rosie!" my mother exclaimed. "You are so festive! Now I'm going to go change into mine!" And just like that, my mother was off.

There is something about the season that makes people happy. There is something about Christmas that connects people. Maybe it's because it is the one time of year people don't have to stress about work, and the kids are off for two weeks. It is the only winter day people wish for snow, because Christmas isn't as special without it. It is the time of year when people exchange gifts and presents with the ones they love. The only day of the year when children voluntarily wake up early instead of sleeping in. Hot chocolate and ice skating, eggnog and tobogganing. Radio stations playing the same songs over and over again, all through December—people love it. Cashiers wish *Merry Christmas* to their customers as they hand over receipts. People are inspired to do good deeds. They donate to food drives and volunteer to help the needy. Something keeps people alive during Christmas. A tiny flame burns inside all of us because it is the time of year we all knew we aren't alone. Almost everyone has a place to go to on Christmas, and if they don't, anyone will welcome them. That is just the beauty of human nature. We all of a sudden like strangers when we realize we share a common interest. But I could never put my finger down on why Christmas is such a happy holiday and why the happiness is so contagious. Did I really feel happier because I knew it was Christmas, or did I only feel happier because I knew the people I loved were at peace? I had no idea. All I could remember is that when I saw Rosie in that sweater, I fell even deeper in love with her.

It was just a sweater, but I couldn't help it. Just like it was just a dimple, but I was madly in love with it.

Rosie held my hand through the entire dinner. My mother was glowing as she sipped on her eggnog. My father looked at my mother as if he were falling in love with her all over again. He held his stomach every time he laughed, which always reminded me of good old St. Nick. My brother was telling good jokes. Even though we knew all of them already, we still laughed really hard. Because that is what we do on Christmas. Rosie, my sweet beautiful Rosie, was having a blast.

I'd sometimes tune everything out and just look at her from the corner of my eye. She clapped her hands every time she laughed, but then she'd take my hand again. Sometimes our eyes would meet as her face held her beautiful smile, and all I could remember thinking was that I was so lucky to have her.

That was the first night she spent at my house. She told me that her parents had decided to go on a Christmas cruise that year. They felt comfortable leaving her because, for the first time, she had someone else to spend Christmas with. Her parents had spoken to mine and requested that she only sleep over on Christmas Eve and New Year's Eve, and of course, my parents allowed only that. I didn't care, though. I was so excited to spend the night with her. When dinner was over, we all helped clean the kitchen. We sat there as my brother begged and begged to open his presents that night. Despite his many attempts, his request was still rejected by my parents.

"Don't worry, kiddo," I said to my brother as I patted his back. "You'll open them in a few hours. Cheer up." Brad shoved me and laughed. The same thing happened every year, but my parents always said no.

"At least you tried," Rosie said. *I love her*, I thought. Just the sound of her voice drove me crazy. We all wished each other good night, and then at last, Rosie and I were alone in my room. She sat on my bed and crossed her legs. She looked down and bit her lip. I wondered what she was doing, so I just watched her.

"Can I change into my jammies?" she asked.

I laughed to myself. "Of course, baby," I said. Her cheeks flushed and she looked down.

"Can you go in the closet while I change?" she asked. I thought it was a weird request but I respected her wishes. And so I walked into my closet, closed the door, and waited. I heard her shuffle around, I heard a zipper open and close. I heard her giggle and then she told me to come out. And when I opened the door and saw her, she was wearing the same clothes. She hadn't changed. What was going on? But she was smirking. She was dying to smile but trying to hide it.

"What's going on?" I asked as I slowly walked out of the closet and looked around my room. "Why are you smiling?" I asked.

"Promise you won't get mad?" she said as she looked down at her feet.

"It depends," I said as I inched closer to her.

"Well," she said. "I know you always tell me to save my money, but I—"

"Rosie," I interrupted, "I told you not to get me any—"

"Hush!" she interrupted me again. "Let me finish," she demanded.

I crossed my arms and shook my head.

She continued. "Anyway, as I was saying before I was so rudely interrupted, you kept telling me to save my money. And I did. I saved my money for you. Because technically, you never said what I should save my money for. You just told me to save my money. So I got you something that you really, really wanted."

I was excited and mad at the same time. I worked full time and she worked part-time while she was in school. She shouldn't have had bought me anything. "What did you get me?" I asked.

She laughed a little and said, "You can't have it that easily. You have to work at it."

"Okay," I said and sat down on the edge of my bed. "What do I have to do?"

"See in my hand," she said. She showed me a bunch of cue cards. "These are all questions you have to answer correctly to get clues. Every clue will lead you closer to your gift."

I couldn't believe she had put so much effort into my gift. "Okay," as I said, and I clapped my hands together. "Let's do it."

She pulled out the first card. "First day we met?"

"June 22nd," I said.

She smiled. "Clue number one: I am in your room. Second question. First kiss?"

"July 17th."

She nodded her head, impressed at how fast I answered her questions. "Clue number two: I am not in your closet. Third question. What day did you ask me to be your girlfriend?"

"July 19th."

"Clue number three: I am underneath something. Question four: First movie we watched together, not including the movie theatre?"

"Uh," I said and thought for a bit. I was trying to remember what movie it was, and then it hit me. When we first started dating she threatened to wear black and white spots until I watched this movie with her. "*101 Dalmatians*," I said cheerfully.

"Excellent. Clue number four: I am not in your hamper, though I am touching something that usually goes there. Question five: First meal we ate together."

"Vlad's hamburgers and fries."

"That is correct. Clue number five: You won't be able to sleep without finding me a home. Question six: I saw a necklace one time at a store that I absolutely loved, what store was it?"

I raised my eyebrow at her.

"Kidding, you would never get that. The question really is, what was I wearing when—"

"Wait a minute," I said, standing up. "You really don't have faith in me, do you?" I asked.

"What do you mean?" she asked.

"You didn't let me answer your question about the necklace."

She laughed. "Yeah right, babe, we've seen so many stores and necklaces. *I* don't even remember what the store was."

I slowly walked behind her, brushed all her hair onto her right shoulder and kissed her neck. She tilted her head back and moaned. I reached into my pocket and placed my gift around her neck. I turned her shoulders to face the mirror and told her to look. Her mouth dropped as she gasped. She placed her hand on the jewel and excitedly jumped up and down. "How? How did you even? When?"

she spluttered. She examined her necklace, then turned around, tears filling her eyes. She wrapped her hands around my neck and kissed my cheek. "You remembered," she whispered in my ear. "I can't believe you remembered."

She was right. We had been to many malls and many stores and seen many jewels. But this white gold necklace with a simple white gold rose charm covered with diamonds caught her eye. And I could tell by the joy in her eyes and the tone of her voice that she loved the necklace. She was about to buy it when she turned over the tag and saw the price. It was the first time I saw her heart break, even if it was just a little crack. I saw it break. I saw the glint disappear from her eyes. She just shrugged her shoulders, pretending it didn't bother her, and went to look around the store. I looked at the necklace too, and I thought it was beautiful. I looked at the price tag and realized why she was upset. It was $919. But without her knowing, I bought the necklace for her. Because I knew I had to keep her happy. I needed to see the glint in her eyes again. And that night, I did.

"So," I said as she held onto me, "I won the game, didn't I?"

It was as if I had snapped her back into real life. "Oh yes!" she said. "I almost forgot." Then she just stood there and smiled.

"So," I said. "Where is it?"

"I gave you the clues, didn't I?"

"Care to refresh my memory?"

"Sure," she smiled. "Wait, I didn't even give you the last clue!"

"So tell me what it is." I laughed.

"You can't sleep without finding me a new home. You can't sleep on your bed without breaking me."

"So if it is touching something that sometimes goes in my hamper, and I can't sleep without moving it," I said as I walked closer to my bed, "it must me under my bedsheets?" I placed my hand on the corner of my comforter and started peeling it away. Rosie brought her hands together and jumped up and down in anticipation. My mouth dropped when I saw the Mac box resting on my bed. At first, I thought it was a joke, and that she had put a set of clothes in the box just to trick me. I looked at her as I grabbed the box.

"Go ahead," she said. "Open it." She couldn't contain her excitement anymore. The box was heavy. With shaking hands, I peeled away the tape and looked in the box. I realized it wasn't a trick. She had gotten me the real thing. She had gotten me a Mac notebook. The one I'd been eyeing for a while. I slowly pulled it out and placed it on my bed. I brought my hand to my mouth and muttered, "Holy fuck."

"Ethan!" she yelled in utter shock.

"What?" I was surprised.

"You said a bad word on Christmas!"

"So?" I laughed. "I'm shocked."

Rosie crossed her arms. "I'll send it back if you don't behave."

She was so cute. I walked up to her and hugged her. I squeezed her and spun her around in the air. She shrieked with laughter. "Put me down!"

I did. "You really didn't have to, Rosie," I said. "Those aren't cheap."

"Neither was the necklace."

"But you don't make as much money as me, baby," I said. "You can return it."

"Money doesn't matter, Ethan," she said. "I love you. That's all that matters to me."

I felt a smile grow across my face. I wrapped my arms around her and kissed her head. "Thanks, babe, I love you so much."

"I love you so much," she said as she nuzzled her nose into my chest. "We'll be in love forever, right?"

"Forever," I said.

"Promise?"

"Cross my heart."

"Good," she said. "Let's sleep now."

She wore my T-shirt and her underwear to bed. She was beautiful. And as we held each other and wished each other good night, I knew then it was certain. My life would never be the same again. She had changed me forever, and I knew I would love her until the day I died.

And I never wanted that day to come.

I asked Rosie if she remembered talking in her sleep that night. I heard nothing on the other line except for her breathing. "Rosie?" I asked. I waited for an answer, but there was nothing. "Rosie?" I said again. "Are you sleeping?" Again there was no answer. "Good night, baby, I love you so much," I whispered into the phone and hung up. I wished she was with me again this Christmas Eve. I wished she was lying beside me with her legs entangled with mine. I wished she was tracing her finger smoothly across my face, whispering how much she loved me. I wished her warm arm was resting on my chest as she laid her head on my shoulder. I would have done anything to have her in my bed in the bitter, cold evening. I really would. But no matter what I said or did, it was up to her. I didn't want to push my boundaries and make her uncomfortable. I didn't want to push her away. I would give her the space she needed from me. But no matter which way I put it—even if I said I was keeping my distance to make her happy—it was never justifiable. I was the one and only person she ever confided in. She took comfort in me. I was her rock. And I hated the way things had turned out. She seemed so alone in the world. Nothing made her happy anymore. And she wasn't supposed to feel that way. She was supposed to feel loved. Because I loved her. But no matter how many times I had promised her I'd love her forever, she would never be the same again. And as each day passed, I was discovering that no matter how much I loved her, and no matter how badly I wanted her to be happy, I couldn't be the one to fix her. All I could do was be there for her whenever she needed me.

And I hope that one day she'd say those three words to me again. I just wanted her to tell me she loved me.

"Can you hear me, Santa?" I whispered. "Make her love me again, please. That is all I want this Christmas, and every Christmas for the rest of my life."

I knew it was stupid. I knew Santa didn't exist. But the tiny embers in my heart kept me hoping. Hoping that Rosie would come to my house tomorrow wearing her Christmas sweater. She'd wrap her arms around my neck and kiss my nose. Then she'd say that she loved me more than Christmas itself. And I would hug her back and kiss her lips. And we would exchange our gifts and have a feast. And I would watch her laugh as she held my hand. And my life would be complete again.

"Merry Christmas, Rosie," I whispered. "I love you so much."

I pulled my covers to my chin and closed my eyes. I felt my teardrops roll down my face and into my ear. The shutters were banging against my window and the wind howled through the trees. *What a Christmas,* I thought. What a sad, sad Christmas it was.

CHAPTER NINE

CHRISTMAS MOURNING

I woke up with an angel in my bed. Her dark hair lay across her pillow like a beautiful halo. The white bedsheets covered her entire body except one leg. Her breathing carried a rhythm, and I badly wanted to turn into a cloud of dust so she could inhale me and I would be a part of her. I had no problem watching her sleep, even if she were to sleep for a whole day. She licked her lips, stretched her arms and yawned. Her eyes blinked open and she realized I was lying beside her. And then she smiled. That smile always melted my heart.

"Good morning, beautiful," I whispered as I leaned in to kiss her forehead.

She stretched again, yawned again and moaned. "What time is it?" she asked as she rubbed her eyes. She was so cute.

"6:52 a.m.," I said as I stretched. "Wanna sleep more?" I asked with my arms up in the air, reaching for the sky.

"You have to tell me about your tattoo," she said, her voice firm and tough.

Suddenly I realized that when I stretched, my tattoo became visible. I quickly covered it with my hand. With her hair a mess, she just sat and stared at me. *There is no way I'm gonna get out of this one,* I thought to myself, *but I'll try.*

"It's nothing," I said, ignoring the problem. "Let's go open gifts!" I quickly got out of bed and put on a pair of jeans. "C'mon, babe! Let's wake everyone up!" And as I looked back, I noticed she had taken off the necklace I had given her and placed it on the nightstand. "Wh-wh-what are you doing?" I asked.

"I'm just gonna go home," she said as she headed for the door.

I got in her way. "Babe?" I said. "What the heck? What's wrong?"

She crossed her arms and stared into my eyes. "How long have we been dating?"

"Uh," I said, "almost six months."

"Okay," she continued. "And in that time, I have fallen in love with you, I have shared everything with you, I have given you my all, and now when I ask about a tattoo of a girl's name, you can't tell me? Every single time we've had sex, you've kept your shirt on. And I've said nothing. Because I wanted you to tell me when you were ready. But if you're not ready now, you'll never be. So I'll just go home." She headed for the door.

I couldn't let her walk out, so I said it. I finally said it. "Leah," I said. She stopped and turned to face me. "Her name is Leah."

"Who is she?" Rosie asked, with jealousy in her tone.

"Cam's little sister." I sat down on my bed. I was clearly upset and Rosie noticed, so she sat down next to me.

"Did you guys date?" she asked.

"Nope." Rosie didn't ask any questions, but I knew I had to continue the story.

"Leah was a year younger than you," I stated. "And she had the biggest crush on me."

Rosie waited for me to continue.

"I broke her heart about a thousand and one times. Yeah, she was cute and I liked her, but she was Cam's baby sister. He told me he didn't mind if I dated her because he knew how much she liked me, but I was a fool. I played with her heart. I didn't want to hurt her, so I always kept her hoping."

"So why do you have a tattoo of her name?"

I took a deep breath and confessed. "She died in March."

Rosie placed her hand on her mouth. "How?"

"Car accident."

"What happened?"

"Cam and I were going out," I said as I ran my fingers through my hair. "And because Leah wanted to spend time with me, she asked if she could come, and because I kept breaking her heart, I said she could. We were driving to a buddy's house to shoot some pool, and some drunk idiot ran a red and hit us from the side." I felt tears gather in my eyes. I cleared my throat. "Cam was driving, I was in the passenger seat, and she was sitting in the seat directly behind me. She didn't even make it to the hospital. She died right away. But I know she saw the car before we did because she screamed. And her scream was the last sound I heard." I cleared my throat again. "Anyway, we went to the hospital. I stayed there for about a week. They had to remove a huge chunk of glass from my arm." I rolled up my sleeve to show her the tattoo. "And because I got the scar the same time she died, I decided to cover up something hideous with something beautiful. A tribute to Leah, if you will."

"I'm sorry, baby," Rosie said as she wrapped her arms around me. "I had no idea."

"Don't be," I said as I pulled her arms off my neck. "It wasn't your fault."

Rosie's sad eyes stared into mine.

"Listen," I said. "This is going to be a very hard Christmas for Cam and his family." I stood up and Rosie did the same. "I think they hate me."

"Who hates you?" Rosie asked.

"Cam and his parents."

"Why would they?"

"Because I didn't even give Leah a chance."

"Imagine if you did," Rosie stated. "Everything would be different."

"I wouldn't be with you."

"Not only that," she looked down. "You would have lost your future if you had given her a chance. They probably prefer that Leah died as your friend instead of your future wife."

"I never saw it that way before," I said. "But I doubt it."

"Why?" Rosie asked. "Technically, you didn't break her heart. You just never gave her a chance."

I had no response.

"You didn't date her, right?"

"No," I said. "I didn't."

"So you didn't break her heart," Rosie said. "So they have no reason to hate you."

"I did break her heart."

Rosie laughed. "Baby," she said. "There is a huge difference between a crush and loving someone. Sure, you probably hurt her, but you didn't break her heart."

I shook my head and laughed. "You don't get it, Rosie."

"So explain it to me," she snapped.

"I slept with her," I snapped back. "I was the first person she was ever with. I was the only person she was ever with. Do you understand how guilty I feel every single day?"

Rosie brought her hand to her mouth and stared at me with empty eyes.

"We did it more than once," I continued. "She thought we would become serious if she gave me what I wanted." I brought my hand to my head. "I couldn't even give her what she wanted." I glanced up at Rosie and she looked broken.

"Wow," she said as she started packing her bag. "Wow." Tears started to fall from her eyes. "I can't believe you." She picked up my Macbook and placed it in her bag.

"What are you doing?" I tried to stop her. "Babe, what do you want me to say? I told you the truth. I'm being honest."

"Being honest?" she suddenly stopped. "You're far from honest, Ethan! You're the type of asshole I have been trying to avoid. But you're a damn good liar, and look, Ethan, you fooled me."

"I have never done anything to hurt you!" I snapped. "Leah is in my past! You don't think I learned my lesson? You don't think that shit killed me every single day? Do you think Cam knows what I did to his baby sister? No, he doesn't. And after the accident, I was so fucked. I was on antidepressants because I hated who I was! Do you think I enjoy keeping this a secret?"

"I can't believe you. It's like I don't even know you anymore."

"Don't penalize me, Rosie. I give myself shit every day, and I sure as hell don't need it from you." I quickly grabbed the bag out of her hand. I didn't want her to leave.

"You're disgusting. Because whenever I'm upset about something and I don't want to talk about it, you flip out. You tell me I should be able to open up to you about everything if I trust you. And now you decide to tell me this? God, Ethan, it's not that I'm jealous of her, because I knew you were with other girls, but when I don't want to talk about a bad day at work, you tell me I should be able to talk to you about anything. And this, *this* is what you decide to keep from me? You're such a hypocrite."

"Rosie, please. At least I told you. I don't know why you're so upset."

"Oh, sorry, Ethan," she said sarcastically. "I'm sorry I'm not jumping for joy."

Rosie turned around and walked away. I wished I could have stopped her. I wished I could have made her stay. I wished I had told her that everyone has a skeleton in their closet. And its bones rattle so loud at night. It dances behind the door, begging to get out. We all dig our faces deep into our pillows and scream to drown out the noise. Everybody's secret wants freedom, and it keeps you up at night, but you just pop another pill and fall asleep, thinking you might let it out another time.

I wished she had known that one day she'd have a secret for me. A secret that would change my life forever.

Christmas morning went by very slowly. My mother made a big breakfast of pancakes, waffles, bacon, eggs, fruit and tarts. Kimberly came over to spend Christmas day with us. I wished Rosie would too. But I had promised her and myself that I wouldn't be the one to call or text her. If she wanted to talk to me, she would contact me. I hated it, but she liked it better that way. I knew her father had had an influence on that decision too. During breakfast, I found myself staring at the front door, hoping she would show up. But I knew she wouldn't. I wanted to see her so badly that my mind created images of Rosie walking through my front door. While we sat in the living room and opened the gifts, I would occasionally look out the window and think she was there. I'd see her all wrapped up in a scarf, wearing her bright red snowman sweater. She'd knock on the window with her knitted mittens and smile and wave. *God, I miss her,* I thought. I really did. And when I saw Brad and Kimberly exchange their gifts, when I saw them laugh and kiss, when I saw the glow in their eyes, I was jealous again. I was constantly reminded that happiness can be the easiest thing to find while being the most difficult thing to achieve.

I closed my eyes and brought myself to a place I hadn't been in a while. Just my guitar and I sitting in the warm sand, strumming all my miseries away. I'd sing in my head a song for her.

> *I want so bad to hold you baby,*
> *But your soul is on fire and I still haven't learned.*
> *Oh, what I'd do to have you in my arms,*
> *But I can't hold on too long without getting burned.*

I dozed off on the couch while we were watching *How the Grinch Stole Christmas.* I awoke to my mother shaking my shoulder. "Ethan," she whispered. "Ethan, honey. Cam is at the door. He wants to speak to you." I rubbed my eyes as I struggled to open them. I wondered how long I had been sleeping for. I looked at my cell phone to check the time. 12:57 p.m. I walked through the kitchen and saw Cam standing there in his winter boots. He looked anxious to see me.

"Merry Christmas," I said as I reached for a hug. He quickly hugged me back. "Ethan," he said. "Have you heard from Rosie this morning?"

My stomach dropped at the sound of her name. "Rosie?" I asked. "No, why?"

"I saw her today."

"Where?" I asked.

"I went to pick up my grandmother. And on my way, I crossed a set of train tracks. And I saw someone lying in front of a tree."

I waited for Cam to continue.

"Well, I thought it was fucking weird that someone was lying in the snow, a few metres away from the road. So I stopped the car and opened my window to get a better look. It could have been a dead person. But it wasn't. It was Rosie."

"Okay," I said, trying not to panic. "She always goes there," I continued. "Well, she used to always go there. It's no big deal."

Cam shook his head. "Dude," he said. "I know I don't know Rosie as well as you do, but I know for a fact she shouldn't be lying down in the snow without a jacket."

I tried my best to deny that anything was wrong. "Maybe she had a heavy sweater," I suggested.

Cam raised his eyebrow. "Ethan," he said. "I know when things can be considered normal. And this shit wasn't normal. It looked weird. And when I stopped my car, she sat up and looked at me. That's when I knew it was her. Her face was red like she had been crying."

Every inch of my body was dying to drive down to the tracks and see what was going on. But I couldn't see her unless she wanted me to. And I knew I could mess any progress we had made if I showed up without a phone call. "Cam," I said. "I believe you, okay. I know it's fucked." I looked around us to make sure no one was listening and lowered my voice. "But I can't just show up at the tracks."

"Why not?"

"Because, man," I said. "I don't want to push things."

"What do you mean 'push things'?" Cam asked.

"When she wants to see me or talk to me, she'll call me. Every single time I showed up unannounced, it never turned out the way I'd wanted."

"Well, no shit," Cam said. "You were wasted all those times."

"All but one," I said. "I can't just go there. She'll hate me, and we'll be back to square one. I know it. Unless she calls me for help, I can't do anything."

Cam looked defeated. "Fuck, man," he said as he looked down.

"Cam, thank you for coming here to tell me," I said. "It means a lot to me. I can tell that you care about her. But I have to sit my ass down in here and fight off the urge to drive to those fucking tracks to see what's going on." I ran my fingers through my hair. "Believe me, Cam," I said. "I would love to see what's going on. But I can't. I just can't." I wanted to avoid his eyes, so I looked down at my feet.

Cam patted my shoulder. "I'm sorry, buddy," he said. "I don't understand what you're going through, but I trust you. And I believe you're doing the right thing."

"Thanks, man," I said as I patted his back. "I appreciate you coming here."

"No problem." He turned the doorknob and stepped out. "But remember this: I'm always here for you. Whenever you need me. No matter what day. I'll always be here."

"Thanks." I watched him walk down the driveway, get into his car, and drive off. I wanted to follow him, but I knew better. Rosie didn't need me until she told me she did. And I had to respect that. So I walked back into my living room, sat on my couch, and watched the rest of the movie. It surprised me. The Grinch turned out to be a completely different person at the end. Everyone he knew completely underestimated him. He changed for the better.

Maybe that would happen to Rosie. Maybe she would change for the better. Or maybe for the worse. My stomach turned at the thought.

We had a late dinner that night because we had to wait for my mother's cousins to arrive. They were always running late. I wasn't looking forward to seeing them because they were all snobby, bratty and annoying. Brad, Kimberly, and I munched on sandwiches my mother made to keep us satisfied. Brad warned Kimberly about our cousins. She laughed at all the stupid stories we were telling about them. As I brought our plates to the kitchen, I felt my phone vibrate in my pocket. I checked the call display.

It was Rosie. "Hello," I answered in a panic.

"Ethan," I heard a man's voice say. It was Phil. I let out a sigh. I didn't know if it was a sigh of disappointment or a sigh of relief.

"Hi Phil," I said in a monotone. "Merry Christmas."

"Ethan," he said again. "Is Rosie with you?"

"No, she's not," I said. "Why?"

"I don't know," he said. He sounded worried. I didn't like it. "She left this morning. She was very upset. She took her car and just left. I've been calling her cell phone, but she never picks up."

I said nothing.

"Ethan," he said. "I know you're upset with me. But it's almost six o'clock and she has never stayed out of the house this long. She didn't even take her jacket."

I remained silent. But I knew he could hear me breathing.

"Do you know where she is?" he asked. "I'm desperate."

"I'll find her," I said. "But I'm doing it for me." And I hung up.

I quickly put on my jacket and headed for the door. I heard my mother ask where I was going, but adrenaline was running through my veins. I didn't pause on my way out to the car she had a chance to ask again. I sped down the street and headed for the tracks. The setting sun blinded me, so I squinted as I tried to see the road. I was hoping and praying that Rosie was still at the tracks. I should have gone earlier when Cam told me about it. She probably wasn't even there anymore. As I sped down the highway, my phone started ringing. I picked it up quickly.

"Hello?"

"Ethan," Phil said. "It's me again." Before I even had a chance to respond, he started talking again. "Ethan, a bottle of whiskey is missing from my liquor cabinet." I didn't understand why he was calling me for this. "She took it, Ethan. She took the bottle."

"What do you mean? How do you know?" I asked.

"I always know what's in my liquor cabinet. And a full bottle of whiskey is gone."

"That doesn't mean it was her," I said, trying to defend her. "Did you ask your wife?"

"Rosie can't drink," Phil said, completely ignoring my suggestion.

"Why not?" I asked.

"She's on Zoloft." I knew exactly what Zoloft was. I had been on Zoloft after Leah died.

"Zoloft is a strong antidepressant," Phil continued.

"I know what Zoloft is," I said. "I'm already looking for her. What else do you want?" I hung up my phone as I approached the tracks.

I parked the car and got out. I heard the snow crunch under my feet. It was cold out. The sun had almost set, so it was very hard to see. I looked to my left and saw nothing. I looked to my right and at first, I saw nothing, but when I squinted my eyes, I noticed something in the snow. I quickly ran up to it. As I got closer, I knew it was Rosie. I dropped to my knees. She was lying on her back with a half-empty bottle of whiskey in her left hand.

"Rosie," I said. "Rosie, are you okay?" She didn't even open her eyes. I began to panic. My first thought was that she was dead. I sat down in the snow and rested my head against her chest, hoping that her heart was still beating. After what felt like an hour, I heard it.

"Rosie!" I yelled as I shook her shoulders. Again, no response. I embraced her. She felt so cold in my hands. And I felt that a chunk of her hair was frozen. I shook her again and yelled her name as tears escaped my eyes.

"Rosie, goddamn it!" I yelled. "Wake up!" I shook her again and heard her murmur a sound. Or a word. "Rosie?" I cupped her face in my hands. I looked in her eyes and waited for them to open. Her breath reeked of alcohol. I rubbed her eyes and her lips with my thumbs. I tried to wake her up. I tried to generate heat on her face. I didn't know what I was doing, but I was trying. "Rosie, baby," I cried as I cradled her in my arms. "Talk to me, baby." I rocked her back and forth, trying to wake her up. She slowly brought her flimsy arm to her face and tried to rub her eyes. She was so weak that her arm barely reached her face before it fell to her side. Her lips were turning blue. I quickly grabbed my phone out of my pocket. "I hate to do this, baby," I said as I tried to control my tears. "But I have to call an ambulance."

I dialed 9-1-1 and it rang twice before I got the operator.

"Hello," I yelled into the phone. "Hello. I need an ambulance. I found her in the snow. She's cold and she drank a lot. She's not talking. Her eyes aren't opening." I was kissing her eyes, hoping that her life wasn't escaping her.

"Sir, I need you to calm down," the voice on the other line said. "Can you tell me where you are?"

"Uh . . ." I looked around. I had suddenly forgotten where I was. "I'm on the train tracks, on Station Road." I was panicking and out of breath. "Please hurry," I begged.

"Okay sir, an ambulance is on the way. Who did you find, sir?"

"My girlfriend."

"Okay, what's her name?"

"Rosie," I said. "Her name is Rosie."

"Is Rosie breathing?"

"I think so," I said as I struggled to bring her nose up to my ear. "I don't know," I cried. "I can't tell. Please, hurry!" I begged.

"Okay, sir," she said. "I need you to calm down. Is she hurt?"

"No," I said. "I don't think so."

"I need you to check if her heart is beating. What you need to do it place two fingers right under the side of her jaw, right beside her trachea. Can you do that for me?"

"Yeah," I said. I tried to pin the phone to my ear. I laid her down in the snow and did as the operator had told me. Her neck was so cold. "Yeah," I said. "It's there. I can barely feel it, but it's there."

"Good," she said. "Now can you tell me if her clothes are wet?"

I patted my hands on her shirt and pants. They were cold but they were dry. "No," I said. "They are just really cold."

"Okay," she said. "I need you to do something for me, okay?" she asked. "Rosie needs heat. Hold her tight against you so your body heat can generate warmth for her body. Can you do that for me?"

"Yeah," I said as I scooped Rosie into my lap and squeezed her against me. Just then I heard the sirens of the ambulance. I dropped my phone into the snow and started yelling. "I'm here!" I yelled at the top of my lungs. "Over here! Please, hurry!" I started waving my arms back and forth, trying desperately to catch their attention. "Over here!" I yelled again. They noticed me. They quickly ran towards us with the stretcher. "Help her, please," I cried as they approached me. Two paramedics started working on Rosie right away while the other one stood me up and led me away from them. "What happened?" he asked.

"I don't know," I said. I wiped my tears. My hands were shaking.

"How did you find her?" he asked. Just then a police cruiser arrived. I began to get nervous.

"I found her here," I began. "Her father called me and said she was missing. So I came here because she always came here when she was upset."

"Okay," he said with empathy in his voice. "Just sit here, we'll try everything we can."

I took a seat on a rock and rested my head in my hands. The police officer approached me and I explained the whole story to him. I kept looking beyond him to see what they were doing. They put one of those breathing tubes in her mouth and started pumping it. They looked really serious. I was so nervous. The officer offered me a ride to the hospital. I took a seat in his car and we followed the ambulance. The ambulance turned on its sirens. It was then that I knew it was serious. I knew it was bad. Very, very bad.

I called Phil from the waiting room. I also called my parents to explain why I had left in such a rush. I was pacing back and forth, back and forth. My nail beds were all chewed up and I wished someone would just come out and tell me she was okay. I saw Anne from the corner of my eye. She noticed me right away and ran up to me. Phil followed her.

"What happened?" She asked with panic-stricken eyes. "Where's Rosie?"

"They're with her now." I was trying to remain calm.

"Where was she?" Phil asked.

"I found her at the tracks," I said, avoiding eye contact. "She'd drunk half the bottle of whiskey and she was passed out in the snow."

Anne brought her hand to her mouth as tears filled her eyes.

"How long was she there?" Phil asked.

"Since before one o'clock." I said.

"That long?" he gasped.

"How do you know?" Anne asked.

"Cam saw her earlier today and he told me where she was," I said. "That's why I knew where to find her."

"Why didn't you go there earlier, Ethan?" Phil asked angrily.

I finally turned to face him. My blood was boiling. "What the hell did you expect me to do, Phil?" I asked, exceeding his tone. "You're the one who told me never to see her again! We're all lucky I was able to find her when I did!"

"*We're* lucky?" he mocked me. "If you cared enough, you would have gone to the tracks the moment you found out."

I felt my anger rush from the core of my soul to the palms of my hands as I shoved Phil into the wall and held him there. "Don't blame this on me, you bastard," I said through my teeth. "She was in *your* house and she took *your* whiskey. You say you know your daughter more than anyone. At least I knew where the fuck she was." I let go of my grip.

Anne stared at the both of us as tears fell down her face. Phil was right. though, I should have gone to the tracks the moment I found out. But what I knew for sure was that I had helped Rosie more than he had that day. And I knew that he would never again get between us. I would never let it happen. It could have cost both of us her life.

CHAPTER TEN

RELIEF

My heart was tired. Deprived. Exhausted. I had no idea how much more my heart could take. I had lived and died over and over again. And I didn't know how much more I could take. My blood felt thin and my will was worn out. And waking from the dead left me with a dreadful feeling. My feet were heavy and my head hung low. It was as if earth's gravity exceeded its own strength, and the stronger the pull, the weaker I got. Earth was using my energy. She was using it all up. She was using it like it was hers to begin with. She was extracting every tiny piece of everything out of my body and my soul. She wasn't picky. She took anything, whatever she could get. And I was feeling it. It was taking a toll on my life. But there was really nothing I could do about it. I couldn't just tell the earth to stop. I couldn't lecture life and explain why I should be left alone. I just needed to remain on my own two feet with solid ground beneath me. Dirt and rock beneath my shoes. The reality was that no matter how much I hated her pushes and her pulls, I needed her to live. I would literally die without her. And as toxic as our relationship was, I needed to stay. She was sucking every little bit of life out of me, but if it kept her alive, I was all for it. Because in the end, all that could ever matter to me was her.

Rosie was diagnosed with acute hypothermia. Thankfully, she hadn't overdosed on her medication, so she was dismissed from the hospital the day after Christmas. The day after I found her. And I couldn't even explain how great it felt to know she was okay. I was unable to mutter any words, let alone make a sound. Phil and I stood in opposite corners of the room, and with a broken heart, Anne stood between us. The only question that lingered my mind was why Rosie had been there in the first place? There could have been many reasons. It was the first Christmas since she had been back and Christmas was always her favorite season. Or maybe she was just wanted to visit memory lane. And then, suddenly, it hit me. I knew exactly why she had been there in the first place.

"You were visiting our garden, weren't you?" I asked. It was December 26th. The bright sun awaited us outside, a great finish to what had been a frightening day for most. Phil and Anne were in the hallway speaking to the therapist. Rosie was sitting on the bed with her head in her hands. She looked defeated. I sat in a chair across from her and just watched her breathe. "Wasn't that why you were there?" I asked again.

Rosie rubbed her eyes. "I don't know what you're talking about, Ethan."

"Why did you go to the tracks yesterday?" I asked.

"Why do you care?" she asked.

I was insulted by the suggestion that I had no interest in her life. She was my life. "Why wouldn't I care, Rosie? I love you." I placed my hand on her knee, but she pushed it away.

"C'mon Ethan," she said. "You don't love me."

I let out a sigh. "You can't just tell me that I don't love you without giving me a reason."

Rosie said nothing.

"Give me one good reason why you think I don't love you."

Again, she was silent.

"What do you want me to do?" I finally snapped. I saw her flinch.

"Just leave me alone!" she snapped back. "I need you to leave me alone! Just get out of here, Ethan."

"I'm not going to do that, Rosie." I said. "I am not going to leave you alone."

I saw tears fall from her eyes and onto the floor. I wanted to stop them. I wanted to stop her pain. I didn't want her to hurt anymore. But she wasn't letting me in. She wasn't letting me help her. I just really wanted her to be okay again. I wanted her to be happy.

My chin started to quiver, and I tried with all my might to hold in my hurt, but my emotions failed me once again. I sat beside Rosie and held her in my arms as we both cried together. I held her head against my chest and kissed her hair. She was warm. "Rosie, baby, please," I said. "I don't want to ever lose you again. I promised you a long time ago. I promised I'd never leave you. Remember?" Rosie began to sob, but her sound was muffled against my chest. "Baby, remember? We planted the garden beside the tracks. The garden of roses. We had such a good time. Remember we went to so many nurseries because we had a hard time finding a rosebush because it was late in the season?" I began to smile at the memory. Her cries were silenced as she listened to me speak. "And then we found this ugly dead bush at some random nursery. Remember the guy was such a weirdo?" I waited for an answer. Rosie tugged at my shirt, signalling me to go on. She liked the story, I thought as I smiled to myself. "But it was the last bush, so we took it anyway. And then we planted it and I laughed at how ugly it looked. It was dry and dying. But you were upset. And when I saw your face and you looked sad, it completely wiped the smile off my face. The following weekend we had planned a picnic at the park. But it was ruined because it rained heavily for three days straight. And baby, you were even more disappointed because you were looking forward to that picnic. Then you took a walk that Sunday night. It finally stopped raining and the sun was shining late that afternoon." I started to laugh at myself. "And then you called me. You called me and said 'Ethan, hurry, come to the tracks!' And I got so scared, so I jumped into my car and went there. And when I got there you were jumping up and down, clapping. You ran up to me and hugged me. I was so confused. You grabbed my hand and led me to our garden. And then I saw it. I saw our rosebush, full bloom and bright with colour. I was so happy! I was ecstatic! And baby, remember what you told me?"

Rosie was looking up at me with a glow in her eyes. She wiped at her tears and nodded her head.

"What did you tell me?"

She cleared her throat. "I told you that we were mean to make fun of the ugly bush. And I shouldn't have been upset that it rained that weekend."

"Why not?"

"Because sometimes things happen. Bad things happen to make good things happen. Bad things happen so the good things can fall into place. The rain ruined our weekend but it saved our garden. And everything was okay."

I smiled and held her.

She slowly sat up and ran her hands through her hair. "But this isn't the same thing, Ethan."

And my heart stopped again. I held my words in my throat until she continued.

"It's never going to be okay again," she stood up and headed for the door. Then she stopped, took a deep breath and turned to face me. She was crying again. "I promise you, Ethan, our lives will *never* be the same." And just like that, she opened the door and walked out of the room. She walked away from me once again.

I sat in the same spot, paralyzed. Every time I got close to her, I was pushed seven steps backwards. I remained frozen in the same spot as I stared out the window. The sun was too bright, so I turned away and focused on the beam of dust particles visible in the sunlight. I wished out loud that I would turn into millions of dust particles. Life would be easy enough if you could just float around and mind your own business. If you didn't care about anyone and no one cared about you. That's all I wanted at the moment. To be nothing. And as I redirected my eyes back to the window, the sunlight burned my eyes. I realized that a sunny day didn't have to be a good day. A sunny day could be the worst day of someone's life. It was all an illusion. People loved the sun and hated the rain. But it didn't make sense to me anymore. *The weather doesn't determine how one's day turns out*, I thought. *The sun is just the sun and the sky is just the sky.* It was all meaningless. It was all worthless. Just like the dust meant nothing to anyone.

And that was exactly how I felt at that moment. Useless. Just like a piece of dust.

I went over to Cam's house later that afternoon. Ever since I had known him, his mother always invited me over for dinner on Boxing Day. It was a tradition that would never change. I rang the doorbell and waited on the doorstep a few moments before his mother opened the door. Gloria was a really short lady. She had short blonde hair and brown eyes. She was always wearing an apron.

"Merry Christmas, Ethan!" she greeted me enthusiastically and wrapped her arms around my body and squeezed me. "I haven't seen you in forever! How have you been?" she asked.

Just as I was about to open my mouth, she interrupted. "Oh, it's cold out, please do come in." Gloria took a step back as I entered the warm house. She moved her head to the right of me and stuck it out. It was as if she saw something behind me. I naturally looked back to see what she was seeing. She quickly shrugged her shoulders and redirected her attention to me. It didn't take long to figure out; I believe she was looking for Rosie.

"Merry Christmas, Gloria," I said, trying to be polite. "The food smells amazing, as usual."

"Oh, thank you," she said as she grabbed my coat. "I made your favorite dessert again!"

"You really love fattening me up," I said as I tapped my belly.

She took my arm and held it. "Don't be silly, Ethan," she said. "You have plenty of room for food."

At that moment, Cam walked into the room sporting a big smile. "Hey there, buddy!" he said as he bear-hugged me. "Merry Christmas!"

I laughed and hugged him back. "Merry Christmas, buddy!"

"Hey, mom," Cam said, turning to face her, "do you mind bringing us some beer and chips downstairs?"

"Oh, sure," she said with a big smile on her face. "No problem, honey."

"Thanks, mom," he said as he leaned in to kiss her cheek.

I hadn't been in Cam's basement since I'd woken up in his washroom with a crazy hangover. The memory hit me hard and reminded me how much of an idiot I was. I shook my head at the thought. But his apartment looked exactly as I remembered it. Modern furniture, a nice TV, and his most prized possession, a pool table. Last time, I hadn't had a chance to admire it.

"Nice table, man." I said, stroking the soft green felt. Then I noticed Leah's name carved into the wood. I rubbed her name on my arm, suddenly remembering the day she died.

"Thanks," Cam said, tracing her name with his finger. "She's a beauty."

I could tell by the way he said it that he wasn't talking about the pool table.

"Well," I said, "she looks bored."

I saw Cam smile from the corner of my eye. "You sure you wanna face the master?" he said as he got the balls ready.

I grabbed a stick and chalked it up. "Master?" I laughed. "Master, my ass." I said sarcastically. "You have never defeated me in a game of pool."

"I may never have defeated you," Cam said. "But I've been practicing."

"All right," I said. "Challenge accepted."

Cam did the first break. Solids. "So," he said as he was aiming for another ball. "Did you talk to Rosie yesterday?" He didn't get anything in. It was my turn.

"Fuck, man," I said. "Her dad called me and he was freaking out. She was still at the train tracks at like six o'clock. So I went to get her and she was passed out drunk and she was frozen."

"Really?" Cam asked, shocked.

"Yeah," I said. "She had hypothermia. I had to call an ambulance."

"Fuck," he said in shock. "Is she okay?"

"Yeah, I guess," I said. "But we were all shaken up." I looked down and placed the stick between my fingers. I pulled it back and forth, back and forth. One more push. I hit the white ball and got a ball in. My turn again.

"Well," Cam said. "Did you guys talk?"

We both heard a knock on the door. "Cam, Ethan," we heard Gloria call. "I have your stuff." Cam and I both turned to face the door. She walked in with a tray full of chips and a small cooler filled with beer. "Now don't fill yourselves up with junk," she demanded. "Dinner will be ready in a few hours."

"Thanks mom." Cam grabbed a beer out of the cooler and tossed it to me.

Gloria just smiled and left, closing the door behind her.

I took another shot and got another ball in. I held a smirk on my face but Cam wasn't focussed on the game at all.

"So did you talk to her?"

"Yeah," I said. I wanted the conversation to end. I attempted another shot, but missed.

Cam sensed my disassociation. He knew I didn't want to talk. "You never want to talk to me anymore," he said as he smoked the white ball and got two solids in. I was impressed.

"I never said that," I said.

"I know," he said as he got yet another ball in. "But you're implying it."

I was about to open my mouth to respond, but I had no chance.

"No," he said. "It's fine. We don't have to talk."

I suddenly felt bad, so I decided to fill him in on what happened. "Fine," I said. "I was at the hospital with her. She was upset, obviously. She wanted me to leave."

Cam took another shot but missed.

My turn. I took a shot, but I missed too. "So I told her the story of our garden."

Cam raised an eyebrow. "Your garden?"

"Yeah," I said. "Long story short: A few summers ago, we bought a rose bush that was pretty much dead, and we planted it at the tracks. That was always her favorite place to go. Anyway, she was upset about how bad it looked. And that same weekend, we had plans to go on a picnic, but it rained for like three days straight and she was upset about that too. But when she went back to the tracks,"—Cam took a shot and missed—"the rose bush was fully bloomed. And she told me that sometimes bad things happen so good things can happen. We need to have bad to have to good and vice versa. I told her that story to remind her that something beautiful can come from something ugly. She seemed like she was enjoying the story, but then she said, 'It's not the same thing, Ethan,' and she promised me our lives would be changed forever."

"Shit," Cam said. "What do you think she means by that?"

"I have no idea," I said as I took a shot. "I have no fucking clue." I watched the red striped ball roll into the pocket.

"Maybe it's a good thing," Cam said.

"How can that be a good thing?" I asked.

"At least she said both of your lives would never be the same again."

"And that's a good thing because?"

"She included you," he said.

"Okay . . ." I didn't know what he was getting at.

"If she had said, 'My life will never be the same,' she wouldn't be including you, which would mean she had already made up her mind to be without you and face it alone."

I was starting to understand.

"But because she said 'Our lives will never be the same,'" he went on, "she is implying that you guys will be together. You're facing it together."

I smiled when I finally understood him. "It makes sense," I said. I took another shot, but I missed. "But do you think she said it on purpose?"

"What do you mean?" Cam asked as he shoved a handful of chips into his mouth.

"Do you think she said that to subtly assure me that she still wants to be with me? Or did she say it by accident?"

"I have no idea," Cam said, chewing. He took another shot and got one in. "You have to figure that out on your own."

"Figure it out how?"

"Well," he said. "You know her better than I do. What do you think she would do?"

I thought really hard about that one. After a few games of pool, all of which Cam won, and a few bottles of beer, I thought about it. I contemplated whether or not Rosie had meant to give me a clue.

Maybe she had hit her breaking point and finally realized that there was no being rid of me. Maybe I had finally convinced her that I was always going to be there. Maybe she finally had faith in us once again. And as I sat through dinner with Cam and his parents, then went down again to play another round of pool, I began to get more hopeful. There was something in me that was starting to believe. I was starting to believe that sooner or later, Rosie would be back in my arms. Obviously, things wouldn't go back to normal; she would never be the same person again. But I was starting to think that "normal" was boring and overrated. And Rosie had never been normal in the first place. She had always been an exciting part of my life. She had always been full of surprises. I was finally convinced that she had meant to say what she did. She purposely had told me that *our* lives would never be the same. The sentence was perfectly executed. It wasn't a mistake or an accident. She had been aware of her words. That was her way of thanking me. She was thanking me for not giving up on her. And she was ready to be "us" again. Oh God, I hoped I was right. More than anything, I hoped I was right about this one.

It reminded me of a dream confused with reality. It felt like one of those moments when I'd wake up in the middle of the night from a dream that felt so real. These dreams were so realistic, so expected and so common. So ordinary. I'd dream about going to work and forgetting my boots. Or about eating my breakfast at the kitchen table. Sometimes I'd dream up conversations with my mother or Cam or Rosie, and I'd be confused when I saw them next. I'd wonder, did I actually talk to them about this? No matter how realistic my dreams felt, I would still always carry doubt. And so I'd ask. And Rosie would giggle and say I was silly. She'd say we had never spoken about it. And then she'd laugh again and joke. And she'd tell me I was losing my mind. But then she'd grip my face and kiss my lips. And she'd tell me she loved me anyway.

I felt that way when I got the text message. I thought to myself, this must be a dream. Without a doubt, it had to be a dream. I looked at my phone over and over again. And my doubt started to disappear. I started to see clearly. There was no way that I was dreaming. I had just left Cam's house. I had finished dinner at his house, and I was heading home. All of that was real, so wasn't this? I felt like hitting my head over and over again. I felt like pinching my arm. It was so overwhelming, I had to pull over. And I re-read it. I double-checked the phone number. And I read it again. It was real. It was her.

I miss us so much. Can we start again?

My heart did a backflip. My heart started to tumble. And then took a bow for its awesome performance. I was overjoyed. I was thrilled. I was in love! She hadn't told me she wanted to see me that moment, but I was already speeding down the road on the way to her house.

She was already there. As if she had had a premonition. She knew I was coming. She was sitting on her porch steps waiting for me. She looked beautiful. Her hair was shiny again. It looked long and strong. Her cheeks were full of colour. And she sat there, finally wearing a winter jacket. I parked my car and got out. She was already walking towards me. But I noticed that she picked up the pace once she got closer. And then she was finally doing a light jog. And when she reached me, she jumped up and wrapped her hands around my neck. I hugged her tightly, and spun her around in a circle. I couldn't believe this was happening, I thought to myself.

And sure enough, she took my face in her hands and planted her sweet lips onto mine. I loved the taste. Oh, I had missed the taste. I held her face in my hands and kissed her back. I felt her gently push her tongue against my lips. I opened my mouth and allowed her to move into me. My hand moved its way to the back of her head and I pushed her into me. She tasted unbelievably delicious. I wanted her badly. I wanted all of her.

Rosie pulled away from me and took a deep breath. My eyes were still closed and I almost lost my balance. When I regained my focus, I noticed tears in her eyes. "No, Rosie baby," I said as I held her beautiful face in my hands. "What's wrong?"

"I'm sorry," she said. "I'm sorry about everything."

"No, baby," I said. "You did nothing wrong. You have nothing to be sorry about."

"I went to see the garden yesterday," she said. "That's why I was there."

"Why, baby?" I asked. "I don't like when you hurt yourself."

"I didn't mean to," she said as she started to cry. "I was just upset. And I wanted not to hurt anymore. So I drank. But it hurt even more. And it was too much."

"It's okay, baby," I said as I hugged her. "I believe you. I love you. And I will always be here with you. I promise you."

I felt her hug me back. She nuzzled her face into my chest. *God, I thought, I never want to let this moment go.*

"I miss you, Ethan," she said. "God, I miss you so much." She tightened her grip around me. And she held onto me for a while. I didn't care how long she needed me there. I didn't care how long it took. The cold wind didn't bother me at all. She could have held onto me for the rest of my life if she wanted. I didn't want to move. I let her be. But she led me to my car and told me to drive. And I did. She held my hand as we drove off into the sunset. As we sang at the top of our lungs.

> *Sweet Caroline,*
> *Good times never seemed so good.*
> *I've been inclined to believe they never would.*

Sweet Rosie. I love you so much, sweet Rosie.

CHAPTER ELEVEN

PURITY

Rosie and I went camping for the first time after a few months of dating. It was the end of August, the last weekend of Rosie's summer holiday before she started her first year at the University of Toronto. She complained that she didn't want the summer to end. She didn't want the days to get shorter. She wanted to always feel the sand between her toes. She wanted to sleep in and stay up late. She didn't like the idea of the sun setting at 5:00 instead of 8:30. She loved the freedom that summer brought her. She loved her new Jeep Wrangler. She took the top off and drove around. She said she loved feeling the wind in her hair. She loved being able to get up and do almost anything she wanted. She could get up and drive to the beach and dip her toes in the water. Or she could drive around in the country for a bit, stop at a little ice cream shop, and grab a vanilla cone. She told me she loved seeing the ice cream melt down the side of her cone. She'd often watch the ice cream droplets as they landed on the ground beneath her. She said summer provided her with endless possibilities. There were no limitations. She was free. She was in love and she was free. And then she looked up at me with sad eyes. The saddest eyes I'd ever seen. And I knew it then. I knew that she saw me as a season. I had blown into her life like a warm breeze. And she thought that I'd leave her once summer disappeared.

"For you," I said as I kissed her forehead, "I'll always be your summer."

Rosie had never been camping before. I thought that was crazy. But I also thought she was hilarious as she frolicked around her room packing the most unnecessary things. A hair dryer, nail polish, and several other things. She threw everything into her giant pink duffel bag. I sat on her bed watching her turn her room upside down looking for another electronic hair appliance. She suddenly stopped when she noticed the smirk on my face. With her hand on her hip, she asked me what I thought was so funny.

"Nothing," I said as I held onto my smile. And with a wave of my hand, I told her to carry on.

She moaned and groaned and stomped her feet. She looked under her bed, she flipped over her pillows, and when she began empting out her closet, I started to feel bad, so I spoke up.

"Rosie?" I asked.

She turned around and looked at me with the look of death. The you-need-to-shut-up-before-I-kill-you look.

Normally, I would have backed down, but it was getting ridiculous. "What are you even looking for?" I asked.

"My flat iron!" she snapped. "I use the stupid thing every day and now when I need it, I can't even find it." It looked like she was going to pull out her hair, so I decided to intervene. I walked up to her and hugged her. "Baby," I said. "If I knew what a flat iron was, I would help you."

"You know what a flat iron is," she snapped again as she escaped my embrace. She started opening her drawers. "It's the thing I use to straighten my hair. I use it all the time!"

"Oh," I said. I knew exactly what she was talking about. "Isn't that it? Over there?" I pointed at her desk, where she got ready in front of her mirror.

She quickly spun around and when she noticed it, she let out a fierce groan, grabbed it off of the desk and threw it into her bag. She took a deep breath and closed her eyes. "I'm forgetting something," she said as she began to pace the room. "I really am."

"Rosie," I said. She didn't hear me. She was looking for something else. I didn't know what, and she probably didn't either. "Rosie," I said again. Again, she didn't stop. "Rosie!" I finally snapped.

She stopped in her tracks and blinked. "What?"

"Why are you bringing so much shit?" I asked.

"What do you mean, *shit*?"

"All this stuff," I said, pointing to her bag. "We're going camping. You don't need that stuff."

She rolled her eyes. "Yes, I do! And you wouldn't understand. You're a boy."

I loved the way she said it. She emphasized the word boy like it was a bad thing to be. Like she was making fun of me for being a boy.

"Okay," I said. "I'll give you that point. But where do you think you're going to plug all this shit in?" I asked as I twirled the chord of her flat straightening thing like a lasso.

"What do you mean?"

I laughed. "Are you planning on inserting this into the trunk of a tree?"

She blinked for a bit and then looked up at me and smiled. "The washroom, silly," she said. She began to pace her room again.

"Babe," I said. "Remember those dirty stinky washrooms we had to use at the beach?"

"Oh my God, yes!" she said, eyes wide with shock. "They were disgusting!"

"Yes, they were," I said. "But that's the kind of washroom we have to use when we go camping."

She froze in place. "You're joking, right?" she asked.

I laughed again. "No, babe," I said. "I'm serious! What did you expect? Fancy washrooms and room service? We're gonna be in the woods, surrounded by nature."

I saw the light in her eyes change from invigorated to disappointed. She slowly dragged herself to her bed, sat down and crossed her arms. She was adorable.

"What's the matter, baby?" I sat down beside her.

"Nothing," she said.

"You don't want to go camping anymore?"

"I didn't say that," she said. "I'm just gonna be ugly when I do."

I chuckled. "That's impossible."

She looked at me as if to say I was lying and inclined to say good things about her appearance.

"I can be ugly with you," I offered. She just looked at me. I put my two index fingers in my mouth, stretched my lips out sideways, crossed my eyes, and made a hideous sound.

"Ew, stop that!" She shrieked and hit my arm. "You're gross!" She rolled over on her bed and giggled. I rolled over on top of her and started to tickle her. She was kicking and screaming, but still laughing. And her laughter was music to my ears. I continued to tickle her, selfishly enjoying the sound of her laugh while she struggled to catch her breath. When I stopped, she took a big breath of air and hummed satisfaction as she looked up at me with her beautiful brown eyes. She noticed that I was admiring her beauty, so she smiled. I nuzzled my face into her neck and kissed her. She tasted beautiful. And I wanted her, badly. I started making my way down from her neck. I kissed her collarbone and started moving towards her breast. Her eyes rolled back and she moaned, but then she opened her eyes and pushed me off. She sat up and turned away from me. "I don't think I'm ready," she said.

I stood up, reached for her head and kissed it. "Take your time," I said. "I'll always be here."

It was a cold night. It was a miserable weekend and the air was crisp; the campfire did us no good. We remained in the tent and lay on top of an air mattress beneath blankets, trying to keep warm. I cuddled up against Rosie, and she laid her head against my chest. I felt her shiver under the covers. Her nose was cold and red. Her foot slowly brushed up against my leg. Up and down, up and down. "Ethan," she said from beneath the covers.

"Mm-hmm," I hummed with my eyes closed.

"You love me, right?" she asked.

"More than anything," I said.

"Even more than," she thought for a while. "Even more than the moon?"

"Yes, of course," I said. "Even more than the moon."

"I like the moon." She shifted to lie on her back. The tent had a mesh top and we were able to see the night sky.

I opened my eyes and inhaled the moon's beauty. "Me too."

"Did you know that you only ever see one side of the moon?"

"Really?" I asked.

"Yep," she said. She was proud to know that fact. "That's why they always call the other side 'the dark side of the moon.'"

"Hmm. I had no idea. That's amazing."

"Isn't it?" she asked. She turned her face towards me. "Do you think I'm prettier than the moon?"

"Baby," I said, "the moon is just a rock. Of course you're prettier than her."

She had no response for me. She just turned to watch the moon for a while.

"Wanna know a secret?" I asked, breaking the silence.

She turned to face me with excitement in her eyes. "Yes, I do!"

"I used to think the moon was the prettiest thing I had ever laid eyes on."

"Really?" she asked innocently.

"Yep," I said. "I remember as a kid, I used to sit at my window and just stare at the moon. I loved it when it was a half moon, or when it looked like a clipped fingernail."

Rosie started to giggle. "I always thought it looked like a clipped fingernail, too!"

"I especially loved it when it was full. She was so bright and she drew me in. She was my first ever experience of real beauty."

"Yeah," Rosie said. "She is really pretty."

"But I don't think she's so pretty anymore."

"You don't?" Rosie asked in pretend shock. "Why?"

"Something else has caught my attention."

"Really?"

"Yep. Something even more amazing."

"Let me guess," she said. "The sun?"

"Nope," I said.

"I know!" she exclaimed. "The ocean."

"Not even close."

"What, then?"

I turned onto my side and kissed her cold nose. "You," I said. "You are the most beautiful thing I have ever had the privilege to see."

A wide smile spread itself across her face. "I love you," she whispered as she leaned in to kiss me.

"I love you more."

We began to kiss each other tenderly. Her lips were sweet and she tasted like a flavor I'd been addicted to my whole life. She was so beautiful. I rubbed her back with my hands, and I slowly reached down and traced her behind. I felt her tense up so I quickly moved my hand away, but she continued kissing me. She starting rubbing my thigh with her hand and moved her way down to my area. I quickly tensed up because she had never done that before. She sensed my tension immediately, so she slowly whispered in my ear, "I am ready. I want to be all yours."

A powerful feeling rushed through my bones at that moment. A strong feeling of passion and fire. But an even stronger feeling of desire and love.

She lay beneath me, her hair a dark halo that contrasted against the snow-white bedsheets. She took off her shirt, and I placed my hands on her breasts. I kissed her neck and made my way down to her bosom, using my tongue to taste her. She locked my hair in her fingers and moaned. She leaned her head back, and the outline of the muscles on her neck looked sexy. It drove me wild. I traced my finger from her neck down to her navel over her silky skin. We were warm enough; the cold air didn't matter anymore. She closed her eyes and winced in pain as I eased my finger into her. I put my nose against her neck and started to kiss her ear. "I love you, Rosie." I whispered as I eased my finger into her once again. She was so warm. I started to rub her as I continued using my finger. I didn't want her to be in pain. I wanted her to feel good. She started to moan as she kissed my chest. "I'm ready for you, baby."

Those were the words. Those were the words needed. So I slowly put myself in her. I didn't want to hurt her. Deliciously torturous moments went by as I went in and out. Slowly and gently. Her nails dug into my back as she closed her eyes. She was so warm. It felt so good. I started to kiss her neck as I went in and out. Faster and faster, I whispered "I love you" in her ear. She held onto my hair as her pain turned into pleasure. I thrust myself deeper into her. She rolled her eyes back again as she started to moan. Our bodies intertwined with each other. My skin was hot and melted into drops of sweat. I watched them fall on her. And the pure white bedsheets melted beneath us like snow. She was beginning to tense up; her fingers dug into my back and her toes curled underneath the bedsheets. She let out a scream and collapsed into me. Not even a moment later, I exploded and fell apart on top of her.

We were both out of breath. We were both gasping for air. She was so beautiful.

It was a difficult concept to grasp. I mean, I had been with different people before, and sex was just sex. It was fun and wild. It felt good. But when I saw Rosie sleeping by my side that night, I had a different feeling. She wasn't just someone I had slept with. She was someone I appreciated. She was someone I loved. She was an angel, pure as gold. She hadn't given herself to anyone before. She had saved herself for me. I was proud of her, and grateful. She confided in me, and it gave me the confidence to believe she knew what she wanted. She was brave. I wanted to spend the rest of my life with her. I wanted to see her beautiful face walking down a church aisle towards me. I'd carry her into our brand new house. We'd buy a Siberian Husky like she'd always wanted. And then I wondered how she would look like while she carried my child. She'd be really round and she'd walk funny. The thought put a smile on my face. I couldn't wait for the day.

"Ethan . . . Ethan, hello, Ethan?" Rosie called my name as I awoke from my daydream. "Ethan, can you please pass me a sandwich?"

I brought myself back to reality. I blinked into the realization that we were at a park having a picnic, and I had somehow dozed off into nothingness. I distractedly handed her a salami and cheese sandwich.

"You okay?" she asked as she suspiciously took the sandwich from my hand. "You were totally zoned out."

"Yeah," I said. "I was just daydreaming." I smiled at her.

"Okay," she said, biting into her sandwich. "Whatever you say."

It was the beginning of April. All of the snow had melted away, and birds were starting to fill the trees and the sky with song. The weather had been mild, but that one Saturday was a beautiful sunny day. So Rosie and I decided to pack up a blanket and a few sandwiches and hide away for a while. We found a perfect place right beside a riverbank. I had drifted off listening to the sound of the flowing water. Things were getting better with time. I still felt timid around her at times, but I always remembered that time had the power to heal all. We spent more and more time together, which was a good thing. I began to notice little things. The little things that shouldn't even matter—but they did. For instance, she was starting to hold my hand naturally. It wasn't planned or thought out; there wasn't one bit of hesitation. She just grabbed my hand because it felt right. She was starting to sing in the car again, too. She had always used to sing in the car, and recently she had been holding back. But when a song she really liked came on, she'd sing it like she was a professional. She wasn't bad—I mean, she could have used some work, but I didn't care. I just liked the sound of her voice. I began to notice the subtle things, too. I used to always have to push and initiate conversation. If I didn't talk, we wouldn't talk at all. Sometimes when I picked her up, she'd talk to me about something ridiculous she had read in the newspaper. Or she would tell me that she redecorated her room that day—which she did quite often. But it's strange what you notice once you've been given a second chance. Once you've lost something and had to learn to live without it. It is bizarre how the simplest things are always the most complex. It was weird that I knew my Rosie was getting better because she started painting her nails again.

One thing that I noticed for sure was that her dimple had started to jump out at me again.

And when it jumped at me, I so badly wanted to catch it. Catch it and never let it go.

"Hey," Rosie said as she poked my nose. I was lying underneath the sun's warmth and dozed off again. I opened my eyes and saw her cute face. "Wanna go for a walk? I'm done my book."

I looked at the closed book sitting in her lap. "That was fast," I said in shock. "Didn't you just buy it yesterday?"

"Yeah." She took a sip from her water bottle. "But Mister sleepyhead here was snoring away, and I had nothing to do. I could have played Frisbee with myself, but I thought reading my book would be more suitable."

"You're cute," I said as I leaned over to kiss her nose. "Let's go, then," I said as I stood up. I reached out my hands and helped her to her feet.

We held hands as we walked down a trail through the park. A warm breeze whistled through the leaves. It was quaint and peaceful. It was a nice feeling, walking through the woods with her hand in mine. The wind was warm and comforting. A great contrast to the winter we had all endured.

"Baby," Rosie said, "maybe one day we can have a house up here."

"Yeah," I said sarcastically. "Do you have a million dollars to throw away?"

"Well, technically, we wouldn't just be throwing it away. We'd get a nice home out of it. I might be rich when I'm done school. I might just make a lot of money when I sell my books."

"That's true," I said. "Do you think you're going to go back to school in the fall?" Immediately, I sensed her mood change. It happened quite often; as soon as we started talking about life and serious things, she'd get upset.

She looked down at her feet and shrugged her shoulders.

"Why not?" I asked. "Didn't the dean give you a huge extension so you could graduate with your class? You need to go in September or he'll revoke his offer."

"I don't think I'll be ready."

"What do you mean?" I asked. "You're doing great! Right? You don't have those nightmares anymore. You're off of the Zoloft. I think you'll be fine."

"It doesn't matter what you think, Ethan," she snapped. I was taken aback by the frustration in her voice. "Can you just back off? I'll go when I know I'm ready. Not when *you* think I am."

I muttered an apology under my breath. It was all I could manage say. I was trying my best. I didn't want to push her, but I wanted to encourage her. I knew she had potential. I knew she was passionate, and I knew if she tried hard enough, she could do anything she wanted.

She immediately let go of my hand and picked up the pace. She never failed to make me aware that she was upset or that I had done something wrong.

"What now?" I asked. I stopped walking. "You don't need to be mad at me. I was just trying to help."

She quickly turned around and shot me a fierce look. "I don't need your help!" she cried. "I don't need your help. I don't need anyone's help!" Tears began to fall down her face.

It felt like somebody had punched me in the gut. I hated seeing her cry. Especially after what she'd been through.

"Rosie." I walked up to her with my arms extended. "Why are you crying? I hate seeing you cry."

She turned away from me and rejected my hug.

"Rosie, please." I wanted her to stop hurting.

"You don't understand, Ethan," she whispered. "You don't understand."

"Well, how do you expect me to know anything when you don't tell me anything?" I said as I turned her around. "You never let me in, Rosie. How do you think I feel? I just want you to be happy."

"How can I be happy, Ethan?" she snapped. "How can you expect me to just forget it all? I want to. Believe me, I wish nothing had ever happened to me! But it did and there is nothing I can do about it. You don't think I want to be happy?" She wiped her face with the back of her hand. "I want to be happy. And I'm trying, Ethan. I really am. But I can't switch it on and off, whenever I feel like it. It's a part of my life now. It's a part of me now."

"I don't want it to just be a part of you, Rosie." I said as I choked back my tears. I grabbed her hand and placed it on my heart. "I want it to be a part of us."

She began to cry harder.

"You're not alone, Rosie. You're safe now." I started to kiss her sweet hands. "You have me. And you'll have me forever. Nothing bad is going to happen to you, because I won't let it. Not anymore." I gently placed her head on my chest and held her tight. "You're okay now, baby. I'm so glad you're okay." I couldn't hold it anymore; a river of tears made its way down my face and onto her hair. "I missed you so much. I hated being without you. I slept with your picture under my pillow. I'd scream your name every night. I thought you were dead. And my parents hated seeing me that way. Everyone treated me differently. I have never felt so much pain in my life, Rosie. My everything was taken from me, and I wasn't certain if I'd ever have her back. It killed me, Rosie. It felt like a thousand knives made their way through to my heart." I hugged her tighter. I felt her tears soak through my T-shirt. "I missed you so much. And I wanted to die. I wanted so badly to die, but something in me kept me holding on. I believed in you. And I couldn't leave this planet without being certain. Something in me told me you were coming back, and that was the only thing that kept me strong through it all."

She pulled away from me and her eyes met mine. She looked like she had just seen a ghost. "I couldn't remember this, Ethan," she said.

"Remember what?"

"Us."

I was confused. "What do you mean?"

"I'm so sorry." She started to cry. "But . . ." She hesitated. "I couldn't remember you."

I was startled by her confession. *What does she mean?* I asked myself. "I don't understand," I said.

She shook her head and kept crying. "I stopped thinking about you, Ethan. And there were so many times I just wanted to end it. I wanted to end my life. I wanted to end it all. But it wasn't you that kept me alive." She looked down at her feet and remained quiet for a moment. "I'm sorry," she finally said.

I didn't say anything to her. I stared at her for a while. Her eyes were locked on mine. I was waiting for something while I stood in front of her. The wind was picking up and clouds were rolling in. I saw her hair blowing with the breeze. She was so beautiful.

"I was so scared, Ethan," she cried. I quickly gathered her in my arms and held her. "I was so alone and scared. As soon as he took me from the parking lot—" She stopped and brought her hand to her face. Her beautiful, swollen eyes looked up at me. "I thought I was going to die. I really did. And as I was trying to fight him off, I saw you. I saw you standing over his shoulder, watching everything happen. And you looked so real. It felt like I could touch you. And I was screaming your name, and you didn't budge. You didn't even move." She pulled away from me. "I knew it was a delusion, but you looked so real. And I felt so hurt and abandoned. You didn't even want to help me." Rosie wiped her eyes and turned away from me. "I tried my best, Ethan. But that image of you was so disturbing. I hated you and I loved you at the same time. And then you turned around and walked away, so I stopped fighting. I gave up. And the man shoved me into his truck. The only person who mattered to me didn't want to fight for me, so I stopped fighting too."

"Rosie, you know I would never—" I began.

"Let me finish," she interrupted. "If I don't tell you now, I never will." She took a deep breath and turned around to face me again. "I just want to apologize, okay? I knew better. I knew with all my heart that if you really witnessed anything like that happening to me, you would have literally killed someone. But I don't know why, Ethan. I don't know why I suddenly lost all my faith in you."

"It was because I didn't fix your car," I confessed.

"Don't be silly, Ethan," she said. "It had nothing to do with my car."

"Let me finish!" I snapped. I immediately felt bad, but I needed to talk about it. "Rosie, I failed you, okay?" I began. "I let you slip through my fingers. I put your needs on the backburner. I failed you."

Rosie started to cry again. She tried to tell me it was okay, but I went on anyway.

"Listen to me, please" I begged. "I was the fucking idiot who told you not to go to a mechanic. I said I would fix your car. I insisted I would." I began to cry. "And you were the beautiful angel who told me not to worry about it, and that you would pay to get it fixed. But I promise, baby," I said as I reached to grab her hands. "My intentions were good. My intentions were for you to save your money, and that was all I wanted. And I gave you excuse after excuse, lie after lie. I was too tired one day, or I was busy the next. I should have done it when your car broke down the second time. But I didn't and I'm so sorry. Believe me baby, if I had any idea what would happen to you, I would have paid for a mechanic myself! I promise you," I cried as I started to kiss her hands. "I'm sorry. And I never wanted to admit it to myself. I was a coward. I wondered why you were so hostile towards me. I wondered why it felt like you hated me. And I convinced myself that you were wrong. You should love me because I love you. But how can I expect you to do such a thing? You have every right to hate me, baby. I'm disgusting. I'm a fool. I am nothing. I feel guilty all the time, you know." I tried to block out her sobs because I needed to tell her. I knew she was hurting, but I needed her to know that if it weren't for my broken promise, nothing bad would have happened to her. I held her face in my hands and stared into her beautiful, crying eyes. "I hate myself, Rosie. I know that I am the reason it happened—"

"No, Ethan, you're not! Please, stop it!" she begged.

"You saw an image of me walking away from a problem because that's all I have ever done!"

She struck my face. She raised her hand and hit me. I felt the sting through my tears. I immediately stopped talking. I choked on my words. I stared at her wide-eyed and shocked as I brought my hand up to my face.

"I will *never* let you convince me or yourself that you were the cause of this, Ethan," she snapped. "You need to stop. Stop wallowing in your own misery. Things happen to people all the time. Bad things happen all the time. It's a part of life, okay? Even if my Jeep did start, do you think if he really wanted me, he would have let me get away? I wasn't random, Ethan. He had his eye on me for a while." She turned away, ran her hands through her hair and let out a scream. "He knew where I lived." She turned back around to face me. "He knew where my parents worked. He knew what time they left the house in the morning and what time they came back." She began to calm down. "He even knew who you were, Ethan. He knew where you worked; he knew where you lived. He'd wanted me for a while, and he found the perfect moment. When I left work late at night, that was his opportunity. So please *stop* telling me this wouldn't have happened if you had fixed my car. Because it would have happened no matter what."

"What a fucking pig," I snapped. "People like him deserve to rot in hell!"

Very quietly, she said, "He is, Ethan. Believe me, he is."

I never stopped to think how Rosie had been affected by his death. She had had to kill him to protect herself. She had to end a human life to save her own. I couldn't even imagine being in the situation. Her conscience was once pure, but now it was splattered with death.

"Where did you shoot him?" I asked. The question made her freeze.

"What do you mean where?" she asked as she turned to face me. The heavy clouds began to release the rain. Rosie and I stood under a shower of despair.

"Where?" I yelled. "Where on his body did you shoot him?" I believed she was crying. I mean, we were talking about the man that she killed—she had to be crying, I thought. But the rain disguised it all. The rain disguised her tears.

"In the head," she snapped back. "I shot him in the head!"

I looked for a sign. I looked for a teardrop, a chin quiver, or a sniffle. I looked deep into her brown eyes. I looked for a hint of guilt. A hint of shame. It was hard to see through the rain, but I couldn't make a clear distinction. Her eyes were like a wolf's, empty but strong. There isn't a hint of guilt in a wolf's eyes as it takes the life of its prey. Not one bit.

"I have no remorse, Ethan," she said. Her words were cold and they made me shiver. "I have no remorse for that man's death," she repeated. She stood still with an expressionless face. "I stood over his dead body and told him to rot in hell."

I didn't like how murderous she sounded.

"If I had a chance to do it again," she continued, "I would." I was about to speak, but I swallowed my words. "But this time I'd spit on him," she went on. "I'd spit on him to shame him. Shame him like he shamed me."

I had never seen this side of Rosie before, but who was I to judge? There was something obviously different about her. She had an essence of power and strength. She had a huge sense of independence. It freaked me out, it really did. But there was something about it that

I liked. Something about her confessing her kill to me drew me in. It was as if we shared a common interest. Something was attracting me to her.

"I didn't kill him out of self-defence," she confessed. "I walked up to him while he was drinking his coffee. I walked up to him, put the gun between his eyes and pulled the trigger."

I said nothing. Her hair was wet from the pouring rain; I saw a fire burning in her eyes.

"I saw him fall onto the floor and die," she continued, "and it was the most liberating feeling ever. I was finally free."

I began to believe that if it had been me, I would have killed him too. Because killing him was liberation. And we both wanted to be free.

CHAPTER TWELVE

INSTINCT

There was a deer eating in the valley below me. It was hard to see. The sun was blinding, but I saw her grazing with her fawn following close behind. The fawn must've been a few days old, a week at most. I sat against a tree with my guitar in my hand, and I realized that life was often cruel. Life felt no empathy towards anyone. Hills and valleys landscaped my visions that afternoon. The trees were full of leaves, flowers were blooming, and just like every year, I was quickly reminded how much I loved spring. Spring was a reward, a promise of sorts. Spring was always there to save us from the cold and bitter winters. It provided nature with new life in the form of vegetation, animals, and humans. I watched as the fawn followed its mother, imitating everything she did. It amazed me how complex and beautiful those creatures actually were. They learned essential survival in the most complicated manner. Nowadays, we need to research how to do everything. We read books, search online, observe, ask questions, and pursue. All the doe needed to do was what she normally did, and without a word, she taught her fawn exactly what to do. Learning how to survive is essential. Animals do it without rationale. They have no idea why they need to eat; they just do it because it's natural. In order for their species to continue living on this planet, only the strongest may breed, and when they breed they pass on their genes, securing another surviving generation. There will always be that definite line that separates civilized human beings from animals. Animals base their lives off of instinct. Once they sense danger, they defend themselves and their young. They do this to ensure the continuation of their species. But men call each other ruthless, crazy, or uncivilized for decisions that society doesn't approve of. Men are condemned for acting in such a way. But I think that when it comes down to people fighting for their lives or for the lives of loved ones, they may find themselves willing to do the unimaginable. Humans also have the instinct to ensure the survival of their species. Many people will cross the line when pushed enough and act out ruthlessly. But we all want the same thing in life. And that is to just live.

I watched the doe suddenly perk up her ears as her fawn hid in the grass. She looked around, licked her nose and sniffed the air. A fox slowly came out of a bush. Regardless of the critter's intentions, the mother doe went on high alert. She walked up to the fox. I watched his fur puff up and his ears fold back. He showed his teeth. But she stomped him with her hooves. I heard him yelp, but she went on. I saw the rage in her eyes. The fox finally escaped. The mother walked away as her fawn followed close behind. Uncivilized? Barbaric? Ruthless? Or just natural?

I felt guilty not being able to look at Rosie the same way anymore. I couldn't begin to imagine what Rosie was capable of doing. It was wrong, and I knew that. She hadn't suddenly turned into a cold-blooded murderer, but I just hadn't gotten used to the news yet.

Friday, April 12th, was Leah's birthday, which Cam and I always celebrated. Every year, we went to a bar in downtown Toronto right on Yonge Street on that day. We always ordered beer and chicken wings, which had been her favorite meal. We dedicated the whole night to her. Cam picked me up at 5:00 that evening. We always played her favorite music on the drive there, which was about an hour and a bit, mostly because of traffic. I used to think Cam was torturing himself with reminders of his baby sister, but people grieve differently. Whatever worked for him, I was all for it. We spent about 25 minutes looking for parking, and when we finally found a spot, we were a 20-minute walk from the lounge. It wasn't a bad walk. The sun was already setting and the wind picked up, making it a chilly evening. We walked into the lounge and found a booth in the corner of the room. The music was loud and the place was packed, which was quite surprising because it was only 6:45 p.m. It was warm in the lounge, so I unzipped my sweater as I took a seat. Cam offered to get the first round of drinks. I watched him walk to the bar and shove his way through a crowd of people. I always looked forward to this day all year, but there was always a place in my heart that hurt me. Leah should have been celebrating her birthday with us. It wasn't fair.

A redheaded waitress walked up to the table and asked me if I wanted anything. Her face was spotted with light freckles and her skin was fair. She was quite tall and slender. Her bright green eyes were warm and inviting.

"Uh, yeah, can I get one pound of the barbeque chicken wings and one pound of the honey garlic?"

She scribbled it on her notepad. "Sure." She smiled. "Anything else?"

"Yeah," I said and thought about it. "A large fries with gravy too."

"All right," she said. "Any drinks?"

"No. My buddy is on that." She turned around just as Cam was walking up with two Coronas.

"Here," he said as he handed me a beer. Cam noticed the waitress and smiled as he took his seat. She smiled back and quickly scurried off.

"She likes you," I said, taking a sip of my beer.

Cam looked back. "Who does?" he asked as he looked back at me.

"The waitress," I said with a smirk.

Cam laughed. "You're full of it."

"I'm serious," I insisted. "You should have seen the look she gave you. You should get her number."

"I'm not gonna get her number. I know she's hot, but she won't like me."

"Oh, God," I said, disgusted. "You sound like a little bitch. Do it for Leah. She always wanted you to find a nice girl."

Cam smiled as he nodded his head. "I'm gonna need more beers, then," he said.

"Cheers to that, my friend," I said as we clinked bottles. "Cheers to that."

"Happy birthday, Leah," Cam said as he took a sip.

"Happy birthday, Leah," I whispered.

The red-headed waitress came back with our wings and fries. It was a night for us to pig out, and I was hungry. "Would you boys like anything else?" she asked as she flashed a smile to Cam.

"Yeah," Cam said. "Onion rings."

The waitress scribbled it down. I noticed her nametag: Mary.

She was about to turn around and walk away before Cam stopped her. "Oh," he said. She turned around quickly and smiled. "Keep the beers coming," he said. Mary just blinked. "Please," Cam added. She nodded her head and was off.

"She is gorgeous," Cam admitted.

I just nodded my head.

"So how's Rosie?" he asked.

"Good," I said. "She's getting, you know, better."

Cam looked at me suspiciously. "Last time I asked about her, you said things were great."

"I know," I said. "They are great. It's just some days aren't as good as others."

"Is she still having nightmares?"

"She told me they stopped," I said. "But with her, you never know." I shifted in my seat. I didn't know what it was, but I was always uncomfortable talking to Cam about Rosie. It wasn't because I didn't trust him, but because I did. I knew Rosie's secret, and I knew alcohol could make me let it out. I chugged my beer nervously.

"What do you mean you never know?" he asked.

"I don't know," I said. "It's like she's bipolar. One minute she's fine and the next she's not."

Mary walked by and brought us more beer. I suddenly felt so thirsty, I swiped the beer out of her hand and began to chug it. "The onion rings will be a few more minutes," she said and walked away.

I didn't want onion rings. I was satisfied with my honey garlic wings and fries.

"Have you guys fought recently?" Cam asked. "You've been trying so hard to be on her good side."

"I know," I said. "And I don't know what's even considered a fight anymore."

"So you guys argue often?" he asked as he licked barbeque sauce off his fingers.

"She has been through a lot," I began.

"I know," Cam interrupted. "And I am in no way undermining what she has been through. But do you think it's fair that she drags you down with every emotional blowout she has?"

"That's the problem, Cam," I said. "I think she's trying to keep me away. She hasn't told me anything that happened. She doesn't talk about it. And I think she just doesn't want to hurt me so she keeps it from me. And I think it's driving her nuts. I can't just tell her to talk to me because she'll freak out. But I know she hasn't told me anything." I suddenly remembered her confession. "Well," I said, "she hasn't told me much." I had already finished my second beer. Mary came back with onion rings and two more beers.

"Mary is your name, right?" Cam asked her. I was relieved that the attention was finally off me.

"Yes," Mary said as she smiled and giggled. "And yours?"

"Cameron," Cam said. He stretched out his hand. He suddenly realized it was full of sauce, so he just closed his hand and bumped her fist. She laughed. "But people usually call me Cam."

She nodded her head. "I'll try to remember that."

"It sucks that you're working on a Friday night," Cam continued. I was actually quite surprised and impressed that he was talking to her.

"Yeah," she said. "I know. But I gotta make money somehow. Someone's gotta pay for school."

"You're in school?" Cam said, looking quite impressed. "Which school?"

"Ryerson," she said proudly. "I'm studying biochemistry."

"Wow," Cam said, winking at me. "We have a smart girl here."

Mary laughed as her cheeks flushed red. "Not smart," she said. "Just dedicated."

"Well, you have to be pretty smart to get accepted into university in the first place," Cam insisted.

Mary laughed and looked around nervously. "I'm done my shift in half an hour," she said. "What do you guys say I have a few drinks with you when I get off?"

"Sure," Cam said excitedly. "By all means, you're welcome to join us."

"Thanks," she said as she gently rubbed his arm. "See you in a bit."

Half an hour soon turned into an hour. Cam and I were pretty tipsy, but he couldn't hide his dismay when he noticed that Mary was still working. "She said she'd be done half an hour ago, man," he whined. "I told you she doesn't dig me."

"She probably had to stay a bit later," I tried to comfort him. "It is pretty busy in here. They are probably short-staffed."

"Whatever, man." He shrugged his shoulders. "I won't find a girl like you."

"A girl like me?" I asked. "Or a girl like Rosie?" I laughed. I knew what he meant.

"You know what I mean, man!" Cam laughed. "You found yourself a perfect girl."

"No one is perfect," I said.

"Rosie is pretty close," Cam insisted. "How is she doing, anyway? We didn't finish our conversation."

"She's okay," I said. "I guess." I felt a little more than tipsy. I could tell Cam was feeling it too.

"I don't believe you," Cam said. "You're already a bad liar, but it's even worse when you're drunk."

"I'm not drunk," I lied. "You're drunk."

"Cheers to that," Cam laughed as he held up his beer. He quickly chugged it back and was on to the next one. "Did she tell you anything more?"

"Tell me anything more about what?"

"About what she went through. Does she talk about it at all?"

"Not really," I lied.

"You know you can trust me, right?" Cam said.

"Of course I know that," I said. "It's just a hard thing to talk about." I really wanted to tell him. I wanted to see the situation from a different pair of eyes. I mean, my opinion of Rosie could be shattered because I loved her. I was biased. And Cam could give me advice.

"The rape?" he asked.

"No," I responded. "She actually doesn't talk about that at all."

Cam sensed my hesitation, so he stopped pushing it. "I'm here if you need to talk, okay?"

"Thanks." I nodded my head and took a sip of my beer. There were a few awkward quiet moments; the conversation had loose ends. He knew I wasn't done. "You know she killed him, right?" I whispered.

"Yeah," Cam chuckled. "Everyone knows she had to. Who cares? He deserved it. The fucker deserved it."

"No," I said. "I know everyone knows she shot him out of self-defence. But what if I told you it wasn't out of self-defence, per se?"

"Okay," Cam said. "So what if she did?"

"You don't think it's fucked?"

"Do you know that for sure?"

"Yes," I said. "She told me he was drinking a coffee when she walked up to him and,"—I hesitated a bit and cleared my throat—"and shot him. Right between the eyes."

"Your point?" Cam looked unimpressed.

"What do you mean 'my point'?" I asked. "Cam, she pretty much murdered him!" I quickly looked around to make sure people weren't listening. They weren't.

"No she didn't," Cam snapped. "What the fuck, Ethan? You're going to look at Rosie differently because she killed on purpose the guy who was raping her?"

I blinked at his response. Maybe I was the only one who was freaked out about it. "You don't think it's scary?"

"No," Cam said. "Not at all. She has balls. That's actually courageous, and I am proud of her for that. I respect her for that." Cam was beginning to make sense. "She decided she'd had enough, and she did the only thing she could have done. The only thing any human being could do."

I had no response.

"And believe me, Ethan. If you were in her situation, you would have done the exact same thing. I can guarantee you."

Mary finally joined us an hour and half later than promised. "Sorry guys," she said as she scooted in and sat beside Cam. "My boss needed me to stay a bit longer."

I gave Cam an I-told-you-so look.

"Well," Cam said. "We're glad you were finally able to make it."

What a charmer, I thought. I saw Mary blush.

"This is my friend Ethan," Cam said as he pointed at me.

Mary stuck out her hand. "Ethan," she said. "I'm Mary. Nice to meet you."

I nodded my head and said, "Nice to meet you too."

"I apologize in advance, lovely lady," Cam said. "But my friend here is drunk. And so am I."

Mary giggled. It was a fake laugh, I thought. I could tell she liked Cam. It seemed like she was trying hard to impress him.

"So what are you boys celebrating?" she asked. She had already brought another round of beers.

"My sister's birthday," Cam said.

"Your sister?" she asked, confused. She started to look around. "I didn't see you with anybody else."

"Oh," Cam said. "Sorry for the misunderstanding. My sister isn't here."

"Oh." Mary smiled. "So she's on the way?"

"No," Cam said. "She's not coming."

She tilted her head sideways and shot him a confused look. Cam just took a sip of his beer and pretended the conversation wasn't happening. Mary looked at me for an answer.

"Leah," I said. "Leah died four years ago in a car accident. We celebrate her birthday every year."

"Oh my," she said. She raised her hand to her mouth. "I'm so sorry." She placed her hand on Cam's knee. "That is actually so beautiful and amazing. So inspiring."

"It's no big deal," Cam said. "She's gone and she won't come back. Who cares?"

I knew Cam didn't mean a word he'd just said. "Actually," I interrupted, "it is a big deal. We both miss her very much. Cam is just drunk and he's pretending like it doesn't bother him. But it does. He just tries to hide it, but I see right through him. And he's kind of hypocritical, because when something bothers me, he feels the need to drill it out of me and be some sort of superman. But when I try to talk to him, there is no use."

"It's a different situation," Cam snapped. "Completely different. There is closure with Leah. We know she is dead. I was supporting you because we didn't know about Rosie."

"Who's Rosie?" Mary asked.

"My girlfriend," I said as I took a sip of my drink.

"Did she pass too?" she asked.

"No," I said. "She was abducted for 11 weeks. She's okay."

"Oh my God!" she shrieked. "Rosie Lutine? The girl from the news?"

"Yes," I said. "Her."

"That's your girlfriend?" she whined. "Oh, you poor thing."

I suddenly didn't like her, but I could tell Cam was drooling over her.

"You guys are so inspiring and brave."

"So why don't you tell us about yourself?" I asked redirecting the conversation. "What's your story?"

"Well," she said, shifting closer to Cam, "like I said, I go to school. I work here part-time. I like going out to have a good time."

"You have nice legs," Cam interrupted as she started to rub her thigh. "I like them."

"Thanks," she blushed.

"I'm assuming that a pretty girl like you must have a boyfriend."

She giggled. "No," she said. "I did, for a long time, but I just recently left him. About two weeks ago."

"Why?" I asked. I don't know why I asked. I really didn't care, but I was bored. And she was entertaining.

"He was an ass," she said.

"An ass?" I asked. "How so?"

"He was mean to me."

"Mean how?" I asked. I felt Cam kick my foot under the table. He shot me a look.

"I don't know," she shrugged her shoulders. "He was always mean, but then he started to hit me."

"He hit you?" Cam asked in shock.

"Yeah," she said. "It didn't happen a lot at first, but then I guess he started to like how powerful it made him feel and he kept doing it. So I left him."

"Sorry to hear," I said, suddenly feeling bad.

"It's no big deal," she insisted. "I mean, yeah it sucked, and I loved the guy, but I deserve better."

"Exactly," Cam said. "And don't let anyone make you feel otherwise."

She just smiled, but she suddenly looked uncomfortable. "I still get scared though."

"Scared?" Cam asked. "Why?"

"He's not in jail," she began. "He lives in Toronto like I do. And he walks around like I do. I have a restraining order against him, but sometimes I feel like he's watching me and when he sees me, he'll kill me, or something." She paused for a bit. "I know it sounds ridiculous, but he's always in the back of my mind."

"Don't think like that," I said, trying to comfort her. "You should just keep it out of your mind."

"I know," she said. "But it still scares me. Like I do see him around sometimes, and he doesn't do anything. He knows I work here and he usually comes in for a few drinks and then he's off. And I know he's harmless in a place like this. I just don't want him catching me alone."

"Don't worry," Cam said. "I'll protect you."

Mary laughed and nuzzled her nose into Cam's neck. "You're so cute," she said.

I saw Cam kiss Mary's neck and I suddenly felt extremely uncomfortable. I hated being a third wheel. "Okay guys," I said. "I'm gonna go now." I stood up.

"Whoa," Cam said. "It's only 9 o'clock, man. Stay, have fun."

"Naw," I said. "It's okay, you two have your fun."

"You didn't drive here. And you're too drunk to drive anyway," Cam said. "You gotta sober up."

He was right. I was way too drunk to drive. Before I even thought about sitting down again, Mary stood up, opened her arms, and shrieked. I was startled and confused. I quickly looked behind me and saw another girl shrieking as she ran up to Mary. They embraced each other and started jumping up and down, squealing and screaming. I was freaked out. What the heck was wrong with them? I asked myself.

"Sorry, Ethan," Mary said as she turned around. "This is Isabella, my best friend. I texted her to come when I thought you were single."

Mary frowned and looked back at her friend. Isabella had dark curly hair, tanned skin, and dark eyes. "He's dating the Rosie chick from the news. Remember her?"

"Oh my God," Isabella said. "Wasn't she like raped and stuff?"

"Bella!" Mary shrieked. "Don't say that stuff around him."

"Sorry," Isabella said, giggling.

I just rolled my eyes and sat down. This was going to be a long and annoying night, I thought.

Isabella sat beside me. I felt her move closer and closer, until I was against the wall. I thought Mary was obnoxious, but Isabella was much worse. Much, much worse. I thought my ears were bleeding. I decided to pull out my phone and text Rosie.

> *Hey*

Not even a minute later Rosie responded.

> *How's it going? Having fun?*
> *Nope. Not at all.*
> *Why not?*
> *Cam is hanging out with a waitress. Her friend came to join us on this imaginary double date. They know I'm dating 'the girl from the news'. But girls are crazy, and loud*

She didn't respond right away. I was immediately nervous. I thought she was upset.

> *Lol*

I knew that Rosie wasn't impressed.

> *I'm too drunk to drive. Can you rescue me? Please*
> *Ethan! I told you I have family over today*
> *I know but I really need to leave*

*Sometimes you are just so irresponsible. I told you not to
   drink if you were driving*
*I didn't drive! Cam picked me up. I'm not gonna take his
   car*
I'm on my way

"Oh my God, Mary!" Isabella shrieked. "I totally forgot to tell you!"

"What?" Mary shrieked back.

"I saw Ty outside!"

"You what?" Mary asked, suddenly speaking in a normal tone.

"Yeah," she said. "Don't worry, I totally gave him a dirty look. You don't have to worry."

"Why didn't you tell me before?" Mary hissed.

Isabella looked taken aback by her friend's anger. "Sorry, girl," she said. "I totally forgot."

"Are you freaking kidding me right now?" Mary said as she shifted away from Cam.

"What's wrong?" Cam asked.

"Ty is here!"

"Ty?" Cam asked. "Who's Ty?"

"My ex. He's been here since before Isabella got here," Mary cried. "He probably watched us the whole time."

I saw the fear in Mary's eyes. The same fear I saw in the fawn's eyes.

"Don't worry," Cam said. "He won't come around you while we're here."

Mary sighed. She seemed relieved. "Yeah," she said. "You're right, I guess."

The fawn hid in the grass.

"I'll protect you," Cam said as he kissed her cheek.

The mother doe.

"Hey, asshole," I heard Isabella say. I looked up to see who she was talking to. A man stood at our table. Dark hair, dark eyes and a strong build. He was wearing a tight white T-shirt and ripped jeans.

"Shut up, you little bitch," he hissed. "Mary, what the fuck are you doing here?"

It was Ty. The fox.

Cam spoke up before Mary had a chance to answer.

Mother doe.

"Leave her alone," Cam said. "You know you can't be here."

Ty slapped Mary on the back of her head. "You little bitch, already telling everyone about me!"

Cam rapidly jumped to his feet and got in front of Ty.

Mother doe.

Ty grabbed Cam by the shirt, turned him around and shoved him into a wall. "Who the fuck are you?" Ty yelled. "Do I know you, you little bitch? How about you mind your own business!"

The fox.

One thing I knew about Cam was that he was naturally a gentle person. He was usually laid back and relaxed. I rarely ever saw his bad side. His temperament was docile and quiet. But once Cam's buttons were pushed, he became completely different. And he was not the type of person you'd want to cross.

I knew I didn't need to step in because I knew exactly what would happen next. And my predictions were correct. Cam punched Ty in the jaw and Ty fell onto the floor. And within seconds, Cam was on top of Ty, continually punching him in the face. Mary was crying and screaming, begging him to get off. Isabella was freaking out. People and bouncers got involved and finally a bouncer pulled Cameron off. Ty wobbled off with a broken and bloody nose.

The fox.

Cam quickly turned his attention towards Mary.

The doe.

Mary smiled through her tears and squeezed his arm.

The fawn.

But because we were all humans, Cam and Ty were taken away by the bouncers and the police were called. Humans are expected to act in a certain way because we aren't animals. We are far from animals. We are smarter than animals. We create civilizations, cities and countries. We create technology. We adapted to make life easier. We are the most successful species.

But we are all still animals. And there is always an instinct that can become so powerful that it overtakes us. And it can change our lives forever.

CHAPTER THIRTEEN

DEFEAT

I was sent home early on a rainy April morning. I always worked whenever I had the chance to, but a day away from work meant a day with Rosie. And that was a day I loved to live. I'd never prayed for rain before, but any waking moment I spent away from her sent burning flames across my skin, and the water was a torturous refreshment. I felt like I could bury my feet deep into mud, deep into the ground, sheltered from the sun. It was cool. And I so badly wanted to grow roots and plant myself in the mud's coolness. I would remain there on my own two feet. And my rose would be planted right by my side.

"You never play your guitar anymore," Rosie said as she fluffed up her pillow and placed it under her head. She was wearing a sweater and hiding under my blanket. A shelter from the brutal storm outside. "It looks dusty."

I was sitting at my computer paying some bills online while Rosie snuggled in my bed and watched Finding Nemo. It had been raining all day and we had nothing to do but stay indoors and watch movies.

"Yeah," I said. "I know."

"Well, why don't you?"

"I want to spend all the time I can with you," I said. I heard Rosie laugh and I turned around to look at her. She was beautiful. "What?" I asked. "What's so funny?"

"You are spending your time with me," she laughed. "You can still play guitar. You don't need to be a charmer."

I smiled and turned back to the computer. "I did write a song for you," I said. "While you were missing."

"You did?" she asked. "Really?"

"Well," I said, "not a whole song. Just a chorus, I guess." I looked back at her and she was sitting up with her arms folded.

"Why not a full one?"

I ignored her question, walked up to my guitar and started playing a few chords. Rosie closed her eyes and leaned her head back. I saw her foot tap to the rhythm of the music. Then I sang.

> *I stand alone in this darkened town;*
> *The streets are bare and no one's around.*
> *My devoted heart knows the truth,*
> *But my desperate eyes still search for you.*

I repeated it a few times along with the chords on the guitar. I watched her as I sang. I saw my lyrics flow through her ears and into her heart. I saw her feel the music. I saw her emotions. I moved her. When I stopped she looked up at me with tears in her eyes.

"I didn't write a full song because I didn't need to," I said. "Because that was all I felt while you were gone."

"It's beautiful," she said. "I love it."

I got off my seat and got under the covers with her. I kissed her head and then I kissed her nose. I felt her legs wrap around mine. She was warm and inviting. I missed her.

"You know," she said, leaning her head on her arm, "my dad doesn't hate you."

I was taken aback by her statement. "That was random," I said as I as I sat up. "Where'd that come from?"

"I know you guys fought," she said. "He told me."

I suddenly got nervous. I didn't want her to know about the confrontations I had had with her father. "What did he tell you?" I asked.

"Everything," she said. She could tell I was nervous.

"Like?"

"He told me about the day I came back, that you told him that you wouldn't leave me unless I told you I wanted you to leave." I said nothing. "And he told me about the time in our driveway, when you told him you know me better than he does, and he was pretty much a crappy father."

"I don't want to talk about this anymore." I started to get up. Rosie grabbed my arm and held me firmly.

"Let me finish," she demanded. "He also told me about the time in the hospital when you shoved him against the wall." I saw a smile grow on her face. "You used profound language."

I was really confused. Why was she smiling? "You think that's funny?" I asked.

"I do," she said as she began to laugh. "I think it's really funny."

"Well, I don't," I said angrily. "It's not funny. Your dad hates me for no fucking reason."

"Temper, temper," Rosie said. "Control your temper, Ethan."

"You and I already know I can't just control my temper. I get angry easily, and I snap. And when I snapped on your dad all those times, I was really pissed."

Rosie was still smiling.

"This isn't funny!" I snapped. "C'mon Rosie, your dad will hate me forever."

Rosie placed her warm hand on my cheek and laughed. "Don't worry," she whispered into my ear. "He doesn't hate you."

"Yeah right," I said as I pulled away. I stood up and went back to the computer. "If it were his choice, I'd never see you again."

"That's not true," she said. She sounded offended. "My dad loves me and he wants me to be happy. That's all he wants."

"So then why does he think you're not happy with me?" I asked.

And to that, Rosie had no response. I was automatically worried. She looked down at her hands and started twiddling her fingers. I saw her bite her lip.

"Rosie?" I said. "Are you happy with me?"

Again, she said nothing.

"Rosie!" I snapped. I saw her flinch, so I took a deep breath and tried my best to relax. "We were fine! Weren't we?" I stood up and walked towards the bed. She was sitting up, but our eyes never met. "You're the one who started talking about your dad. What was your point to all of this, Rosie? Did you want to put me on the spot? Did you want to show me what kind of asshole I am?" I started pacing the room. "I mean, what kind of boyfriend talks to his potential father-in-law like that? Right? Is that what you wanted to do? Make me feel bad?"

I noticed she was crying and I immediately felt terrible. I felt worse than dirt.

"Fuck!" I said under my breath. I ran my hands through my hair. "I'm sorry," I said. I reached in to grab her hand but she pulled it away. "I'm sorry baby, I really am."

She never made eye contact with me.

"I'm sorry," I whined. "I am, baby! I am sorry." I reached again for her hand, but again she pulled away.

"Can you just stop?" she cried. "Please, Ethan. Just stop!"

"I'm sorry," I whispered. "I really am."

She suddenly stood up and faced me. "Sorry doesn't always cut it, Ethan! Sorry isn't going to save you every time. And saying sorry should never give you any reason to act the way you do!"

"Act the way I do?" I repeated. I was getting upset.

"You're so hotheaded. You get mad at everyone and everything. Sometimes you just need to relax!"

I laughed to myself. "This is fucking pathetic," I said.

"Stop it!" she yelled. "Why do you have to swear every minute? Why do you feel the need to add the word *fuck* to every sentence? Is it so we all know you're mad? So that we can say 'Oh no, Ethan said *fuck*, we'd better all be worried'. You know it gets frustrating having to deal with that all the time!"

"Deal with what?" I asked. "The word *fuck*? Is that what bothers you so fucking much? That I get angry and I swear?"

"Yes, Ethan," she said. "It does bother me."

"Well fuck me then," I said. "I'm sorry for that too!"

Rosie rolled her eyes.

"Oh, fuck, sorry," I said. "I can't say sorry anymore. I apologize. Is that better?"

"You're being stupid," she said.

I'd been called stupid before, but hearing it from Rosie felt like the stinger of a scorpion. It hurt once it hit me, but the venomous word ran through my bloodstream, and the pain was lasting.

"I'm taking you home," I said, destroyed and fed up. "Let's go." I grabbed her arm, but she pulled it away from me.

"Let go of me!" she yelled. "You have to stop treating me like I'm a little girl!"

I was beginning to get really frustrated. I felt like punching a hole through my drywall. "When do I *ever* treat you like a little girl, Rosie?" I snapped.

"All the time!" she yelled back.

"Please," I said. "Enlighten me. Tell me how much more of an asshole I am!"

"You always want to look after me. You always want to take care of me. You want me to be safe. You don't like when I drink, you don't like when I smoke, you hate it when I go out. I mean, you treat me like my father does! And your empty promises are getting annoying. You can't promise me the good life, Ethan! You can't promise me safety! You can't promise me happiness!" Tears of frustration began to erupt from her eyes. "You can't promise me love! And you most definitely cannot promise me *us*!"

I felt a lump in my throat. I tried to hold in my tears. I had nothing to say.

"You've made so many promises. You promised me I'd never get hurt. Look at me, Ethan!" I did. And she was a beautiful mess. I could never love anyone in the world as much as I loved her. "Does this look like someone who's happy?"

I looked down at my feet.

"You promised me I'd never get hurt. I got hurt. You promised me I'd never cry. I cry every single day. You promised me I'd be happy forever, Ethan."

I looked up at her.

"I don't remember the last time I was."

I felt hot tears burn the skin on my face.

"And then you wonder why I cringe every time you promise me love. Open your eyes, Ethan. Nothing is ever guaranteed."

And just like that, she walked out of my room, out of my house and into the rain.

The torturously refreshing rain.

I had promised her many things in life. I couldn't lie; I was guilty of that. I had made her promises that no man could keep, no matter what. Promises about things that were out of my hands. I really couldn't guarantee her happiness. I couldn't protect her all the time. I couldn't promise her that she'd never get hurt. My intentions were golden, I could guarantee that. And I did always want the best for her, whatever it was. I wanted her to be happy. But she was right. I had absolutely no right to guarantee anything that was out of my reach. She had been naïve; she was a child when we fell in love. Of course she'd believe everything I told her. And now she wouldn't believe a word I said. She had learned that she couldn't believe me. She trusted me and I let her down. As badly as I wanted to get up and drive to her house and fix it, I knew I couldn't. We were broken, but there was nothing I could fix. There was nothing I could do to make it better. I tried, I really did. But I couldn't try anymore. I had tried everything. I tried to give her space and I was there when she needed me. I took things slowly. I was patient. I was calm. I tried to make her happy. If I wanted to take her out but she wanted to stay in, we did. If I wanted to stay in but she wanted to go out, we did. I had confessed my most sincere apologies. I had admitted to failing her. I acknowledged my mistakes. I told her I was a fool. I made sure to tell her I loved her every day. I told her she was beautiful. I smiled when she smiled, I laughed when she laughed. Things were great when she was happy. We had picnics and bike rides. We went to dinners and movies. But when they weren't good, they were horrible. I fought against her, I fought with her and I fought for her. I fought and I fought and I fought. But no matter the battle, I always failed. I had put in my all. My efforts were never good enough. There was nothing more I could do. I was physically, mentally and emotionally exhausted.

I gave her love. It was all that was left of me, and I gave it to her. I loved her with all my heart. But in reality, some broken things can never be fixed. And the burning embers were finally drowned out by the torturously refreshing rain. But I was cold without a flame. I was cold without Rosie. My sweet, sweet Rosie.

I suddenly remembered Rosie hadn't driven to my house, which meant she was walking alone in the rain. Before I knew it, I was driving in the pouring rain, looking for her on the sidewalks. When

I spotted her, I started honking my horn. She looked back and when she realized it was me, she rolled her eyes and began walking faster. I parked the car on the road, got out and ran up to her.

"Rosie!" I yelled. "Let me drive you home."

"Go away," she said. "I'm fine."

"That's great," I said. "I'm fine too. But you'll get sick out here! Please!"

She quickly turned around to face me.

I stopped in my tracks.

"And you want to convince me that you don't treat me like a child?"

I realized what I had said. "You are unbelievable," I said. "You are absolutely ridiculous and unbelievable. Why does every little thing have to be something with you?" We were both absolutely drenched at that moment. The rain got heavy, quickly.

"Listen!" she snapped. "I didn't ask you to come here and pick me up! I'm fine!"

I grabbed her arms and shook her. "What do you want from me, Rosie?" I cried. "I am begging you for an answer or a reason or anything. Please! Rosie!"

She started to cry.

I held onto her arms. "Can't you see that I love you? I waited for you every single day for three months! I didn't give up on you! Can't you see that? Everyone tried to convince me to move on. They said it was time to go. The chances were slim. You weren't coming back. I couldn't move, Rosie. For the goddamned life of me, I could not see past your fucking eyes! Your beautiful fucking eyes!"

She began to sob. So did I.

"I am only human, and I have faults. Everything I have promised you was out of good intentions. I promised you that *I* would never hurt you. I promised that *I* would make you happy. I promised that *I* would protect you. You think if I was in that parking lot that night,

I wouldn't have killed the fucking guy? And I'm sorry I'm not Superman. I can't be everywhere at once. I couldn't be there to keep you safe. I am just a man, Rosie. I'm just Ethan. And I do love you, I really do. I wouldn't be here if I didn't. But I'm exhausted, Rosie. I will be the first one to admit it. You wore me out. I'm tired. I'm sick and tired, every day. I want us to be better. I want you to be better. And I know I'm not perfect. I get mad. I swear. I yell. But I never hurt you. I never hit you. I've been the best person I can be. I have been the best for you. I don't know what else I can offer. I don't know what you want from me! What do you want from me?"

I looked at her and she said nothing.

I took a deep breath. "I don't know what you want from me because you don't talk to me. You don't open up. You don't tell me anything. You haven't even told me you love me since you came back. I've been pushed enough, Rosie. I'm only human. I'm sorry I'm asking for something more from you, but I need it. And if you don't want to love me, or to be with me, you have to let me know. It's not fair for you to string me along like this. I can't sit here and watch you go back and forth. I can't have another minute of you having a great day with me to you walking in the pouring rain trying to get away from me. I'm sorry, but there is only so much I can do. I think you're trying to be happy with me. We've had good days. I really believe that you're trying. But we're broken, Rosie. We are." I brought my hand up to wipe my face. "I want to fix us. I think we can be fixed, but I can't do it on my own. I can't believe I'm saying this. It's breaking my heart, Rosie, it really is. But I need you to tell me something. Tell me you love me, please!" I begged. "Tell me you love me. Or tell me you want to try. Just tell me something, please! I'm begging you. Tell me something."

We both stood drenched in the rain. I was cold and shivering. My teeth were chattering as I spoke. I looked into Rosie's eyes. I looked for something. I looked for an answer. What did she want?

She closed her eyes and shook her head. "I can't," she said. "I'm sorry, Ethan. I just can't. I can't be the person you want me to be, Ethan. I can't be the Rosie I was. And I don't want to hurt you anymore." She shook her head again and looked down. She sniffled. "It will never be the same again. I'm sorry."

I don't know why I thought she'd say something else. I don't know why I thought she'd admit to loving me. I have no idea why I'd gotten my hopes up when I knew they'd come crashing down again.

Rosie turned around and walked away from me. I wasn't sure of it, but I thought my hand suddenly reached for hers, attempting one last rescue. Asking for one more chance. But again, I wasn't sure. It probably didn't happen. It was time that I gave up on her. I needed to give up on her just like she had given up on me. I knew it wouldn't be easy, but fuck me, I was going to try.

I never put a label on our circumstances. I didn't tell people we were broken up, but when they asked, I shrugged my shoulders, indicating that things weren't the way I wanted them to be. Besides, I couldn't just sit there and tell myself we were broken up because if I said we were broken up, it meant we really were over, and there was a part of me that didn't want to accept that. Rosie was the best thing in my life for three whole years. I wasn't ready to close that book yet. But as I sat there alone in my room, staring at my ceiling, I considered Rosie and what she had been through. I knew I needed to take it easy on her. It dawned on me, however, that I didn't know much about what had happened. Of course, I didn't want to bring up the topic and remind her of the tragedy, but I didn't even know the guy's name. She had never explained anything to me in detail. All I knew was that she had been kidnapped from the parking lot where she worked. He beat her and raped her. He knew where she worked, where she lived, where her parents worked, where I worked and I where I lived. And he was drinking a coffee when she picked up a gun and shot him in the head.

I guessed she didn't want to talk about it, and I'm sure if I were ever in her shoes, I'd understand why, but still I wished I knew more. She must have been keeping things from me. And I was confused. Was it my love for Rosie or my desire for the truth that kept me holding on? *I don't think I'll ever know,* I thought. *I never will.*

The end of April was nearing. I hadn't spoken to Rosie in two weeks, and it was taking a huge toll on me. The guys at work noticed, Cam noticed, my parents noticed and even Brad noticed. But I was tired and I had lost all my will. I was a coward. I gave up. I did exactly what I had said I wouldn't do. But I had no choice. I couldn't hold on to something that wasn't even there. I had to either let go, or she had to grab on. It was slowly killing us both. I tried my best to keep my head up and move on with life.

My foreman was sending Cam and I to another job site for a week or two. I was at the local hardware store picking up a few supplies when I ran into Phil. I tried to hide behind a skid of drywall, but he spotted me and called out my name. And like a six-year-old child, I dragged my feet up to him and sloppily shook his hand. I was ready for the worst.

"Hey," he said. He must have been working because he was wearing old ripped jeans with grass stains and a dirty white T-shirt. "It's nice to see you."

I nodded my head, trying my best to be polite.

Phil nervously looked around and then leaned closer to me. "Listen," he whispered. "I'm sorry."

I put my hands up and said, "It's fine. You got what you wanted."

"No," he said. "Let me finish, Ethan. I was wrong, okay? I was wrong and this is not what I wanted."

"So what did you want?" I asked. I was getting frustrated.

"I didn't want this. I know I pushed you. I made it harder for you. And when you shoved me into the wall at the hospital, I knew I was being an idiot. I was wrong about it all. Rosie does need you, Ethan. I promise you this, she does need you. Anne and I saw such a huge improvement with her when she started seeing you on a regular basis. She seemed happier and brighter. She was different. And it was refreshing to see. She's not like that anymore, Ethan. I know it's hard, and she hasn't been the easiest person to deal with, but she does need you."

I felt hurt and confused. "So why did you try so hard to push me away?" I asked.

"I thought it would help. But it didn't. You are the reason for my daughter's happiness. It's just hard, you know. Rosie was always my little girl. She used to tell me I was her best friend until you came around. And I know that's not your fault, it always happens, but I'm putting my pride aside. I'm putting away my dignity. I can tell you I was wrong. Please, I beg of you, please don't give up on her. Not now, Ethan. She does need you."

I ran my hands through my hair. "What do you want me to do, Phil?" I asked. "I don't know what to do! I'm at the end of my rope. I've tried and tried. Something always escalates into something else. She won't let me in. There are no guarantees with her. It's hard, Phil. I try so hard to keep her happy, but nothing seems to be working. No matter what I do, nothing works." I began to get upset. "It gets frustrating!"

"I know, Ethan," Phil said. "I know. I face it every day with her. But she needs you. I can promise you this, she does need you. She's just trying to keep you away to protect you. She does actually love you."

"Protect me from what?"

Ignoring my question, Phil said, "Just give her a call, please. I have to go. I'm on a job right now. But call her. Or better yet, go to the house. Please, Ethan. I was wrong and you're exactly what she needs. But you're suddenly doing what you promised me you wouldn't do."

He turned around and was proceeded to the exit when I called out to him. "Phil, wait!"

He looked back and said, "I have to go, Ethan. Please do something about her."

He walked out of the store, leaving me bewildered and disappointed. What the hell was I supposed to do?

I pulled up in her driveway later that evening. I had taken a trip to the tracks to clear my head, and I noticed that our rose garden was beginning to bloom again. I had stood and stared at it for a while. I realized I was being stupid. We had planted this garden as a vow of our everlasting love, and I was so quick to throw in the towel and dry my hands. Our love had just taken a break, like the roses had. The winter environment was too cold for the garden, so it went away. That was exactly what had happened to us. It wasn't the right time for us. But the roses were back now, and I knew Rosie had to see them. Phil's truck wasn't in the driveway, and neither was Anne's car. Rosie's Jeep sat alone on the pavement, and I suddenly got nervous. What was I even going to say?

I walked up to her front door, and just as I was about to knock, the door opened. I found myself staring into Rosie's beautiful eyes.

"What do you want?" she asked.

I stood there shocked, trying to find something to say.

"C'mon, Ethan," she said. "What do you want?"

"Can I show you something?" I asked.

She rolled her eyes. "Ethan, I don't have time for this."

"What do you mean you don't have time?" I asked, feeling brave. "You're not doing anything."

She pursed her lips together. She didn't look impressed.

"Just come with me to the tracks, I have to show you something."

"I know, Ethan!" she snapped. "I know what's there. You don't think I go there? I know the roses are blooming. I already know that."

"Why are you getting so mad?" I asked.

She leaned against the open door and sighed. "Nothing. I'm not getting mad."

"I'm sorry about the other day, Rosie. I was just—"

"I know. You don't need to apologize."

I reached in to grab her hands. "I miss you so much."

She turned away from me and I saw tears fill her eyes.

"Rosie," I said. "There is no reason for you to be sad anymore." I stepped into the house and embraced her. "You don't need to cry anymore. We used to be so happy." I pulled away from her. "Why can't we be the old Rosie and Ethan again?"

She wiped her eyes and turned away again.

"Baby, please," I begged. "Aren't you dying a little bit every day without me like I am without you? I know what we had was real. I can bet my life on it. That's why I just can't allow myself to believe this is it for us." I searched her eyes. Her beautiful crying eyes weren't saying anything. "You still love me, right? You do?"

"Ethan, please," she cried. "Just go."

"I'm not going, Rosie," I said. "I'm begging you, Rosie, just tell me something."

She said nothing.

"How can you look me in the eye and pretend there was never magic with us? How can you face me and pretend we didn't love each other? Rosie, how can you turn me down, time and time again? I don't know what you're trying to do. I don't know if you're trying to push me away. I don't know if you're trying to make me hate you.

I don't know why you're not letting me in. But Rosie, come on! Just tell me something! I'm begging you."

"I already told you something, Ethan!" she cried. "I can't be what you want me to be!"

I took a deep breath. "The only thing I want from you is for you to be mine. Is that too much to ask?"

Rosie closed her beautiful eyes and I watched the tears fall down her face. She nodded her head. "Yes, Ethan," she whispered. "It is. It is way too much to ask." She looked up into my eyes. "I'm sorry, Ethan. I'm not okay, and I will never be okay. We're not made for each other. You need a nice girl. Someone different from me."

"I don't need anyone but you!" I cried.

"You don't know what you need, Ethan."

"And you do?"

She disappointedly shook her head. "No, you're right, I don't," she said. "Just like you don't know what I need. I know what I need. And I need you to leave. For the last time, Ethan, I need you to leave. We can't pretend anymore. It's done."

She closed the door before I even had a chance to catch my breath. I don't remember if I ever caught my breath. That was the day that I stopped breathing. My heart made my body believe that living was useless. I was starting to believe it too.

CHAPTER FOURTEEN

CHANGE

I sat near my bedroom window with my arms resting on the windowsill. The night was cold but the light from the full moon made me feel warm. I watched Brad and Kimberly holding hands on a bench in my backyard. She rested her head on his shoulders and he rested his head on hers. A few years ago, my father hired Rosie's father to landscape our backyard. We had a wide lot, and there was room for everything my mother wanted. A trail of cobblestones from my back door made a path through the whole yard. Solar-energized bulbs lit the path of dark stone, making for a pleasant walk. A pond with a waterfall in the back left corner of the yard was my mother's simple wish. A bench made of stone rested amidst the flowerbed, which looked out onto the pond. My mother spent her days sitting on the bench, reading her books and feeding the fish. Towards the right end of the backyard, a paved road to the garage was where the boys of the family hung out. After persistent efforts, my father finally convinced my mother to allow us to install a basketball net above the garage door. Each of my parents had their own escape, but still they remained in the same yard. My mother often found peace in the serenity of the garden, while my dad spent his time in the garage working on his car. It amazed me how a couple so in love could need time away from each other, yet were never out of sight of one another.

I wanted to feel joyous when I saw them, Brad and Kimberly. I wanted to feel love, but I was beginning to forget what it felt like. I was starting to forget what it meant. I was no longer envious or enraged. I wasn't happy for my brother, but I wasn't jealous of him, either. And I knew that that meant it was all slipping away. It was like sand falling through my fingers. I loved the feeling of the grains massaging my hands, but I knew once I had nothing left, it would hurt more than anything. But I wouldn't know until I got to that point. At the moment, I was frightened. My sights weren't clear and I didn't know what lay ahead. I had always believed that I could never fall out of love, and that Rosie would forever mean the world to me. But as I sat down and stared at the moon, I realized how small and irrelevant I was. I was simply a grain of sand falling through God's hands. Perhaps he'd close his hands fast enough to save me, or he might just let me fall through because he liked the feeling.

It scared me how small I was. It scared me how small we all were. I was suddenly realizing that I didn't matter. I had no reason or purpose. I was just the outcome of a bunch of atoms grouping together to make molecules. I was just part of science. And there was no meaning to any part of my life. I was simply made to live and die. I couldn't wait to do either one of them.

As I tried to fall asleep that night, I heard a knock on my bedroom door. I ignored it, but it was my brother, and for some reason, he knew I was awake. I opened my eyes to see Brad standing in my doorway asking me to wake up. He held a basketball under his right arm and asked if I wanted to shoot some hoops.

"Where's Kimberly? I asked as I rubbed my eyes.

"I took her home," he said. "She wasn't feeling well."

"What time is it?" I sat up.

"It's like almost 9:30. C'mon man, it's a Friday night. Let's go shoot hoops."

"Fine," I said, putting on a sweatshirt. "I'll meet you outside."

Brad was already getting some baskets when I walked into the backyard eating a banana. Brad passed the ball to me before I had a chance to put down my peel. I caught the ball but watched my peel fall to the floor.

"Chill, man!" I said as I shot the ball into the hoop.

Brad laughed to himself.

Brad and I hadn't spent a lot of time together since his return from school. I had secluded myself from my family while Brad and Kimberly were getting really serious. He spent most of his time with her. He seemed really happy.

"Can I ask you something?" Brad asked as he aimed for the basket. I watched the ball bounce off the backboard and onto the floor.

"Yeah." I picked up the ball and tossed it into the net. "Anything."

"I know this is really soon," he said. "But I was thinking of getting Kimberly a promise ring. Maybe in a few months."

"A promise ring?" I asked. "Why? Haven't you guys only been together for like three months?"

"Four, almost five," he said. "But that doesn't matter, man." He passed the ball to me and I took a shot. I was disappointed that I missed.

"Okay," I said, passing the ball to him. "Why are you telling me this?"

"I don't know." He shrugged his shoulders. Then he stood on his toes and aimed. He got the ball in. "I guess I just wanted your advice. Do you think it's a good idea?"

When I got my hands on the ball, I dribbled it a bit and took a shot. Swoosh. "I don't know, Brad," I said. "I don't think you should be asking me for advice."

"Why not?" he asked as he swiped the ball out of my hand and spun around, defeating my attempt to steal the ball back. He tossed the ball into the basket smoothly.

"Well," I said, "I managed to fuck everything up with Rosie. Obviously I got it all wrong."

"Don't say that," he said as he aggressively threw the ball towards my chest. I caught it. "You didn't do anything wrong."

"Yeah, right," I said sarcastically as I tossed the ball into the basket. "Then explain why I'm here."

Brad smiled as he grabbed the ball. "'Cause this is where you live," he laughed.

"Fuck off," I said. "You know what I mean." I couldn't help but smile at Brad's smart-aleck remark.

"Kimberly is different," Brad went on. He grabbed his water bottle and took a drink. He tossed it to me. The water felt cool as it went down my throat. Absolutely refreshing. Brad tossed the ball into a bin, indicating that the game was over and he wanted to sit and talk. He sat down on the ground and leaned against the garage door. I took a seat right next to him.

"I love her," Brad said as he used the back of his hand to wipe the sweat off of his brow. "I've never met anyone like her before. I've never looked at anyone the way I look at her."

I started smiling.

"I don't know," Brad went on. "It doesn't matter how much I tell you it's different because you won't believe me, anyway. And I'm not gonna sit here and tell you that I think a ring is a good investment because I *know* she loves me, because I'm not a mind reader. She tells me she does. And I can tell she cares about me. But I know that a ring will put a smile on her face, and it may be the way to tell her she means a lot to me. I really see her in my future."

I gently punched him on the arm. "Way to go, man," I said, grinning from ear to ear. Hearing of my brother's delight made me feel happier than I had in a long time. "I can tell," I continued. "That she is a really nice girl. And I can tell how happy she makes you. Believe me when I say this," I said. "She is crazy for you."

I saw Brad's eyes light up like the sunrise in the morning. "Really?" he asked. "How do you know?"

"Rosie used to look at me that way," I said. I took a deep breath. Suddenly the memory of Rosie strummed a set of painful strings in my chest.

"I'm sorry," Brad said. He put his head down. "I'm sorry about you guys."

"No, man," I said. "You don't have to be sorry. It's life. Shit happens."

Brad was still looking at the floor. "Can I be honest with you?" he asked.

I looked at him. "Yes," I said. "Of course."

He cleared his throat. "Sometimes I feel guilty."

"Guilty?" I asked.

"Yeah," he said. "Guilty."

"Why?" I asked.

"I haven't talked to you much lately," he said. "It's not because I'm mad at you or anything, but I feel bad. I don't think it's right that I can be happy with a girl while you're torn apart about one."

I nodded my head and before I had a chance to speak, Brad continued.

"Listen," he said with a firm tone. "I'm just telling you how I feel. It's hard for me to be around you. It's hard for me to talk about Kim or ask you for advice or tell you how happy I am."

"Then why did you ask me for advice today?" I asked curiously.

"Because I saw you," he said.

"Saw me?"

"I saw you looking out of your bedroom window."

I brought my hand up to my face in sheer embarrassment.

"I saw you for the first time in a long time. And the look in your eyes told me that you're broken. And I tried to put myself in your shoes. I tried to see through your eyes. I know you're devastated but I'm your brother. I'm your only brother and if I can't be here for you when you need me, I'm a piece of shit. And it made me realize that talking to you shouldn't be a bad thing, regardless of the topic. I guess what I'm trying to say is,"—he cleared his throat—"sometimes in life, we don't necessarily need answers. We just need someone to talk to, and especially someone to listen."

I simply nodded my head in agreement.

"So you don't mind if I talk to you about Kim?"

"Not at all," I said as I ran my hands through my hair. "I don't want you to ever feel guilty. Don't suppress your happiness because you're afraid of hurting me. I'll be more offended if you stop living your life because of me. I just want you to be happy. And don't you forget that."

"Thank you," he said as he aggressively wrapped his arms around me, embracing me in a bear hug. "That means a lot."

"I'm always here for you," I assured him. "No matter what."

We spent the rest of the night sitting in the backyard talking about stuff. We talked about life, love, work and just about anything we could think of. I understood it then. Not everything, but I at least understood what I hadn't before—what I had been unable to understand. I had pushed away those I loved the most. My intentions were not to hurt anyone, but I had been doing more harm to others than to myself. Brad had said it himself: he had feared me. He didn't want to upset me with his love life. I suppose he sensed my jealously and bitterness towards him. I had assured him that the last thing I wanted was for him to be happy. And when I thought about it, I felt sick. I felt anguish in the pit of my stomach. I was disgusted. I stood in front of a mirror and I could not bear to look into the eyes of my reflection. Into the eyes of some man. A man that wasn't me. What had I done to myself? What had I done to my family? What had I done Rosie? Of course she didn't want to love me. I was a fool! Like a child, I threw tantrums when I could not get my way. I yelled at her. I yelled at my family. A man does not raise his voice to the ones he loves. And just like everyone else, Rosie must have noticed that I was immersed in a downward spiral. I had missed it. I didn't see it. When she reached out to take my hand, I had turned away. No wonder she turned away from me now. She was already fighting her own battles; the last thing she needed was a child to take care of. She needed a man who was stable on his own two feet. I had never proven to her that I was. All I had shown her was that I spun around in circles, stomping my feet and throwing fits because life hadn't turned out the way I wanted. How selfish of me! I had nothing to complain about. I had no right to be upset. Especially after what Rosie had endured. I was pathetic. Rosie was trying with all her might to stand up on her two feet, and I came around and tried to knock her over. Of course she couldn't love me. I didn't even love myself. I wasn't a man; I was nothing but a boy. A child. I was worthy of no one. My behaviour had been atrocious, and I needed to change.

And for Rosie's sake, I would do just that.

The next morning I woke up feeling refreshed and exhilarated. I suddenly wanted to call Rosie and tell her how I felt. I wanted to apologize and tell her I had been wrong. I wanted to hug her and kiss her and hold her. I wanted to remind her that I was her summer, and that I'd always be her summer. But I knew I was in way over my head. I needed to relax and calm down. I couldn't step on the fragile floor and risk everything collapsing. I needed to talk to someone. I needed to talk to Cam. And so I called him.

I was in my garage rummaging through junk, looking for something I planned to give Rosie when Cam showed up, catching me by surprise. "What are you doing?" he asked. I almost jumped out of my own skin.

"Holy shit!" I quickly turned around. "You scared the shit out of me!"

Cam laughed as he hugged me. "Sorry," he said. "What are you looking for, anyway?"

I turned my attention away and started looking through a box. "When my mom changed up my room, she got rid of a lot of stuff, and I'm just looking for something to give Rosie."

"Okay," Cam said, shuffling his feet. "Can I help?"

"It's a blue box. It's small and it has cue cards in it. Cue cards she used as a game on our first Christmas together."

"Okay," he said. "Why? Are you guys talking again?"

"No," I said as I grabbed a box and pulled it off of the shelf. "That's the thing, Cam, I know it was me!"

"What was you?" he asked nonchalantly.

I stopped what I was doing to face him. I was out of breath. "I'm an asshole."

Cam laughed. "We all knew that."

"No," I said. "I'm serious." I continued searching for the box. "She doesn't want to be with me because I'm an asshole."

"I'm sure that's not why," Cam said. "She's been through a lot."

"No," I said. "Listen. I'm fucked up. I was never the man she deserved. I didn't take into account what she went through. It was always what I wanted. I was so selfish."

"So what's your plan?" he asked as he pulled out a chair and sat down.

"Found it!" I exclaimed as I grabbed the little blue box. I opened it and there they were. The cue cards. I redirected my attention to Cam. "My plan is to give this to her."

"And what purpose does that serve?" Cam asked.

"What do you mean?" I asked.

"What do you expect to happen once you give her this box?"

"I don't know," I admitted. I grabbed a chair and sat down. "Actually," I said. "I really don't know." I suddenly felt defeated.

"Yes, you do," Cam said. "You were looking for that box for a reason. And you expected something out of it. So what is it?"

I ran my hands through my hair. "Maybe she'll realize that I do care?"

"Why is that a question?"

"Because I'm not sure."

"Just talk!" Cam yelled. "This is your problem! You act like you know what you want all the time. You act so sure of yourself. And then when it comes down to it, when it comes down to Rosie, you lose yourself. You told me one day that you would never give up on her. And that is exactly what you did. You gave up on her. And now you suddenly have an idea and you're going to go back to her house and show her what you found and you're going to break her heart all over again."

"It's hard!" I snapped. "Cam, it's so hard! I do care for her and I do love her! And I know I promised her and myself that I would never give up on her. But she pushed me away. She was pushing me off of an imaginary ledge. I couldn't help but fall off."

"Do you hear yourself?" Cam asked. "You just told me you realized that you were selfish, yet you still say you walked away because of Rosie. Why did she push you away?"

"I don't know," I said. "She pushed me away because she fell out of love with me. She doesn't want me anymore because I failed her. I'm not the man she needs."

"I don't think so," Cam said. "I have something to tell you. And I know you'll probably hate me for not telling you before, but I couldn't."

In an instant, my heart fell into my stomach. What did he know that I didn't? I felt my heartbeat speed up, and I was suddenly extremely nervous. "Okay." I swallowed the pool of saliva that had built up in my mouth. "What is it?"

"I spoke to Rosie's dad a while back," he began. "And I know it was none of my business, but he called me and we met up."

I was suddenly infuriated. He must have noticed the rage burning in my eyes.

"Ethan, I'm sorry," he continued. "Just let me finish before you decide to break my jaw."

My fists were clenched. But I took a deep breath.

"I don't know how he got my phone number, and I didn't even answer the phone call. He left me a voicemail saying he needed to talk to me about Rosie and you, so we met up at the bar, the one by the airport. Anyway, it doesn't matter where it was. I went because I care about you, Ethan. I didn't do it for any other reason."

"Okay," I said. "Go on."

"Anyway, we sat down and he bought me a drink. We didn't do much small talk; he got straight to the point. He asked how you were doing."

"When was this?" I asked.

"A few weeks before Leah's birthday. Anyway, he told me he never thought you weren't good enough for Rosie. He said he knew you loved her and he knew she loved you, too."

"So why was he pushing me away?"

"I'll get to that. He said he never doubted what you guys had. He said it was hard to have his only daughter go missing and come back completely different. I don't need to mention what she went through; we all know. But he said the only reason he was pushing you away was because he wanted to protect you."

"Protect me from what?"

"Her."

"Why would I need to be protected from her?" I asked as I stood up. Enraged, I furiously kicked a bucket.

I saw Cam shake his head. He stood up and started to walk away.

"Where are you going?"

"I don't know, Ethan," he said. He turned back around to face me. "I thought you were ready to hear this, but you're being the same old Ethan. Are you satisfied now that you've kicked the fucking bucket?"

"Fuck off," I said.

"No," Cam snapped. "You need to fuck off! The shit you don't know about Rosie might just drive you to kill someone. So until you learn how to fucking control yourself, no one is going to want to be a part of your bullshit!"

"Fuck," I muttered to myself. "I'm sorry." I sat down. "I'm sorry. You're right."

Cam took a deep breath. "I'll make this clear. Rosie has been trying to push you away because she is afraid of you."

I tried to pretend I hadn't heard him correctly. I tried to pretend I hadn't just heard that the love of my life feared me. I tried with all my might, but I couldn't. I couldn't push away the thought because I knew it already. It was always in the back of my mind. The way she'd suddenly flinch when I yelled too loud, unexpectedly. I'd make her cry sometimes too. And I didn't want to believe it. She always came back to me, she always forgave me once I apologized, but I didn't want to believe it. I didn't want to be the bad guy. And since she'd come back, I had been able to allow myself to believe she was wrong. But I was wrong.

"You don't seem surprised," Cam said.

I just nodded my head.

"She's not only afraid of you, she's afraid of hurting you too."

"Okay," I said. "Cam, is there more? Can you please just tell me what her dad told you?"

"She can't have kids."

"What?" I said. I was completely confused. What did that have to do with anything we were talking about? "What the fuck are you talking about?"

"The man who abducted her hurt her, Ethan. He hurt her badly, to the point that her uterus is so damaged and scarred she is now unable to have children."

I couldn't find words to speak.

"I know this is hard to hear, but Rosie knows how much you wanted to start a family with her. You guys had dreams. You picked out names, didn't you?"

"Yeah," I laughed. "Brian for a boy and Perdita for a girl."

"Perdita?" he asked.

"Yeah," I said. "Don't ask. Rosie liked that one."

Cam walked up to me and patted my shoulder. "I'm sorry," he said. "I'm sorry that you have to go through this."

"Is there anything else?"

"That is all he told me. She doesn't even know that I know."

I took a deep breath. "What do I do now? I don't know what to do. I'm so lost for words."

"I don't have an answer for you, Ethan," he said. "I'm sorry, but I don't."

"She can't have kids," I whispered to myself. I felt my eyes fill up with tears. "She always wanted to be a mother. She always wanted a baby," I looked up at Cam. "She has such a big heart, she would be an amazing mother." Before I knew it, I began to cry. "Cam," I said. "This isn't fair. Why does this happen?"

"I don't know, Ethan," he said. "I don't know why shit like this happens. It just does. I'm so sorry."

"I have to see her," I said. "I have to see her."

"Go," Cam said. "Go tell her how much you love her."

"I will," I said as I wiped my face and grabbed the box. "Thanks!" I ran right past Cam to the driveway. I got into my car and drove off.

In a flash, I was standing at her front door, frantically ringing the doorbell. The door quickly opened and I lost my breath when I saw her standing in front of me. She was wearing a white bathrobe and her wet hair was draped over one shoulder. She looked beautiful. "What took you so long?" she asked.

"Wh-what?" I asked as I almost lost my balance. "What took me so long?"

"Yes," she said as she began to cry. "What took you so long to come back? I missed you so much." She wrapped her arms around my neck and buried her face deep into my shoulder. I wrapped my arms around her back and held onto her. She smelled sweet. She smelled delicious. "I'm sorry, baby," I whispered in her ear. "I love you so much, and I miss you."

I heard her cry into my shoulder. She grabbed onto my shirt and pulled me into her house, then closed the door behind her.

I looked around. "Where are your parents?"

"They went away for the weekend," she said. "They're not home."

I turned around to face her. My breath caught in my throat when I saw she had dropped her bathrobe and she was standing in front of me completely naked.

"Whoa!" I said. "Wh-what are you doing?"

"Do you still think I'm beautiful?" she asked.

"Yes," I said, afraid of getting close to her. "Of course I do."

"Are you sure?" she asked as she inched towards me.

I took a step back. "Yes."

"Then why are you walking away?"

"I'm not," I lied. "I'm just a little shocked, that's why. Why are you doing this?"

She looked disappointed. She picked up her robe off the floor and put it on. She walked right by me and up the stairs. I followed her. When I walked into her room, she was sitting on her bed, crying. I sat down beside her.

"What's wrong, baby?"

"I thought you hated me," she confessed. "I thought you left me because you hated me."

"No," I said. "Baby, I could never hate you!"

"Did Cam talk to you?" she asked.

"Yes," I said. "Just now, why?"

"Like today?"

"Yes."

"Oh," she said as she wiped her eyes.

"Why?" I asked. "I'm so confused. Did you tell him to talk to me?"

"No," she said. "My dad told me that he spoke to Cam and I thought he'd told you before. I thought you knew. I thought that's why you didn't come back. I thought you didn't want me anymore. I was mad at my dad! I couldn't believe he did that!"

"Did what?"

"He told Cam! Of course Cam was going to tell you!"

"Baby," I said. "Why didn't you just tell me?"

"How could I just tell you?" she cried. "How could you expect me to just tell you?"

"Rosie," I said. "I don't care about that. I just want you in my life. I don't care about anything else."

"I care!" she cried. "I care about it, Ethan. Why did he have to take that away from me?"

"I know," I said. "I'm sorry. I'm sorry, baby." I embraced her, and I held her head tightly against my chest. I kissed her head.

"He ruined my life. I thought you wouldn't want to be with me once you found out. I know how much it meant for us to—" she stopped. It was probably difficult for her to go on. "I know how much we wanted our own children, and he took that away from us."

I couldn't cry in front of her anymore. I needed to be strong for her, even though it was hard. It was hard watching her lose her mind.

"Don't leave me ever again," she said. "Please, Ethan. Don't leave me. I need you. Especially now, I need you more than ever."

"I will never leave you," I promised. "I will always love you." I exhaled. I smiled. It was the first time in a long time Rosie had admitted that she needed me. She was back. My Rosie was back. I knew then that I'd have my happily ever after with her.

I was naïve, but I believed that it was it. That that moment was the beginning of the rest of our lives. That Rosie was back for good. She needed me now more than ever. We were okay.

CHAPTER FIFTEEN

It was May 16th. It was a hot day, and while I was working, the scorching heat made my job almost unbearable. I felt sweat pour down my face from underneath my hard hat. The heat was distracting, and in a job like mine, any distraction could be dangerous. I thought about Rosie for most of the day. I was excited to see her later on. I found myself glancing at my watch every few moments, hoping I'd see the end of shift. And it felt like the more I looked, the slower time moved.

"Ethan!" I heard my name being called. I turned around and noticed my foreman walking towards me. "Hey, I need you to do me a favour," he said.

"Sure," I said. "What's up?"

"Can you go to the bottom floor and clean up a bit? The big boss is coming and we can't show him a job site like this."

"Yeah," I said. "No problem."

I took the elevator to the bottom floor, where the sun was hidden. It was dark and cool, and it felt wonderful. The coolness slipped its way into my skin, causing me to instinctively close my eyes and embrace the moment. I began by picking up pieces of scrap wood and metal, and taking them over to a bin. Then I found a broom and started sweeping the floor. There were loose screws and nails everywhere and I realized my foreman was right; the big boss would have been horrified if he had seen his job site like this. It felt like I had been working for a while but when I checked my watch, I realized I still had more time to kill. I didn't enjoy cleaning. The coolness was refreshing, but I was suddenly jealous of my old self. Sure, he had been up there working up a sweat, but at least time was flying and he was doing work that he was good at. I didn't get this job to clean, I thought.

I walked around the column to see if there was anything I had missed. There I noticed a piece of broken wood on the floor with a bird sitting on it. I quickly stopped in my tracks when I saw the bird. He was big and black. A raven or a crow, perhaps. I jumped in an attempt to scare him, but he didn't move. I took a few quick steps towards him to frighten him, but he just opened his wings and flapped them, as if my presence made no difference in his life. Then I had the idea to go back to the bin and pick up another piece of scrap wood to throw at him. That would definitely scare him off, I thought. I picked a small piece of lumber and chucked it towards him. I didn't intend to hit him, so it landed just to the left of him. He watched the wood fall at his side, and then he looked back at me. *Is that all you got, Ethan?* I let out a frustrated laugh. You've got to be kidding me, I thought. I walked back to the bin to find something smaller—a small stone, perhaps. My new plan was to actually hit him, but I still didn't want to kill him. I found a small piece of old metal. "Perfect," I mumbled to myself. "All right bird," I said as I toyed with the metal in the palm of my hand. "You leave me no choice." I threw it at him. It hit the side of his body, just under his right wing. He jumped up and flapped his wings, and for a moment I thought I had finally met success, but in just a matter of seconds, he was back on the piece of wood. I felt a heat flash, and being in a cool dark place no longer felt friendly. I was working up a sweat. I wanted to walk up to the stupid bird and kick it, but the way that bird looked me in the eye sent an eerie chill through my senses. He could probably claw my eyes out. How hard could it be to get rid of a stupid bird anyway? I thought. I needed something that could reach him while keeping me at a distance. And that was when I thought of the broom.

I grabbed the push broom and started to sweep the floor in front of him. I noticed he was watching the broom carefully. He was ready to defend himself when he needed to. I held a tight grip on the broom as I met his eyes. His eyes were dark. They were cold and heartless, unforgiving eyes. And while his eyes were locked on mine, I raised the broom slowly into the air, and without hesitation, with all my force, the broom came crashing down on him. I heard his bones crush under the weight of the broom. When I looked at him, he was broken and mangled, lying lifeless on the floor. I took a shaky breath, suddenly not believing what I had just done. I poked him with the broom one more time to make sure he was actually dead. I slowly walked up to him. When I was close enough to see his eyes were still open and spewing blood, I immediately took a step back and headed the other way. It felt like he was watching me leave.

May 16. I had to take Cam to the hospital that afternoon. He nearly lost his thumb after falling on top of sharp metal. He had used his hands to brace his fall. I saw the metal go through his skin just like a knife would. I wasn't sure, but it looked like it had gone deep enough to have cut bone. We all stopped working when we heard Cam yell "Holy shit!" loud enough for the entire street to hear. I was immobile when I noticed the blood dripping down his arm. I was unable to see the wound. All I remember seeing was a stream of blood. My foreman ran up and asked Cam if he was okay. Cam held onto his hand for dear life with his eyes closed tight. "Do I still have my finger?" he asked. The foreman grabbed Cam's hand and looked at it. "It looks like it may have severed the bone," he said. He demanded that someone call an ambulance. I offered to drive Cam; the hospital was just down the road. The foreman sent everyone back to work while Cam and I walked off the job site. He wrapped his hand in a cloth. It was different, looking at Cam the way I looked at him that day. He sat in my car and I watched the sweat dripping from his temples. He was pale and I saw fear in his eyes. "I can't lose my thumb, Ethan," he said. "I won't be able to work." "Don't worry," I said, "I'm sure it will be fine." But Cam never settled. He wouldn't wait for people to tell him bad news; he always had to find out himself. It was almost a self-inflicted torture.

The night Leah died, Cam escaped his hospital bed and pressed his nose against the window. He tried his best to hear what the doctor was telling his parents. And when he saw his mother collapse into the arms of his father, when he saw them slowly slide down to the floor, when he witnessed the breaking of their hearts, he knew that Leah hadn't survived. He slowly turned away and climbed back into his bed. Guilt was written all over his face. He thought I had been asleep the entire time. Ever since that night, I knew Cam would always be close to me. We had both endured a tragedy for which both of us, one way or another, blamed ourselves. I took comfort in the fact that I had not expressed my feelings to him, nor had he done to me, but when we saw each other, we knew.

Cam slowly unwrapped the blood red cloth. It slipped off like a satin ribbon, ever so gently exposing his wound. He raised his hand slowly, and I gasped when I saw his thumb dangling, just a hair away from being completely detached. Cam quickly covered it up again. He gently wrapped the cloth back around his hand. I saw him wince in pain. I swallowed hard. This couldn't be happening. Not to Cam. I waited for quite some time in the emergency room after Cam was rushed into surgery. I tapped my feet anxiously along with the song playing over the PA system. Last time I'd been at the hospital was when Rosie was admitted the night I found her at the tracks. Another memory struck me hard when I saw Cam's parents rush into the emergency room with panicked looks on their faces. Life worked in mysterious ways. I always imagined that parents became less worried once their children grew up. They were called out of work when their children fell ill at school. They impatiently tapped their fingers by the phone, expecting a phone call when their children didn't arrive home from school on time. They needed to meet every parent of every friend before they allowed their children to have sleepovers. It was supposed to get easier as children grew older. They were supposed to be smarter and more responsible. Parents were supposed to worry less. But when the Fitches received a phone call from the police notifying them that their children had been in a car accident, and that their daughter had died, a parent's worst nightmare instantaneously became a reality. I suppose parents expect life to get easier. They might loosen their grip, slowly letting go of their worries. But life happens, and unexpectedly, some of them might lose everything before they can clench their hands back together again. I suppose a parent never stops worrying. A parent never stops loving.

When the Fitches walked up to me, I assured them that Cam would be fine and I highly doubted that he'd lose his thumb. They both sighed in relief. I told them that I was going to head off and promised that I'd be back later. As I was heading towards the exit, I noticed a gift shop to my left. Because I had nowhere to be, I decided to take a look around. Get well balloons greeted me as I entered the shop. When I looked to my right, I noticed a nervous cashier dealing with a rowdy customer. I simply rolled my eyes and turned the other way. I walked into an aisle with greeting cards. Most of them were birthday cards and anniversary cards, which I found inappropriate for a hospital. I found a section of cards welcoming new babies into the world, right next to the cards for the loss of a loved one. And finally, at the end of the aisle, I found the get well soon section. I was browsing through the cards when I felt my phone vibrate in my pocket. It was a text message from Rosie.

I cut my hair.

Rosie had always had random thoughts and suggestions. She was becoming more and more spontaneous, and I found myself becoming more grounded.

That's nice. Can I come see it?

I quickly grabbed a card for Cam and walked back to the counter. I noticed a small flower shop across the hall. I rushed to pay for the card. I ran through a stampede of people, and when I entered the flower shop, a sweet aroma gently hit me.

I hate it.

I looked through the selection. Suddenly, a display of roses caught my eye.

I'm sure it looks fine.

I grabbed a bouquet of a dozen red roses. She'd love them.

I cut it all off. I don't have hair anymore.

I placed the roses down at the register and paid for them. They smelled sweet.

Why did you do that?

I grabbed the roses and headed towards the exit of the hospital. I rummaged through my pocket looking for my parking ticket.

I'm ugly.

I found the ticket and quickly paid the attendant. I got into my car and sped off.

Don't say that, you're beautiful.

I was reading street signs in an attempt to find the quickest way to her house.

I hate when you say that. It makes me sick.

I hid my phone in my lap and sped down the road.

Are you okay?

I turned my car onto her street. I sped up to her house and quickly parked in the driveway.

I will never be okay.

I felt weary. Something wasn't right. In my defense, however, nothing was ever normal with Rosie anymore. But while things weren't normal, they were still okay. Something in my gut was telling me Rosie wasn't okay. I grabbed the roses from the backseat and exited my car. I didn't even knock—I just opened the door. I called her name, but I heard nothing. I looked around her house as I closed the door behind me. I noticed movement in the kitchen, so I made my way there. I saw her sitting at the kitchen table with her back to me. Her head was resting on the tabletop, and there was a big pair of scissors in her hand. I noticed the chunks of hair littering the kitchen floor. Her sobs were muffled. Her head rested on her sleeve. I stood quietly in shock.

"Why are you here?" Rosie asked as she lifted her head.

I knew I needed to remain collected. I had to act like nothing that I was looking at was a problem. Nothing was serious. It was all okay. "I brought you something," I said as I inched towards the table. I placed the roses down on the table as I slowly took the scissors out of her hand.

She wiped her face and looked up at me. Through her tears I could see her pain-stricken eyes. Her soul was lost. "Why?" she asked. She didn't even look at the roses.

I slowly pulled out a chair and sat down beside her. I gently placed my hand on hers. I was surprised when she didn't pull away. "You love roses," I said. "And I thought they were beautiful."

"Well you know what?" she snapped. "Things change, okay? I don't love roses. I hate them."

I was taken aback by her honesty. I swallowed hard. I felt like I was watching my entire life pivot on a ledge, and any move I made could send it over the edge. "Why don't you talk to me?" I offered. "Tell me what's on your mind."

She ran her hands through her newly short and choppy hair. "I'm hideous," she whispered. "I'm a monster."

"No you're not," I assured her. "You're beautiful."

"Stop saying that!" she yelled as she grabbed the roses from the table and threw them on the floor. "Just stop it!"

I looked at the roses on the floor. Petals and hair were mixed together, but I still did not feel part of that chaotic mess. I looked back at her and that was when I noticed her hand. "Your hand is bleeding." I stood up and headed towards the sink. I grabbed a tea towel from a drawer and ran it under the water. "Here." I offered her the cloth. Her makeup was smeared and her falling tears were black. She was still beautiful. She grabbed the cloth and wrapped it around her hand.

"Don't look at me," she demanded as I stood in the same spot.

I simply turned away and took a seat at the table. I made sure not to face her.

We both sat there in silence. I'm not quite sure how long we sat there, but it seemed like a long while. But then again, when it is quiet and there is nothing to do, time usually passes slowly. Painfully slowly. I was afraid of doing anything. I didn't want to move. I didn't want to make any sound. There was an itch in my throat that was driving me insane, but I feared even clearing my throat. I folded my arms on top of the table and rested my face on them. I still hadn't looked at her. I might have fallen asleep; I wasn't too sure. I wanted to touch her. I missed her embrace. I wanted so badly for the struggle to end. I wished we could be normal again.

Why had Rosie gone from happy to sad in a matter of minutes? It was always unexpected. When things were great, I feared for the worst to occur. I knew what Rosie was capable of, but I presume that love can sometimes be cruel. The love I had for Rosie had blinded me. I knew what she was capable of, but I had always believed that we'd be okay again. I was wrong. I was always wrong, and no matter how much I reasoned it would happen again, I had never believed it. I couldn't believe it.

"You make it so much harder for me, Ethan," Rosie said, finally breaking the silence.

I cleared my throat. "I'm sorry, Rosie," I said. "But I don't know what you mean."

She laughed to herself. "You want to know what the worst feeling is?" she asked.

"Yes," I said. "I do."

"One of the worst feelings is when I look in your eyes and I feel hatred. I make you feel like dirt. And then I ask you to bring me home," she began to cry. "And when I'm alone at home I realize you are my home. And that I don't love my home anymore. And I sit here and wait for something. But then I realize I can't wait for anything because I have nothing. Absolutely nothing."

I remained quiet.

"And you know what, Ethan?" she began again, talking through her tears. "Sometimes I just want to die. Sometimes I just want my pitiful life to end. I think about it a lot, actually. And sometimes I'll sit in my room and argue with myself. A part of me wants to grab the gun out of my dad's closet and just do it, but then another part of me assures me and promises me that my life is valuable and worth living. And so the dark part of me starts to believe what the other part is saying. And then things are great. And then out of nowhere, the darkness takes over again. And I find myself alone in my room, wanting so badly to end it. I want to end it all. But then I look at the frame on my nightstand. It has a picture of you in it. And you're smiling. When you smile, I don't even need to look at your mouth to know you're smiling. You know why?" she asked.

I shook my head.

She laughed again. "Because your eyes smile. When you smile, your eyes become a little bit smaller, and it looks like they're smiling too. And when I see that, I realize that I shouldn't feel the way I do because I have that man in that frame. The man who can smile with his eyes. And I know that he is smiling because of me. And then I realize that the part of me that doesn't want me to die isn't actually me." She paused to take a breath. "That part is you, Ethan."

I started to cry.

"The little being in my heart that saves me from myself every single day is you. And no matter how hard I try, I know that you will always win. You will never let me hurt myself. You will never let me die. And I know if I do grab Daddy's gun and place it against my temple and pull that trigger, I won't only be killing myself—I'll be killing you. I could never kill you." She brought her wounded hand up to my face and gently touched my cheek. Her touch felt so powerful and beautiful. "And that is what I mean when I say you make it extremely difficult for me. I could never die without you, Ethan."

I took her face in my hands. Through my sobs I tried to tell her I loved her. I wasn't sure if she heard me, but God, I knew she understood. She pressed her head against mine as she cried with me. It was an invigorating cry, and through our soulful tears, our definite love was established. Written in stone, carved on a tree. It was there, without a doubt. The love we had for each other was stronger than it had ever been before. And through the journey called life, our hearts would forever be intertwined. We were no longer alone in the world. And we never would be.

I was awakened by a vibrating sound on the table. When I lifted my head and my eyes regained their focus, I realized it was my cell phone. I was alone at the table. Rosie was not with me. I grabbed my cell phone and saw that it was a text from Cam.

My thumb and I have been reconnected.

Before I even considered responding, I wanted to know where Rosie was. I walked into her living room to see if she was on the couch. She wasn't. I looked at my phone again and the time read 3:12 p.m. I quickly went upstairs and walked to her bedroom. It was a relief to see her curled up in a ball under her bedsheets. She was sound asleep. I walked up to her and kissed her forehead. "Sweet dreams, my love," I whispered into her ear. "I love you so much."

On the way to the hospital, I took out my phone and replied to Cam. *Glad to hear, buddy. I'm coming back.* When I reached the reception desk, I asked the nurse if she knew where Cameron Fitch was. "Room 212, second floor, right passed the section with the vending machines."

I thanked her and was on my way. I got into the elevator and waited as it took me on a short trip to the second floor. When I left the elevator, I looked to my right and then to my left. I noticed a few vending machines to my left, and so I was headed off into that direction. I immediately saw Cam's father talking on his cell phone in front of the room. Not wanting to interrupt, I simply nodded my head and entered. Cam was lying in bed watching TV as his mother flipped through a magazine.

"Hey," I said as I walked up to Cam and patted his head. "How are you feeling?"

"I've been better," Cam said. "Can't complain, I guess."

I laughed. I turned towards Cam's mother, Gloria, and greeted her. She hugged me, and with her heavy accent, she said she'd be outside. I sat down on a chair and looked at Cam. "What the hell happened to you?" he asked. "I just got out of surgery and you look shitter than I do."

I laughed and nodded my head. "Nothing," I said.

Cam showed me his hand wrapped in a cast. "The doctor said it should heal perfectly fine, and I probably won't lose my thumb."

"That's good," I said. "Glad to hear it."

I saw his eyes dance with excitement. "I thought I was fucked."

"I know," I laughed. "I could only imagine."

"So did you get me anything?" he asked.

The card. "Oh shit," I said. "I did. But I forgot it in my car. Rain check?"

"It better be a stripper," Cam joked.

"Well," I said. "It kind of is. It's a card with a stripper on it. Is that okay?"

"That will do," Cam said. "For now."

I nodded my head.

After a few quiet moments, Cam asked if I had seen Rosie.

"Yeah," I said. "I just came from her house."

"How is she?" he asked.

I shrugged my shoulders.

"You don't know?" Cam asked. "Well, is she happy?"

"I don't know," I said. "It's fucked."

"Okay," he said as he turned to face the TV. "I'm here to listen to you whenever you need me to."

"Thanks, buddy," I said. I noticed he was watching the Three Stooges. We both sat in silence as we watched the comedic trio do what they always had done.

It was weird how fine I felt. Rosie had spilled her heart out to me, and even though I didn't like what she had said, I felt at peace. She had reassured me that she wasn't going anywhere. I didn't enjoy hearing how hurt she was and I definitely didn't like how she contemplated death day after day. But I respected her. She was brave. I didn't want to begin to imagine the sort of battles she faced daily. Her dignity had been snatched from her. She used to tell me that she loved the fact I was the only person she had ever been with. That secure feeling had been brutally taken from her. Sometimes I'd sit alone and think to myself. I'd try to imagine the moment the man showed up in the parking lot. She obviously hadn't thought he was a threat because she had allowed the conversation to go on. But when did she get that feeling? The feeling that the man wasn't who she'd thought he was. Maybe he offered her a ride home and she knew right away not to take it. He must've been upset when he was rejected, and that was when he hit her. And as I sat down and tried to imagine, my heart dropped into my stomach. Because that was the moment Rosie knew she was no longer safe. That was when her instinct kicked in and that was when she started fighting back. But she was no match for him; he probably had 120 pounds on her. She tried to get away, boy did she try. But she couldn't fight him off. And when he shoved her into his truck she must have thought he'd kill her. I got a sick feeling in my stomach. Imagine coming to the realization that your life was over. Rosie should never have felt that way.

Thankfully, he didn't kill her. He wanted to keep her for himself. I guess from Rosie's eyes, at the moment, she thought that was worse. She probably would rather have died. For 11 weeks, she lived alone with this man. Alone. She was probably stuck in one room for 24 hours a day. She had to be there when he wanted her. When he wanted his fix of sex. The man would just take it from her whenever he wanted. But on top of that, he'd beat her and humiliate her, making her feel like dirt. I didn't know how she had felt. Words probably couldn't express how she had felt. She was alone and out of her element. During those 11 weeks, I had felt alone and scared. I felt out of my element. I didn't want to talk to anyone, I didn't want to think and I didn't even want to feel. But Rosie, my sweet Rosie, all she could have wished for was to be back in her room. Back with her parents. Back with me. Back in her old life. It saddened me every day to just *imagine* what she had endured. But she had lived it. It had been her life for 11 weeks. It was her reality. I couldn't bear to think of it any longer. I really didn't know how she had done it. My brave Rosie.

At around six o'clock that evening, Cam was released from the hospital. His parents drove him home while I made my way back to Rosie's house. When I pulled into the driveway, I noticed that Anne and Phil were home. Phil opened the door.

"Hey, Phil." I shook his hand. "How are you?"

Phil gestured for me to enter. "We've seen better days. Did you talk to Rosie at all today?" he asked as I took off my shoes.

"Yeah," I said. "I did."

He looked behind his shoulder as Anne walked into the hallway.

"Hi, Ethan," she greeted me. She looked upset. "How are you, sweetheart?"

"Like Phil said, I've seen better days."

"So you know what Rosie did to her hair?" Phil asked.

I simply nodded my head.

"I don't understand why she would do that!" Anne exclaimed, clearly upset. "I mean, she looked beautiful with her long her. She loved her hair."

"It's okay, honey," Phil said, rubbing her back. "It's okay."

"I don't know," she continued. "I don't understand how she could be doing so well, and then all of a sudden, she does something like this! I just can't understand what goes through her mind."

"I don't think we'll ever understand her," I said. "She's been through hell and back. I don't think any one of us will ever know what is going on."

"We just want her to be happy," Anne said. "That's all."

"That's what we all want," Phil added.

"I know," I said.

And it was true. I didn't think we'd ever know what was going on with her.

"Is she upstairs?" I already knew the answer.

Rosie was sitting alone in her room wearing dark grey sweatpants and a white hooded sweatshirt. She sat on her floor cross-legged, staring at herself in the mirror. I noticed in her reflection that she was watching me walk into the room. "Where did you go?" she asked as I sat down on her bed.

I cleared my throat and crossed my legs like her. "I went to see Cam at the hospital."

"Why was he in the hospital?" she asked with her eyes locked on mine in the reflection of the mirror.

"He cut his hand at work," I explained. "He almost lost his thumb."

"Oh," she said as she looked down at her own hands.

I could hear her breathing. I took comfort in the rhythmic sound. "What's up?" I asked. I decided to get more comfortable by lying down on my back.

"Nothing," she said.

I sighed. I wanted to talk to her and ask her what was on her mind, but I didn't want to push her away like I had always done. Losing her again was a risk I wasn't willing to take. And so I sat there, staring at her popcorn-finished ceiling, imagining fictional figurines. At first I was looking at a rabbit, and then a turtle. My tired eyes were beginning to get weary when I saw a baby on the ceiling. I quickly closed my eyes and re-opened them, and I was still staring at the imaginary image of a baby. I took a deep breath. Everything at that moment seemed unreal to me. I hadn't expected to have been hit with such bad news. My dreams for a family with Rosie were crushed and there was simply nothing I could do about it. I still didn't believe it. I was having a hard time believing that something so miraculous, beautiful and natural could have been lost. Lost in time, lost in the wind, lost into nothingness. The ability to bear children wasn't itself tangible, so I was having difficulty believing that the ability could be lost. I didn't like to think about it. I closed my eyes and began to drift off into sleep, into a dream telling me it wasn't real. Telling me that Rosie would one day be a mother.

May 17th. I woke up in the exact same position I had dozed off in. I looked at Rosie's alarm clock. It was three minutes past midnight. I wondered if she was still sitting on the floor in front of the mirror. When I sat up and saw she wasn't, my heart dropped into my stomach. Where was she? I quickly stood up and looked around the room. Then I noticed a Post-it note smack dab in the middle of the mirror. The messageIt was written with a trembling hand: *I'll be at the tracks.* I had no idea what was going on, but because she left a note, I knew she needed me to meet her at the tracks.

And just like I promised I would, I got into my car and was on my way.

When I arrived at the tracks, the first thing I noticed was a burning flame. The flame was really close to, if not exactly where Rosie and I had planted our garden. Immediately fearing the worst, I quickly got out of my car and ran towards the fire. The night air was cool in my lungs, but when I neared the fire, my skin tingled with warmth. Rosie sat before the flame's light with a vacant expression. The only sound I could hear when I got close enough was the crackling of the fire. I kept my distance. I had no idea what to expect. I looked at Rosie. She knew I was there, but she refused to look at me. She played with a lighter in her hands.

"What are you doing?" I asked her in a panic.

She looked up at me with sad eyes. Her silence burned right through me.

"Rosie!" I yelled. "What are you doing here?"

And very quietly, she responded, "I'm burning roses."

I looked at the flame when it suddenly hit me. She was burning the garden. Our garden.

"Why would you do that?" I asked. I quickly took off my shirt and began beating the flames in an attempt to put them out.

She shrugged her shoulders as she toyed with the lighter in her hands.

"Don't lie," I said. "You know exactly why you decided to set *our* rosebush on fire." My attempt at putting out the fire failed, so I dropped my shirt on the ground. I prayed for rain.

She quietly laughed to herself. "You're blind, Ethan," she said.

"Rosie!" I yelled. I was getting frustrated. "What are you talking about? Can't you just talk to me?" A cool gust of wind blew by us as tears fell from Rosie's beautiful eyes. She stood up and faced me, wrapping her arms around my neck. She buried her face in my shoulder as she began to cry. Thunder crackled across the sky, sending her on a hysterical rampage.

She pushed me away from her, nearly knocking me off of my feet. "I can't talk to you, Ethan!" she yelled. Gentle raindrops began falling from the sky. "How am I supposed to?"

I was completely caught off guard. I felt a lump in my throat, and I begged God to stop me from crying. "Please," I begged as tears started to escape from my eyes. I took a step closer to her, but she took a step back. "Please," I whispered again.

"It's gone, Ethan!" she yelled. "It's gone!"

"What's gone?" I begged for an answer. "What is going on, Rosie?"

She quickly wiped her eyes and screamed. She fell onto her knees as if all of her strength had just escaped from her mouth. With her face nearly in the dirt, she began punching the ground. She then sat up and yelled to the sky, "I hate you!"

I tried to get closer. I wanted to grab her and hold her and hug her. I wanted to make it stop. I just wanted to make all of her pain to go away. Forever. But I couldn't move. I stood away from her and became immobile. My breath caught in my throat when I saw it. Through the dim firelight, I saw the engraving in the tree: *BP*. I nearly lost my balance, and finally caught my breath.

"BP?" I asked quietly. Rosie didn't hear me. "BP?" I asked again. Rosie was still crying with her face in the dirt. "Rosie!" I yelled. "Why BP?"

She looked up at me with red, swollen eyes. "I'm sorry," she said.

"No, Rosie," I begged. "Start talking, please!"

"I was pregnant!" she cried. "I was pregnant and I lost the baby!"

"Oh, my God," I said in disbelief.

"Ethan," she cried. "I was pregnant. I was really pregnant."

"Holy shit," I said as I turned away from her. I tried to catch my breath.

"It was November 29th," she began with a trembling voice. "He caught me trying to escape through the basement window."

I was listening.

"I was almost free. I almost got out. I was so close. So close I could taste it! But he grabbed me. I didn't think he'd be awake, but he grabbed my leg and pulled me in. I tried to hold on. I tried so hard, but he was too strong, and he pulled me in. I fell onto the floor, and I remember when I fell, the wind was knocked out of me," she stopped to take a deep breath. "I remember hitting my head and everything was fuzzy. But I saw his blurry figure standing over me. He yelled something, but I couldn't hear him. And then he kicked me, right in the stomach. And it hurt. I felt like vomiting and coughing. I couldn't breathe. And when I finally caught my breath, I thought the worst was over. But it wasn't. He kicked me. Again and again. I tried to get away. I was screaming loudly, hoping someone would hear me," she began to cry again. "But no one was around to hear me. All I could think of was the baby. He knew I was pregnant, but it didn't stop him. He just kept kicking me and kicking me. And I heard the baby crying out, I swear to God Ethan, I did. I heard the baby crying out, *Mommy, Mommy*. He was killing the baby. I tried to block my stomach, but I couldn't even feel my arms. He kept kicking me. He kept going. I wanted him to stop. He was killing the baby!" she cried. "I wanted him to stop. And after one last blow to my head, he finally left me alone.

I don't know how long I passed out for, but when I woke up, I could tell it was daytime. The sun was shining. But I was in so much pain that I couldn't even move. I didn't know what day it was or what time it was. He didn't come to check up on me, he just left me down there. I wet my pants because I couldn't even get up to use the washroom. I felt so alone, Ethan. I felt so alone and scared. I felt so hurt and used. I felt so humiliated. I don't know how long it took me to finally get my strength back. Maybe another day. I was in so much pain. And when I could finally crawl to the washroom, I did. And I stayed there for a while because I had terrible cramps. I knew it then. I knew that I had lost the baby. I knew that he had killed the baby. I took off my pants and my underwear. I was lying down on the cold floor. My ribs and my stomach were bruised. But I was scared when I saw all the blood. The blood was in between my legs and in my underwear. I started to scream, but I quickly stopped. I knew no one was going to help me. I was so scared. There was so much blood, I thought I was going to die. And as I sat there alone, I felt something pass through. And when I looked down onto the floor, there was even more blood. And that was when I noticed it." She started to cry again. "It was the baby. And I didn't know what to do because it was still attached to a cord. It was so small. It fit right in the palm of my hand. There was no hope, I could tell it was broken. It wasn't right. And I sat there and I cried alone. I cried and I cried. My physical pain was gone. But my heart broke in half.

I found a pair of scissors in the washroom and cut the cord. I found an old shoebox and put the baby in there. I put on my clothes and used my last bit of strength to get up the stairs. And when I opened the door, that was when I saw him sitting at the table, drinking his coffee. I found his gun in the living room. I walked up to him and before he could even say anything, I put that gun right between his fucking eyes. And before he could even beg for his life, I pulled the trigger. And that sound of the gun going off was the most refreshing and exciting sound I had heard in a very long time." Rosie paused to take a deep breath. It was still raining lightly. She then slowly lifted up her hand and pointed behind the tree with the carving. "The house where he lived was down that way. I don't know how and I don't know why, but I walked right to this spot. It was the first thing I did. And with my hands, I dug a hole right here," she pointed to the pile of ashes that had once been our roses. "And I put the shoebox with the baby inside. Then I walked to the road and I was lucky enough to see a cop. I don't remember getting close to him. I passed out before I even got to see his face. December 1st, Ethan," she said. "That was December 1st."

I took a deep breath. I couldn't find words to speak. I couldn't find anything to say. I couldn't comfort her no matter what I said. But I said the first thing that came to mind. "I'm sorry, Rosie," I said. "I'm so sorry you lost your baby."

Rosie looked at me like she was completely confused. "My baby?" she asked as she stood up and slowly walked closer to me. I could tell she was fighting back her tears. "Ethan," she cried. "It wasn't just my baby. It was *our* baby."

I almost fell over. "Our baby?" I gasped. "How?"

"Ethan!" she cried. "I found out I was pregnant the day I went missing. I was six weeks pregnant."

"Oh, my God," I cried.

"Ethan," she trembled. "It was *never* his baby. It was *always* our baby! And he took that from us, Ethan. He killed our only child, and he stole the chance of us ever having another one."

Her words felt like a bunch of flaming arrows shot through my heart. I fell to my knees and screamed to the heavens. "Why?" I cried. "Why did you do this?"

Rosie fell onto her knees and collapsed into me. "I'm sorry, Ethan!" she cried. "I'm sorry I couldn't save our baby!"

"No!" I said. I grabbed her face with our noses nearly touching. I looked deeply into her eyes. "This wasn't your fault, baby. This was not your fault. Don't you ever say sorry," I cried. "Don't you ever say sorry again."

She nodded her head. "The baby's due date was today. May 17th. That's why I came here. We would have been parents. BP," she said. "Brian Perdita."

I nodded my head in agreement as she dug her face into my shoulder. Her sobs carried out into the night. And as the rain began to pour, the burning roses were finally put out. I thought of my baby underneath the pile of burnt roses. I didn't want to believe what was happening. And so I just held onto to Rosie as our cries carried themselves into the night. I held onto her for dear life. I could never let her go.

CHAPTER SIXTEEN

DREAM

I woke up on a riverbank surrounded by wildflowers and tall grass. The blue skies above me held fluffy white clouds. The sunlight felt warm against my skin. I inhaled the freshest air. The sounds of the river flowing and splashing water meeting the bank sent me into a daze. I felt lightweight and free. I felt no pain. With every breath, I felt as if I were going to float away. I closed my eyes again as I rested under the warm sun. I was interrupted by a sound. I heard two tiny pairs of feet rustling through the grass. Their giggling drew a smile onto my face. Be quiet, I heard one tell the other. With all my efforts, I tried to hide my smirk, and as soon as I felt that they were close enough, I jumped up and yelled, *boo*! They shrieked with laughter as I chased them into a field of bright green grass. They fell onto their backs as I began to tickle them. They were laughing with joy, kicking and fighting me off. I finally stopped and allowed them to catch their breath. I looked down into two pairs of big, beautiful, dark brown eyes.

Brian and Perdita had dark brown hair, just like their mother. They had the biggest, brightest eyes that I had ever seen. Brian's wavy hair rested just above his ears, covering most of his forehead. He wore a white short-sleeved button-down shirt and white shorts. Perdita had longer hair, just past her shoulders and parted in the middle. She wore a white dress that went down to her knees. They both began running around in their bare feet and their joyous laughter filled the air.

I heard the voice of an angel from behind me singing my name. I turned around to greet the love of my life. She, too, was wearing a flowing white dress that ended at her knees. Her cute little feet walked right past me as she turned and reached out for my hand. "Are you coming?" she asked me. *Of course*, I thought to myself. I'd go anywhere with them, and that was the truth. I had no desire to spend one second without my family.

The four of us walked, hand in hand, through a field of bright grass. Birds flying high above us entertained us all with song. Brian and Perdita were always restless, so they ran ahead as I held onto Rosie's hand. We carefully watched the children play while carrying out our own conversation. "Everything is perfect," she said. All I could do was smile in agreement. She smiled back and I saw her dimple dance across her face. Brian came running back to us with a beautiful rainbow-coloured rose in his hand. "Give this to mommy," he whispered in my ear as he handed me the flower. I thanked him and he was running off ahead, trying to catch up with his sister. I looked into Rosie's eyes and reminded her how much I loved her. I placed the rose in her hair and kissed her forehead. She looked absolutely beautiful. I noticed a crystal tear fall from her eye and her smile grew wide. She told me that she had never been happier in her life. I grabbed her hand and we were off. We were floating in the sky, soaring through the clouds. The feeling of the wind blowing through me was the feeling of freedom. Brian and Perdita were soaring alongside Rosie and me. We grabbed their tiny hands and held on tight. "This is so fun," they both shrieked. "Mommy," they called out. "Daddy," they called out. "This is so fun!" they both shouted with joy. It was an amazing sight to see, watching my family looking down on the land below. Rosie and the kids were amazed at the wondrous joys the world had been blessed with. We flew above beaches and through mountains. The beautiful African deserts and the famous Egyptian pyramids. Big oceans and small lakes. We flew above volcanoes and floated through dark, cool caves. We saw waterfalls and valleys. Light and dark. We saw it all, and the most amazing thing I witnessed through it all was the smiling faces of my beautiful woman and children. What amazed me the most was the fact that I lived in a world full of beauty and magic, but all I ever noticed was them. Brian was growing up to look exactly like me, and Perdita, just like her mother. I didn't care where we were. We could have lived on a snow-capped mountaintop or within the deepest valley of our planet. But none of the world's treasures were as beautiful and mesmerizing as my family. I loved watching them smile. They kept me living.

After our exciting flight, we landed on top of the Mediterranean Sea. Each one of us, souls without soles, walked on top of the cool blue water. Brian and Perdita excitedly watched as the fish below danced around underneath their feet. Rosie held my hand as she rested her head on my shoulder. Brian and Perdita dipped their tiny hands in the water, sending splashes all over Rosie and me. "Sorry," they said. "We just want to catch the fishies," they explained. I didn't mind, and I knew Rosie didn't either. "They remind me of you," she whispered in my ear. "Their excitement and passion must come from you," she said. "No," I said. "They love life, and the only person I knew who loves life just as much as they do is you," I said. I felt her squeeze my hand. She liked what I told her. Rosie suddenly lifted her head up and her wide eyes looked into mine. She had an idea. She caught the children's attention. She brought her hand up to her face and plugged her nose. While smiling, she counted to three, and we all jumped into the water.

The water was warm and matched the colour of the light-blue sky. Brian and Perdita wore snorkels and goggles. They splashed their feet around as they dipped their heads into the water, examining the ocean floor. Rosie's hair was wet. She swam up to me and kissed my head before she dove headfirst into the water. She came back up to catch her breath. "Come on in," she said. "The water is great." She grabbed my hand as I slowly submerged myself into the salty sea. I was having difficulty kicking my arms and legs, propelling myself in the water. Rosie and the kids laughed at me, and when I looked up at them, they each had a mermaid tail. "Daddy!" Brian shrieked with laughter. "It's like this," he said as he swam effortlessly down to the ocean floor. Perdita and Rosie followed him, but I swam near the surface, struggling to keep up. I tried and I tried with all my might. Finally, swimming felt so easy. I looked at my legs and saw I had a mermaid tail too. Rosie and the kids were at the ocean floor, clapping and cheering as I made my way towards them. "Good job, Daddy!" Perdita shouted. "You did it!" Brian exclaimed. Rosie swam up to me, kissed my cheek and whispered, "I knew you'd pull through." We swam along behind our children, holding each other's hands. I traced my finger along the warm sand on the ocean floor. It was soft and smooth. Rosie must have noticed that I had closed my eyes and smiled, because she asked if I liked the feeling of the sand. "Of course I do," I said. I love sand. Before I knew it, we were on the white, sandy shores of a beautiful beach right on the Pacific Ocean.

Perdita sat in the sand carefully constructing a kingdom of sandcastles and other buildings while Brian ran back and forth to the shore bringing back buckets of water. Rosie was stretched out on a towel next to me, bathing in the hot, bright sun. She had a notebook and a pen. She was humming a soft tune as she scribbled her heart and soul onto a piece of paper. It was nice to watch her; she was in her zone, in her moment, working in her own time. Nothing else mattered when she wrote. She used the sharp tip of the pen to cut straight through her heart while courageously letting herself bleed out onto her notebook. A warm breeze blew by, flipping her pages. She tried to stop them, but the wind quickly picked up her book and sent it sailing through the air. She quickly stood up and tried to catch it. The open notebook was spewing out letters and words as I ran behind Rosie trying to catch them. The sand was covered with letters from Rosie's writing. I stopped running. I stopped moving.

Standing amidst her words, I felt her. For the first time in my life, I was able to see through her eyes. Her words and soft whispers danced around my ears. I felt her love and her pain. I felt her bravery and her loneliness. I felt all of her. I wanted to stand there and enjoy the moment, but Rosie finally caught the book and slammed it shut. I felt gravity push against me and the wind picked up. All the letters spun around in a vicious tornado, flying straight past me. Letters hit me at full speed and sliced through me as they fell back into Rosie's notebook. When all of them were returned to her possession, she put the book away and demanded that we leave the beach. Brian and Perdita, with their heads hanging low, walked right past me. "But we're not done playing," they both complained. Rosie grabbed their hands and walked them across the beach as my broken and battered body followed close behind. But no one seemed to notice.

The wind started to pick up and I noticed dark clouds following us. "I think it's going to snow," I told them. They looked back at me and Rosie told me to catch up. She had an idea. I quickly caught up to them and she led us into a dark cave. I saw Rosie smile as she looked ahead into the cave, but I couldn't see what she was seeing. She touched the wall and suddenly there was a light in the cave. It was as if someone had turned on a lamp. "Do you see them yet?" She asked us. Brian and Perdita excitedly jumped up and down with joy. Four dogsleds, side by side, each equipped with its own team of sled dogs. Siberian Huskies. "Get on, guys," she said. She jumped onto her sled and I noticed she was wearing a white snowsuit. The kids did exactly as she did, and now they were all wearing white snowsuits. When I got onto my sled, I, too, was wearing a white snowsuit. "Mush!" Rosie yelled. The dogs began to run on her command. Before I knew it, we were being pulled through a land full of snow. We were surrounded by tall mountains, and the cold winter air felt refreshing in my lungs. Rosie's face was lit up as she guided the dogs through the snow-filled valley. I looked at Brian and Perdita and they were enjoying themselves just as much as their mother was. The dogs ahead of us were all barking with excitement, doing exactly what they had been bred to do. When I looked back at Rosie, she was looking right at me. She mouthed the words *I love you* and then she blew me a kiss. I watch an animated pair of red lips fly towards me, and when they hit me, I tasted strawberry lip balm. Her kiss sent me backwards onto the cold groundbeneath me. Brain and Perdita leaped off of their sleds and landed in my arms. Rosie did the same. We all erupted in laughter and lay on the soft, cold snow. "That was fun," Brian said. "I had a lot of fun," Perdita added. "Mommy, did you have fun?" Brian asked. "Yes I did," Rosie replied. "What about you, Daddy?" Brian asked. "Yes, I replied. I had a lot of fun."

I closed my eyes and when I re-opened them, we were all standing at the top of a mountain, looking over billions of acres of forest. An eagle soared through the sky above us. I couldn't focus my eyes on just one thing because there were so many things I wanted to look at. Rosie directed the kids and me down the mountain, all of us hand in hand. We came across what appeared to be all known species of animals on earth. A monkey stole Brian's hat while Perdita sat down to pet the belly of a wolf. I cradled a small bear while Rosie allowed a snake to slither down her arm. The animals werc all friendly to us and showed no signs of aggression. Perdita rolled onto her back as the wolf, along with her puppies, started to lick her face. "It tickles, Daddy!" she yelled. Rosie took my hand and led me to a smaller opening, away from the thick forest. As we walked further and further into the opening, the temperature went from cool to extremely hot in seconds. "Watch your step," Rosie said as she held onto my hand. I took a step onto a dark platform made of rock. Brian and Perdita were quite a bit hesitant about following, but sure enough, they were right behind me. It was harder to breathe in the hot air. I felt my hand in Rosie's begin to sweat, so I pulled it away and placed it in my pocket. I felt beads of sweat pour down my face and I tasted the saltiness on my lips.

When Rosie asked me to close my eyes, I was a bit apprehensive, but I completely trusted her, so I closed them. I heard a river flowing nearby and immediately felt at peace. When I opened my eyes again, I was amazed by what I was looking at. A beautiful, crisp, tropical waterfall poured into a river of molten lava. Brian and Perdita were ready to jump in when I warned them not to. "It's fine," Rosie said. I held my breath as I watched Rosie and the kids jump into the river of lava like it was a swimming pool. "Come in, Daddy," they called out. Something in my gut told me that swimming in lava wasn't normal, but neither was anything I had experienced that day anyway. I took a few steps back and then I ran towards the lake. I jumped into the air, flipped forward and landed an amazing cannonball. The lava was thick and warm, but it wasn't hard to swim in because the lava was heavy enough to keep you afloat. I felt like I was treading through warm pudding, as odd as that sounds, but it was the best way to describe it. I loved the warmth against my skin. Brian and Perdita were throwing balls of lava at each other. I thought they were okay, but Rosie demanded that they get out. I told her they were fine, but she shot me a vicious look, and to that, I kept quiet. It's time to go, she told the kids. Daddy can stay by himself, she said. I didn't like that she said that, especially in front of the kids, but I couldn't move. The lava quickly hardened into rock and I was stuck. I tried to break through it; I tried with all of my effort to get out, but I simply wasn't strong enough. Before Rosie disappeared off into the darkness, she looked back at me with crying eyes. Then she turned away from me and was lost in the darkness.

Before my eyes, the rock I was trapped in opened up below me and I was freefalling into nothing. After a minute of falling, I landed in soft grass.

When I stood up and dusted myself off, I looked into the distance and saw a crowd of people. I squinted my eyes to get a better look, but the only person I could make out was Rosie, so I headed in her direction. When I was close enough, I realized the crowd of people were all my close family and friends having a picnic. "It's nice of you to make it," my father said. Everyone turned their attention to me. "I like your costume," Cam said. Leah was standing by his side, smiling at me. "My costume?" I looked down and found myself staring at a pair of oversized red shoes. Below my feet there was a puddle allowing me to see my reflection, and what was staring back at me was not what I expected. A yellow hat sat atop a rainbow wig on my head. On my face was the makeup of a sad clown. I was wearing a rainbow jumpsuit, and a tiny daisy hung in my shirt pocket. When I looked up, I saw Brian and Perdita giggling while clenching their stomachs. "I like it," they said. "We all have to finish our meals or we are going to be late," Anne said. "Late for what?" I asked. "We're going to the zoo," Brad responded.

The zoo was a fun place to spend the day. However, this zoo was different. There were no caged animals; all of the animals were free. It was a bit chaotic watching everyone find an animal they loved. Within the craziness, I realized I couldn't find Rosie. I began my search for her where I thought she'd be, but when I got to the wolves, she was nowhere to be seen. I went back to where everyone else was and they told me they all wanted to go swimming with the dolphins and the whales. They were all wearing swimsuits and one by one, they jumped into a tank. I was still looking for Rosie when I thought maybe she was in the tank already, swimming. I was the last one to jump in the water but I was still wearing my clown suit, which made it extremely difficult to swim. I was swimming underwater and calling Rosie's name when I swam headfirst into a glass barrier. I didn't expect to be stopped because the rest of this world seemed endless. I saw a figure moving beyond the glass. I pressed my hands against the glass, blocking out any reflections from the light. It was Rosie. She was standing there alone, talking to a shark with scrawny legs. I asked everyone why Rosie was talking to the shark, but no one seemed to know. I pressed my face against the glass in hopes that my vision would be cleared. I couldn't make out what was happening, but Rosie didn't look comfortable. I knocked on the glass hoping that I'd catch her attention. She looked at me with weary eyes and then turned back to face the shark. He started to push her towards a wall. She tried pushing back, but she looked exhausted. What was the shark doing? "Brian and Perdita are standing behind her," Anne said as she peered through the glass with me. I noticed my children were behind Rosie as the shark pushed her into the wall. "He's squishing them," Anne said. I wanted to stop the shark. I saw Brian and Perdita standing behind Rosie. They were both being crushed behind Rosie. They cried out and asked for help. They asked for me. "Isn't anyone going to do something?" I asked Anne. When I heard no response, I looked to my side and noticed she wasn't there. I looked around and realized I was alone in the tank. There was no one was around. I looked back at Rosie and she was screaming for help. I began banging my fists against the glass and shouting her name. She couldn't hear me. Suddenly, I couldn't breathe underwater anymore. My breath caught in my throat and I knew I needed to surface or I'd drown. I was losing them and there was nothing I could do. When I surfaced and gasped for air, I was no longer dreaming.

I had awoken from my dream and was lying comfortably in my bed.

I was sitting at my kitchen table dipping bread into egg yolks when Rosie took the seat next to me. Her washed hair was neatly wrapped in a green towel and she wore a pink bathrobe. "Good morning, handsome pants," she whispered in my ear as she kissed my cheek.

"Handsome pants?" I asked as I looked down at my lap. I was only wearing boxers. "But I'm not wearing any pants."

Rosie smiled, leaned into me and gently bit my ear. "I like that better," she said and then winked at me.

"Easy there, tiger," I said. "You have to go to school today. I stood up, grabbed my plate and placed it in the sink. "And I have to go to work."

Rosie frowned and looked down at her feet. "I don't want to go to school," she whined. "I really don't." She looked up at me with cute, sad eyes.

I laughed as I walked up to her with open arms. I embraced her and kissed her head. "Why not?"

"Because," she said. "I'm going to miss you."

I laughed. "I know, and I'm going to miss you too," I assured her. "But this is your last semester and then you're done. You get to graduate and get a job. And then in July we are going to have an amazing wedding." She smiled and I kissed her dimple.

"Thank you, Ethan," she said, rubbing the ring on her finger. "I wouldn't have been able to get back on my feet without you."

I kissed her forehead. "Believe me when I say this," I said. "There is no point in living if I can't see your beautiful face every day."

Rosie gently punched me on the arm. "You're not the first person to say that," she joked. "And you probably won't be the last."

I wrapped my arm around her and started to tickle her. "Oh, okay," I said. "So it's like that?"

"No, please!" she begged as she burst out laughing. She tried to wriggle out of my arms, but I didn't want to let her go. "Okay, okay, okay," she begged. "I give up, please!"

I finally let go. I watched her catch her breath. "I love you," I said.

"Liar," she joked. She rewrapped her hair in the green towel. "I'm going to get ready. I'll see you later, babe," she said as she walked up to me and kissed me on the cheek.

"Bye, baby," I whispered as I watched her walk out of the kitchen. "I love you." I finished my coffee and made my way to work.

That morning marked the second anniversary of Rosie's abduction. After two long difficult years, Rosie had finally come around. She was off all of her medications and she no longer needed to see a therapist. She stopped having nightmares and random outbursts of manic sadness. She was happy. She was finally happy. I had always said that I wanted to have Rosie back, that I wanted to be the old Ethan and Rosie once again, but I was wrong. I had grown so much since Rosie came back. I'd learned a lot about myself and who I was. I learned who my true friends were and how much my family meant to me. Through all the tragedies and triumphs, I learned that I was strong enough to make it out alive. The love I had for Rosie was the flame that burned brightly in my heart. Rosie and I had never been stronger as a couple. A lot had changed between us, but the one thing that remained the same, the one thing that had never changed was my ability to fall in love with her, all over again, every single day.

If I had a choice, I wouldn't change a thing. I was the happiest that I had ever been. I couldn't imagine being any happier.

CHAPTER SEVENTEEN

July 28th. It was a sunny Saturday morning. The Saturday morning that was to be the start of the rest of my life. I had spent the night in a hotel room with Brad and Cam celebrating and saying goodbye to my last night as a single man. Brad and Cam got wasted during a poker game while I nervously sat and watched. I was the only one who had woken up early enough to take advantage of the free breakfast the hotel offered. I silently left my room and made my way down to the lobby. I wanted to grab coffee and toast and hurry back to my room before anyone else spotted me.

While I was pouring delicious-smelling hot coffee into a small Styrofoam cup, the doorman greeted me. "Hola Señor," he said. "How are you this morning?" He was neatly dressed in black pants and a white button-down golf shirt. His hair was slicked back and he wore a cheery smile.

I placed my coffee back down on the counter and shook his hand. "I'm good, Pablo," I said. "How are you doing?"

"Hey," he said, "you know, I working here, can't be too bad."

"That is a great way to look at it," I said. "Coffee?" I offered.

"Oh, no," he said. "Señor, I cannot take coffee when I work, sorry."

"Not a problem," I said. "Are you coming today?"

"Señor Ethan," he said. "I cannot miss such an important day. I will be there to see you marry your beautiful, young bride."

I smiled. "She is beautiful," I said. "Isn't she?"

"Oh," he said as he raised his hands up. "Beautiful? Señor Ethan, she is what we call *rosa* in my culture. She is as beautiful as *la rosa*. The most beautiful thing on this world."

"*Rosa*," I repeated. "And what's that?"

"It is a rose. A rose is the most beautiful flower in the world."

I couldn't have agreed more. "Thank you," I said. "I appreciate your kind words."

Pablo laughed out loud. "Ethan," he said. "Don't mistaken me. I say your bride is beautiful, I don't say you are beautiful. You are what my people call *burro*."

I laughed. "What is a *burro*?"

"It's what you people call an ass."

I laughed. "Oh, okay," I said. "Thank you, Pablo. Remind me to kick *your* ass later."

"Señor Ethan," he said. "You know I just play joke. You are very handsome man and you have a very beautiful bride. I want to wish you both all the happiness in the world."

"Thank you," I said.

"I must go back to work, I will see you later."

"Have a good one."

Pablo waved back at me as he headed out the door.

I grabbed my coffee and my toast and headed back to my hotel room.

Brad and Cam were just waking up. "Good morning, gentlemen!" I greeted them loudly. I just wanted to mess with their heavy heads.

"Shut up!" Brad yelled as he brought his pillow over his head. "You're so loud."

"Hey," I said. "I told you guys not to overdo it last night." I placed my coffee and toast on the table and started eating. "I need you guys to be in perfect shape. We need to be ready and out of here in less than two hours."

"It's not like we're girls," Cam said as he sat up in bed. "I can be ready in fifteen minutes."

"Yeah," Brad added with his head still under his pillow. "Chill out."

"Okay," I said. "Whatever you say."

"Have you been working on your vows?" Cam asked.

"Uh . . ." I shoved the last piece of toast in my mouth. "Yeah, I have."

"How are they coming along?"

"They are perfect now," I said. "But I know when I'm up there, I'm going to be so nervous that I'll forget it all and look like an idiot."

I heard Brad laugh from underneath his pillow. "I can't wait to see that."

"Shut up, you dick," I said. "I'll send you back home."

"Are you going to let me hear them now?" Cam asked.

"Nope," I said.

"Why not?"

"Because you can only hear them when I actually need to say them."

"Why?"

"Because my vows are only meant for Rosie's ears. She needs to be the first person to hear them."

"Does anyone smell cheese?" Brad laughed from underneath his pillow.

"You better watch out," I threatened. "Before I come over there and suffocate you with that pillow."

232

Brad laughed and sat up. "You know I'm just kidding, right?"

"Yeah, yeah," I said.

"I'm serious," he said. "I'm very happy for you. And today is your day. Cam and I will do whatever you ask us to."

"Cam and I?" Cam laughed. "You're on your own with this one."

"Stop being a prick," Brad said. "This is Ethan's day."

"Okay, guys," I said. "Enough with the nonsense. Can you just get up and shower. My dad is going to be here soon."

"You can go first," Brad offered as he put the pillow back on top of his head. "I need more sleep."

Cam shrugged his shoulders and walked into the washroom.

I went the window and studied the beach. In just a few hours I would be marrying Rosie right by that beautiful Caribbean shoreline.

I had just finished putting on my tie when my father walked into the room wearing a tan tuxedo, just like the rest of us. Brad was fixing his hair in the mirror while Cam was busy looking for his left shoe.

"Good day!" my dad announced as he walked in with his arms open wide. "Come here, my son," he said, wrapping his arms around me. "I'm so proud of you. Your mother and I both."

"Thanks," I said. "But can we save the mushy stuff for later? Where's the gift you promised me?" That caught Brad and Cam's attention. "You said it was amazing."

"Yes," my dad said as he reached into his jacket pocket. "Your gift." He pulled out a case of Romeo and Juliet Dominican cigars. "But it must be shared with your friends here, and of course, with your old man." My father patted my back as he handed me the pack of cigars.

"Of course," I said as I took the package from his hand and placed it in my jacket pocket. "I'll save these babies for later."

My father looked down at his watch and smiled. "You guys ready to go?" he asked us.

Brad and Cam both said yes. I couldn't speak.

"All right," my father said. "I'll meet you guys down in the lobby. For now, I need to have a man-to-man with Ethan."

Brad and Cam nodded and left the room.

My father sat down on the bed and offered me a seat. I sat down beside him. "So this is it," he said. "This is the day you've been waiting for."

I nervously rubbed my sweaty palms on my knees. "Yes," I said. "Yes, it is."

"What's going through your mind right now?"

I took a deep breath. "I don't even know," I confessed. "It's going 100 kilometres an hour right now."

"Ah," he said as he patted my back. "That's normal."

"Is it really?" I asked. "Because I haven't felt this nervous since the first time Rosie and I went on a date."

My father laughed quietly.

"It's not funny, dad," I said. "I'm freaking out here. How the heck do people do this all the time?"

"Don't worry," he said. "It's normal to be nervous on your wedding day."

"But why?" I asked. "It's not like I'm meeting her for the first time. I know Rosie. I love Rosie. Why is today different?"

"It's different," he said. "Because the two of you are showcasing your love for one another in front of a crowd of people."

"I don't think that's it," I said. "I think if I were alone I'd still be freaking out."

"Let me tell you a story about your mother and me. I was always nervous to meet her. Your mother's father, your grandfather, was a really strict man. If it had been his choice, I don't think your mother would ever have gotten married. Not to me, not to anyone else. Anyway, when I took my old beat-up Chevy to pick her up, I, too, was a nervous wreck. I thought I was scared because I was scared of her father. But once I'd picked her up and we were driving to the fair, I realized she was the one who made me nervous, not her father."

I laughed.

"I remember exactly what she was wearing, too. A black-and-white polka-dot skirt with a pink sweater. And her hair, don't even get me started on her hair. She probably used three cans of hairspray; I thought I was going to die if I didn't open the window in the truck. I didn't think she was nervous. She was acting so cool. She turned the radio dial on my truck like it was her own vehicle. She took out her cigarettes and shuffled around her purse looking for a lighter. She put that cigarette in her mouth and lit it up without a care in the world."

"Mom used to smoke?" I asked in complete shock.

"Yes," he said. "She said it kept her skinny. Anyway, when I saw her smoke her cigarette, I was nervous. She was smoking cigarette after cigarette. I immediately felt like an idiot."

"Why?" I asked.

"Because she was way out of my league. Guys like me didn't date the cool girls who smoked. My mother tied my tie that evening, for God's sake, and there I was, hanging out with the most beautiful woman in the world huffing and puffing her cigarette in my old, beat-up pickup truck."

I laughed. "That's too funny."

"We went to the fair that evening and I offered to play a game for her. The prize was a giant teddy bear. I needed to score three baskets, and I knew that would be easy because I loved playing basketball, and I was quite good at it. But she didn't want the teddy bear."

"Really?" I asked in shock.

"Nope," he said. "She took my hand and walked me towards the biggest roller coaster at the fair. She pointed at it and told me she wanted to take a ride."

"You hate roller coasters," I said. "Don't you?"

"That is the exact reason why I do."

"What happened?" I laughed.

"I didn't want to go on the ride, but your mother was smoking hot, and I didn't want to mess it up. All my friends were counting on me and if they heard that the date was ruined because I didn't have the balls to go on a roller coaster, they would kill me. So I took a deep breath and went on the ride. I remember how sweaty my hands were when the roller coaster was on the climb. It was bumpy and uncomfortable and I was so scared. You mother was screaming hysterically; she was enjoying herself. But not me. I was actually fighting back tears and praying to God to let me make it out alive. I should have prayed for something else, because before I knew it, the ride was over and I was clutching your mother for dear life. She asked me if I had been crying, but it was obvious because my eyes were sensitive to the wind. I hated it. I absolutely hated the ride. But she just kissed my cheek and got out. And I was struck. I followed her around for the rest of the night, trying my best to keep her happy."

"You actually cried?" I asked.

"No," he said. "My eyes were actually sensitive to the wind."

"Yeah, right," I said. I didn't believe him. "You probably cried. I can see that."

"This stays between us," he demanded. "Or I will kill you."

"Not a problem," I said. "Your secret's safe."

"Thanks."

"So what happened after?" I asked.

"She fell in love with me."

"What?" I asked. "Really?"

"Yup," he said. "I wasn't the roller coaster, man, but I sure knocked her off her feet later that night in the bed of my truck."

"Wait, what?" I asked. "You and mom? First date? Ew! Dad! Don't tell me this shit!"

My dad tilted his head back and laughed. "High five for your old man?" he asked as he raised his hand up.

"I guess," I said, hesitantly tapping his hand. "I still don't wanna know that stuff."

"Anyway," he continued. "Back to my original point. Yes, you may be nervous, but I can guarantee that Rosie is just as nervous as you, if not even more."

"How can you guarantee that?" I asked.

"Because your mother was a nervous smoker."

"What do you mean?" I asked.

"She smoked a lot on our first date because she was really nervous."

"Yeah, right?" I said. "And she told you this?"

"Nope," he said.

"Okay," I said. "Then how do you know?"

"I learned it about her. She only smoked a lot before a job interview or a meeting or a public speaking."

"So she was nervous to meet you too?" I asked.

"Very nervous. I'm surprised at how well she kept herself together. To this day, I haven't seen her smoke the way she did on our first date."

"Interesting," I said. "So you think Rosie is with the girls right now, freaking out?"

"I can guarantee it," he said. "100 percent."

"Okay," I said. "I still don't feel any better."

"I know," he said as he stood up. "You're not supposed to."

I glanced at my watch and stood up too. "It's time to go," I said. "It's time for me to get married."

"After you," my father said, letting me walk ahead of him. "This is the first day of the rest of your life."

I walked out the door, shaking my head in disbelief. I still couldn't believe that in a few more minutes, all my dreams would finally be coming true. I'd finally be marrying Rosie.

I stood nervously at the altar by the sandy shores. The salty wind blew through my hair as I toyed with a hankerchief in my pocket. Brad, my best man, stood to the left of me, and Cam stood to the left of him. Rosie's maid of honour was Kimberly, Brad's girlfriend. They had become extremely close over the past two years. Coincidently, Cam's new girlfriend, Sofia, was Rosie's cousin, whom she had selected to be her only bridesmaid. Kimberly and Sofia walked down the aisle wearing short pink dresses, each holding a bouquet of flowers. My breath jammed up in my throat when I heard the wedding march begin to play. Rosie began walking down the aisle alongside her father. She held a bouquet of red roses in her hand. She was smiling up at me as she made her way towards the altar. My God, I thought to myself. She looked beautiful. An angel in a white dress was making her way towards me. I knew then that I was the luckiest man in the world. Brad nudged my side and whispered into my ear, "She's beautiful, brother. I'm proud of you." I knew I was smiling like a goof; I could tell by the way the crowd looked at me. Rosie laughed to herself and looked down at her feet. She was walking elegantly like an angel straight from heaven. When she reached the altar, she kissed her father on the cheek and I shook his hand.

"Take care of my little girl, Ethan," he whispered into my ear. "She's yours now."

"Thank you, sir," I said. He walked to his seat.

Rosie took my hand and stepped up to the altar. She was glowing. I was so excited I felt all my nerves jump up in my throat. "Hi," she said in the cutest voice I had ever heard.

"Hi," I whispered back.

The minister asked us to hold hands. "We are gathered here today to witness the beautiful union between Ethan Hobbs and Rosie Lutine," he began. "And with the presence of your loving family and friends, the two of you are about to begin a journey to last a lifetime. Your lives will change after this day. The two of you will be taking on responsibilities, but your joy will be multiplied. We ask God to bless this young couple in their matrimony and to bless them in their future. And when death separates them both, we ask that they be reunited in the afterlife. Ethan, do you take Rosie to be your wedded wife, to love her, to comfort her, to honour and keep her, for as long as you both shall live?"

"I do," I said.

"Rosie, do you take Ethan to be your wedded husband, to love him, to comfort him, to honour and keep him, for as long as you both shall live?"

"I do," she said with a smile on her face.

"Repeat after me," he continued. "'I, Ethan, take you, Rosie, to be my wedded wife, to have and to hold, for better or worse, for richer or poorer, to love and to cherish, from this day forward.'"

I repeated his words.

"I, Rosie," Rosie repeated. "Take you, Ethan, to be my wedded husband, to have and to hold, for better or worse, for richer or poorer, to love and to cherish, from this day forward."

I was still smiling like a goof.

"This young couple before me have also asked to exchange their own vows. Ethan, you're first."

I cleared my throat and readjusted my stance. I took a deep breath as I looked into Rosie's beautiful eyes. "Rosie," I said. "I don't even know where to begin." I nervously took another deep breath. "Ever since the first day I met you, when you accidently got into my car thinking I was your mother,"—everyone laughed—"I knew there was something special about you. I thought you were ridiculously beautiful right away. I thought you were adorable and funny. You were quirky and outgoing. You were just fun to be with. And the more I got to know you, the more I realized you had me wrapped around your finger. I thought about you all the time. You made me so happy. The guys at work started to make fun of me when I smiled like an idiot while reading your text messages. From day one, you changed me, without really knowing it. And I still don't think you realize how much you actually mean to me. You mean the entire world to me, Rosie." I stepped in and took her hands. Her eyes were beginning to water. "And I know as I stand up here on this altar that I am making the smartest decision of my life. I prayed for this day to come, I dreamed for this day. And soon enough, I'll be lucky enough to call you my wife. And after everything we've been through, I'm glad to say I know we will make it. You are everything to me, Rosie Lutine. And I just want to thank you will all my heart. Thank you for making me the happiest I ever could be. Thank you for agreeing to be my wife. And finally, thank you for being the best wife a man could ever ask for. I love you so, so much."

"Ethan," Rosie began with a trembling voice. "You are my light, my rock, my shelter. You mean everything to me and I cannot express that well enough. You make me so proud every single day. You are such a strong person, inside and out. You're a hard worker and you fight for what you want. I remember, when I first looked at your hands, I noticed they were hard-working. They are rough but strong. Old scars and new wounds cover the surface. But your hands tell a story." I felt her rubbing my hands with her fingers. "And from the first time I saw them, I knew I wanted to spend the rest of my life holding them. With your enduring hands you hold my heart, sheltering it from darkness. In your hands, my heart remains in its forever home. I love you so much, Ethan Hobbs."

My eyes watered when the minister faced me. "Do you have a ring for the bride?" he asked.

I turned to face Brad. Brad excitedly handed me the ring.

"Place it on the bride's finger," he said. "And say, 'With this ring, I thee wed.'"

I gently slipped the ring on her finger. "With this ring, I thee wed."

The minister then turned to face Rosie. "Do you have a ring for the groom?"

She turned around and Kimberly handed her the ring.

"Place it on the groom's finger and say, 'With this ring, I thee wed.'"

Rosie placed the ring on my finger and said, "With this ring, I thee wed."

"Let this ring be given as a token of your affection, sincerity, and loyalty to one another. In as much as Ethan and Rosie have consented together in wedlock and have witnessed the same before this company, and pledged their vows to each other, by the authority vested in me by God, I now pronounce you man and wife." The minster turned towards me. "Ethan, you may kiss your beautiful bride."

Without missing a beat, I took Rosie in my arms and kissed her lips like they were a drink of water after a year in the desert. Everyone stood up and cheered as she took my hand and walked me down the aisle.

I was finally Rosie's husband, and I couldn't be happier.

The weather was perfect for a beach wedding. There was not one rain cloud in sight. After the ceremony, all of us took pictures by the shore. I was so happy. Everyone was having such a great time, especially Rosie. I was happy to be able to share this day with her. She was glowing with happiness, and every once in a while, she'd look at me and blow me a kiss. We all took off our shoes and began running barefoot in the sand. It was so refreshing. I ran up to Rosie and grabbed her, cradling her like every groom does to his bride. "You are so beautiful," I told her. "You make me so happy."

She kissed my nose. "I love you," she said. "I love you so much."

After all of the pictures were taken, we all sat on a patio for the dinner service. Rosie sat by my side and I was proud to be her husband. She placed her hand on my knee and squeezed it. She leaned into me and whispered in my ear. "I'm so excited," she said. "I am so happy."

"Me too," I said. I kissed her cheek. "Me too."

"Can I tell you a secret?" she whispered.

"Yes, baby," I said. "You can tell me anything"

"Are you sure?" she asked.

"Yes," I said. "I'm sure."

Her eyes grew wide and filled up with tears of happiness. "Ethan," she whispered. "You're going to be a daddy again."

I thought when I married her I was the happiest that I could ever be. I thought I had reached my limit of happiness. I didn't think I could be so ecstatic. But I was wrong. I wasn't expecting the news. It had happened by surprise and I was completely caught off guard, but as a believer in miracles, I thought it all began to make sense. Everything happened for a reason, and I believed Rosie and I were selected to be a part of each other's lives for a reason. We had a purpose. She had saved my life and I could only hope that she felt the same about me. Life sometimes can be difficult to bear. Life always throws curveballs. Sometimes it can feel like the whole world is against you, because life knows you can't dance with a broken leg. You can't sing with a broken voice. You can't fly with broken wings. You can't dream with a broken heart. But I learned to always remember that any obstacle can be overcome. I learned to have faith because flowers grow in mud, the deaf can make music, and even miracles make babies.

My beautiful baby.

I love you, Rosie Hobbs.

ABOUT THE AUTHOR

Katarina Alexa Arruda currently lives in a city outside of Toronto and attends a local university, where she is studying English literature. She has always enjoyed writing in her free time. She spends her time reading and writing romantic dramas. This is her first novel.

CPSIA information can be obtained at www.ICGtesting.com
Printed in the USA
LVOW131913280113

317586LV00002B/43/P

9 781481 702911